THE MURDER CLUB

SAM BARON

Storm
PUBLISHING

To request permissions, contact the publisher at rights@stormpublishing.co

Ebook ISBN: 978-1-80508-419-8
Paperback ISBN: 978-1-80508-421-1

Cover design: Henry Steadman
Cover images: Shutterstock

Published by Storm Publishing.
For further information, visit:
www.stormpublishing.co

ALSO BY SAM BARON

FBI Agent Susan Parker

The Therapy Room

The Safe House

for
May
&
Sheila,

my
alpha
&
my
omega

and

for
Leia

my
tau

"I believe the only way to reform people is to kill them."
  —*Carl Panzram, serial killer*

ONE

He knows they're watching.

He knows it's a trap.

He goes in anyway.

The need to kill is too great tonight. It will not be denied. If that means he must endure the watchers, then so be it.

The house is a small one, modest even for this low-income subdivision on the less desirable side of the Santa Carina Valley. The interstate is within earshot, the rumble of eighteen-wheelers a constant background noise even now, at this unearthly hour. It's a single-story cottage with a roof that needs fixing, an untended front lawn, and a rust-eaten old Ford pickup in the driveway.

The occupants are a single mother and three kids.

She's a big-boned, brassy blonde with a husky voice that some men find sexy, and an unattractive temper, foul mouth, and quick hand that her children have learned to fear. A recovering, on-off alcoholic and sometime heroin user who has been hauled up for solicitation on more than one occasion and currently works the late shift waitressing at the Original All-American Diner, she has no real friends. Her most frequent visitor is Child Protective Services, whose mandatory supervision of her parenting was a condition of her probation after her last arrest.

She reminds him of his mother.

Which is the reason he chose her.

From his surveillance and the cameras he installed a month ago, he knows she often forgets to lock the side door to the garage. It's a mistake she won't live to regret, he thinks, as the knob turns in his gloved fist.

He stands for a moment in the back hallway, breathing in the smells of a house with three young children below the age of ten. Mac 'n' cheese, fish fingers, dirty diapers, all underlaid by the sweetish odor of marijuana smoke. Through the sliding glass doors, he can see a tricycle on its side and several toys in the scraggly back yard. Something small and furry scurries away through the uncut grass and a gap in the fence, red eyes glinting.

He moves through the kitchen.

The sink is piled with unwashed plates. A half-eaten chicken nugget and congealed ketchup is on the top one.

He eats the nugget, biting off the head of the dinosaur. The familiar breaded taste puts him back in his own seven-year-old self in a house not unlike this one.

The mother is in the larger bedroom, lying on her stomach, snoring nasally. The youngest child, almost a year old, sleeps in a crib beside her bed. The other two children, five and eight, are in the next room. They each have different fathers, all of whom are absent.

He pulls the nylon clothesline taut between his fists as he leans over her.

It is double-braided, a tougher brand less likely to fray under pressure. The simple single-strand ones have a tendency to snap, as he knows from experience. This particular brand is tried and tested—twice before, to be exact—and will crush her throat within seconds, stopping just short of severing her spine.

It will be violent, and she will struggle in her death throes, but he has the advantages of surprise, weight, strength, and skill.

For a moment he considers carrying the crib out to the hallway to avoid the toddler being woken by her mother's dying struggles, but decides against it.

Even if the baby does wake and cry, all she and the other two children will see and remember is the Halloween mask he has on. They will believe the Boogeyman killed their mother.

But in fact, he is the opposite of a Boogeyman.

He is their savior.

As it turns out, the children sleep through it all.

There is a moment when she drums her feet on the bed, kicking a plastic rattle to the floor, and he thinks the baby will surely have heard that, but the infant sleeps the deep contented sleep of the innocent, legs and arms splayed in four bracketing Vs, as his mother dies beside him.

Afterwards, he sits at the kitchen table and eats a bowl of cornflakes.

The milk is on the verge of sour, and the expiry date on the jug was three days ago, but he consumes it anyway.

It is his ritual.

When he is done, he leaves the bowl and the Kellogg's box on the table, to be found by the police.

He then takes a few minutes to remove the cameras he himself installed two weeks ago when nobody was home. They are tiny, impossible to spot by the untrained eye, and fit into his jacket pocket.

When he reaches the last one in the garage, he pauses, looking up into the tiny glass eye.

He smiles.

"I know you're watching," he says softly. "I hope you enjoyed tonight's show."

Naturally, there is no answer.

They cannot hear his words—there is no microphone—but

he knows they see him. He's known from the very first day they hacked into his wireless connection, bypassing his firewall, and hijacked his feed. He chose to let them. As he did the earlier two times.

Reaching for the camera with a black-gloved hand, preparing to kill the feed, he taps the lens, grins, and says:

"You're next."

TWO

My name is Susan Parker, Special Agent in Charge at the FBI's LA office and I'm in hot pursuit of a dangerous felon in the Santa Carina Valley, my hometown.

I'm on a high-speed chase, racing headlong down a road with deadly, hairpin turns.

The suspect I'm pursuing is within sight, hurtling away at breakneck speed.

We're both approaching a particularly hairy curve that forces the suspect to slow down. I use the opportunity to pull up alongside, yelling, "FBI! Pull over!"

The suspect just laughs at me.

She hears me just fine, despite the revving engines and screeching tires, but chooses to ignore my command. She takes the curve at breakneck speed.

We both go around together too fast, swinging dangerously close to the edge.

Time for drastic measures.

I yank my steering wheel to the right, slamming hard into the side of the suspect's vehicle. It's a risky move but I'm trained in high-speed driving and time it well enough to give her vehicle a glancing blow, not enough to topple her over but just enough to force her to slow down.

My timing is perfect.

She spins out of control, slamming against the barriers and bouncing back. As she struggles to point her vehicle forward so she can get away, I prepare to hit her one more time. Second time's the clincher.

I have her now.

That's when someone rams into me from behind, taking me completely by surprise.

I lose control, spinning around to turn a full one-eighty and end up facing backwards.

As I fight to regain control, I see the person who hit me.

It's my own partner!

Grinning devilishly, delighted at their success.

I yell, "You're gonna pay for this!" just before I slam into the side barrier. I'm facing backwards, angled in such a manner that by the time I manage to turn around and get going after the suspect, she'll have gained too great a lead.

It's the end of the pursuit for me.

I'm done.

I turn my head to watch in disbelief as the traitor races away from me to join her partner in crime. They slow to a halt after the finish line, leaping out of their vehicles and celebrating their victory in a high five.

It was a pre-planned betrayal, brilliantly executed.

Despite my failure, I'm impressed.

I unbuckle my seatbelt and climb out of the go-kart, taking off my helmet and shaking my hair free.

"Traitor!" I call out to my ex-partner as I walk over.

The seven-year-old traitor grins proudly at her accomplishment, then puts her hands on her hips, wiggling them from side to side as she sticks her tongue out at me. "Sore loser!"

"I thought you were supposed to be my backup," I say in a pretend-whiny tone.

My daughter, Natalie, shrugs. "I'm a rogue agent!"

I look at the suspect I was pursuing, who's actually my sister-in-law, Lata, or as I call her, my sislaw.

"Rogue agent? How did she pick up that concept?" I ask Lata.

Lata grins. "You're asking me? You're the one who's always telling her stories of your exploits at bedtime!"

I shrug as we exit the go-karting track to let the next batch of players in. "That's just stuff I make up. You don't expect me to actually tell her my real war stories?"

Natalie, my seven-year-old daughter, thumps me on the hip. "I heard that!"

When Natalie says she "heard" it, she means she lip-read it. And when she speaks, it's through ASL, American Sign Language. Natalie's deaf. She was born with the condition. Lata and I both sign to her when we talk, although Natalie can read lips, too.

I bend down and hug Natalie. "You did great, sweetie. Rear-ending me at the last minute was a genius move!"

She raises her chin in pride and does her elbow dance. "I'm gonna be a daredevil stunt driver when I grow up, Mom, just wait and see."

"Well, you have to be old enough to get a license first, which is not for at least ten years, so let's keep our options open."

She keeps her chin up, pointed at the sky, which is her way of saying she means it.

I tousle her hair affectionately and kiss the top of her brown tangle, which is so much like mine. "Now shall we go get lunch? I'm famished!"

A few minutes later, we're across the street at the new Indian restaurant and grocery store, digging into our curries and naans, samosas and dosas. Natalie chats gaily about school and trying out for soccer. I listen and nod along appreciatively, asking the occasional question. Being a participant in my daughter's life, getting to hear the smallest details, is one of the highlights of my day. I treasure these moments and am always grateful that I was the one chosen to be Natalie's mom.

Lata sees someone she knows and goes over to say hi. The woman laughs at something Lata says, and I get the sense of something between them.

Natalie slaps my forearm. "Mom! You're not *listening*!"

"I am, sweetie. You were just telling me about how Taylor was one of the good girls before, and now she's not."

"Yeah. She's gone bad, and I don't think I want to be friends with her anymore."

She scowls as she says it. Taylor is her best friend.

I nod sympathetically, knowing that this is one of several turnarounds over the past couple years of elementary school. I'm pretty sure that Natalie and Taylor will like each other well enough again by the time one of their birthdays rolls around, and all will be forgiven and forgotten—until the next falling out. But I understand that, at the moment, it feels like the end of their relationship with Natalie. I comfort her as best I can.

Lata returns a few minutes later with a particular look on her face that I know all too well.

"So, who was that?" I ask casually.

"Oh, just someone I know." Lata says it with the careless tone that tells me she's playing it cool.

"Know as in *know*-know?" I ask.

She nods slightly. "Kinda."

I want to know more but my phone pings with a message. It's Naved.

Free to talk?

Naved, or Detective Naved Seth of the Santa Carina Valley

Police Department to give him his full title, was my partner on my last case, the Splinter serial killer investigation. He's also the only person I've confided in about my late husband's death. He wouldn't be pinging me on my day off if it wasn't important.

I look at Natalie.

She's happily digging into her meal, enjoying the Indian food. She's trying to use a plastic spoon to pick up a piece of paneer which keeps falling off and splashing back into the curry.

She glances up, sees me watching, then switches over to a fork and uses that to snag the paneer and eat it up with a sheepish grin.

I reach out and ruffle her hair.

I love my daughter so much it hurts, at times.

But this job, hunting down killers, is also something I love in a different way.

It fulfils a need in me that nothing else can.

Maybe it's because of my messed-up childhood and past, or maybe I'm just built this way. It's barely been three months since my team and I put Splinter behind bars, but it's felt like forever.

My fingers fly to reply to Naved's text.

Sure, call.

Because if it's a murder investigation, I want in.

"Hey," he says a moment later. "Sorry to disturb you on your day off."

"It's cool. Just grabbing lunch. What's up?"

There's a small pause during which I hear the sound of a truck horn in the background. It sounds like he's on the freeway or very near one.

Naved says, "I think we might have another one. A serial."

THREE

The back of my neck prickles.

"Where are you?" I say, glancing at Lata who's already cottoned on to the fact that this is a work call.

She nods, smiling to encourage me. God bless Lata. She always has my back.

Beside her, Natalie signs: "Go ahead, Mom. It's cool."

"Thank you, sweetheart," I sign back.

"Texted you the address," Naved says as I hear my phone ping with the incoming text tone.

"I'm on my way," I say, sliding out of my seat and waving bye to my family.

I feel a thrill course through me as I walk out to my long-suffering Prius.

I think we might have another one. A serial.

It's only been three months since Splinter. Three months of recovery, as much for my family as myself.

For the first few weeks, Natalie couldn't bear to let me out of her sight. She'd burst into tears unexpectedly for no apparent reason.

The families of victims' experience PTSD, too. Or as our

family therapist calls it, Complex PTSD. C-PTSD.

I have promised my daughter a thousand times that I'd do my best to stay out of harm's way, and that she isn't going to lose me as she lost her father, my husband Amit, that we are going to have a long, happy life together.

Promises I can't be sure I'll be able to keep.

The address Naved texted me is less than five minutes away.

That's one of the many things I love about Santa Carina Valley, or SCV as we call it. You can cross the entire length or breadth of it in twelve minutes, give or take a few. Though there was a time when that same drive took half as long.

This sleepy valley settlement a couple hours from Los Angeles is fast becoming a magnet for young couples from the city looking to raise families in someplace less hectic, intense, and crime-ridden, while staying within commuting distance of their workplaces, the entertainment hubs, restaurants, theaters, and other big city attractions. Traffic increases steadily every year, but it still retains most of its small-town vibe.

My map app pings to let me know that my destination is approaching.

I've never actually been to this part of SCV before, though I've driven past it plenty of times. It's mostly trailer parks and low-rent bungalows, single-story houses that have seen better days, vacant grassy lots littered with trash, needles, and used condoms. It's the SCV equivalent of LA's Skid Row.

I see Naved's Camry parked on the side of the street and park behind it.

The driver's side door opens and he gets out, raising a hand to greet me.

To my surprise there's a young woman with him. She's oddly familiar. I've seen her before.

FOUR

"Urduja, meet Special Agent in Charge Susan Parker," Naved says, introducing me to the young woman.

She's about my height, skin tone a little darker than mine, on the large side, in a purple turtleneck graphic sweatshirt, non-skinny bootcut jeans over Converse sneakers. A roundish face with a charming, gawky grin.

"Hi." She gives me a small wave. She sees me trying to place her and chirps out, "Pizza delivery for Brine Thomas?"

I picture her in a blue tee with a matching blue ball cap, red lettering spelling out Top Dog Pizza, and it comes to me. Top Dog Pizza is right across the street from our Command Center, and really the only option if my team and I are working late at the task force headquarters in SCV.

"Urduja! Of course."

"You guys tip really well!" she says.

That credit goes to Brine, the youngest member of my team, who loves making sure everyone's fed and well hydrated. "Thanks. So, what's going on?"

Naved gestures at the house behind us. "A woman was murdered here last year."

"Last year?" I frown, recalling a murder reported on SCV news. "You mean the dead addict mom? That can't still be an active crime scene."

"Right," Naved says. "New tenants living here now. SCV released the property a week after the murder. I pulled the file. It's in the car."

"O-kay," I say. This is not the kind of case I was expecting: a small local murder which, as I recall, raised no federal red flags at the time. "Suspects?"

He shakes his head. "None. The case is still unsolved, but I looked at the stats for last year, and it looks like they somehow managed to misfile it under 'death by misadventure'."

"So that it counts as closed and bumps up their stats," I say. It's a typical local PD trick to make their closure rate look better than it is. To be fair, big city departments have been known to do it, too.

"What makes it worth looking into now?" I ask.

Naved looks at Urduja. "She does."

A hefty guy in a dirty once-white cotton vest with hairy armpits and a permanent scowl comes out of the house and stands on the porch, breathing heavily as he stares at us. He glares at us with the hostility of someone who's been in enough scrapes with the law to know cops when he seesthem.

Naved glances back over his shoulder,spots the guy, and says, "Let's get in my car. I'll explain."

Urduja sits in the back of the Camry, Naved and I in front. He takes ac folder off the dashboard and hands it to me. I glance at it. It's an SCVPD case file and as they go, it's pretty thin. Almost nothing there.

I'm a little disappointed that Naved would call me in to what appears to be a cold case investigation with flimsy evidence. It's not what my team and I usually do, and he knows that.

"Help me out," I say. "What are we looking at here?"

Naved nods. We haven't worked together long but he knows me well enough to understand that I like to get to grips with a case immediately.

"Urduja does a true crime podcast on the internet. She's been covering a series of mysterious deaths of women living in Santa Carina Valley over the past eight or nine years. She believes they're the work of a serial killer. This is the most recent killing."

"What's the connection between the killings?" I ask.

Naved glances over the back of his seat to include Urduja in his response. "All the women were mothers of at least two or more kids. All had issues, either alcohol or drug addiction, depression, bipolar disorder, suicidal tendencies, arrests for solicitation, reports of child endangerment, neglect. In every case, the father or fathers were absent, the women were involved with a string of boyfriends or live-in partners, and every one of them had been investigated by Child Protective Services for suspected negligence and/or child abuse. They were all strangled in their beds at night."

I nod, trying to see the larger picture. The problem is, the deaths and the victims he's describing are a textbook litany of low-income working-class women in America.

Still, I'm unconvinced.

"Sounds pretty standard. Where's the serial connection? Any hard evidence? DNA? Forensics? Witness statements?"

Naved looks back at Urduja.

"I know a friend who used to live in the neighborhood of one of the murders," she says brightly, "and she says the kids talked about a Boogeyman who came in the night and killed mothers while they slept. She said he only killed mothers who were bad and abused their kids."

I look at her then at Naved.

I'm starting to get a little irritated now.

A true crime podcast by a young pizza delivery driver, the death of a woman in a seedy, low-rent neighborhood, a story heard from a friend who heard from kids in the area about a 'boogeyman'? *Boogeyman*? Really? What is this, a Freddy Krueger story?

A knot of tension has formed in my forehead. I rub it with my fingers, trying to smooth it out.

I was expecting a real, active murder investigation, the kind with flashing sirens and a multi-agency task force, search parties and a ticking time clock. What I seem to have been handed instead is amateur hour.

Naved starts to say something, but I stop him.

"Okay, look," I say, "I appreciate you guys calling me in on this. I can see that you've done some groundwork here, and you've got a working theory. But I'm going to need a lot more than just hearsay, kids' stories about boogeymen, and a bunch of similarities."

Naved nods along with me.

"Yes, of course, we get that, Susan," he says gently. "And I know what we're presenting to you here looks very thin on the surface."

Thin? I'm tempted to retort. *More like* non-existent.

"But I really think we have something here. Urduja's put in a lot of time and effort on this one. She's spent years, literally, and she's found evidence that's so compelling that she has a whole posse of young women assisting her in this investigation. They take turns watching."

"Watching what?" I ask. I'm getting alarming visions of teenage girls playing Nancy Drew and posting pictures and videos of next-door neighbors on social media.

"Houses of possible victims, potential suspects..." Naved trails off. "She'll explain it."

"I have a scrapbook," Urduja says from the back seat. "It's

like an actual scrapbook, not a virtual one. It's at my trailer. I can get it and show you."

I take a moment to think. The knot in my forehead is even tighter now. Naved starts to say something, but I hold up a hand to stop him. He subsides and waits.

I'm probably going to regret this but even though we've only worked together on one case, our time and experience together was intense enough that I would trust him with my life—and I know the same goes for him.

Besides, he's the person I chose to depend on to solve the one case that continues to defy my own efforts.

That's the mystery surrounding my late husband's death. I believe it was murder, not suicide as the coroner ruled. During the Splinter case, Naved offered to take that burden off my shoulders and look into Amit's death. He hasn't found anything yet, but that's not for want of trying.

That's a huge favor for any detective to do for his partner. It means I can focus on the case at hand while he continues to burn away on Amit's murder in the background, slowly but relentlessly. If there's something there, I know he'll find it.

Either way, I owe him just for trying.

So, even though I suspect I might end up regretting this, I finally say, "Okay, let's go look at your scrapbook, Urduja."

Urduja issues a little squeal of delight. It makes me smile despite myself. The joy of being that young and passionate!

I tell them I'll follow Naved's car and go back to my Prius.

Naved pulls out and I follow.

In my rearview mirror, I glimpse the shirtless guy on the porch of the house shooting me the finger as I drive away. He goes back into the ramshackle house. Still glancing in the rearview, I notice that the house next door has a realtor's sign on the front lawn. It's vaguely familiar.

I'm making the turn back to Soledad Canyon Road when my cellphone buzzes.

DD Connor Gantry calling.

It's my boss, the deputy director of the FBI.
Why is Gantry calling me on my day off?

FIVE

I answer my phone.

"Parker, I know you're not due back until tomorrow, but something's come up."

That's my boss. No hi or hello, straight to the point. Brusque as a hardtack biscuit without gravy.

"Sir?" I say.

My phone pings.

"I just texted you an address. Head there ASAP. Your team's already en route."

I look at my phone screen as I pull up at a stop light behind Naved's Camry. We're waiting on the turn into Arroyo Canyon Road.

The address Gantry just texted me is a good twenty miles from my present location.

"Sir, that's outside SCV city limits."

Gantry makes a sound of impatience. "In case you've forgotten, SAC, we're the FBI. Not small-town police. Now, turn your vehicle around and head to the location I gave you. Chop-chop."

"Sir, may I ask what it's about?" I don't intend to make it too easy for Gantry. I'm not the kind of agent who jumps every time he calls and from time to time, I like to remind him of that.

A slight pause. I can hear the deputy director recalibrating his tone in the wake of the brief blast of publicity the Splinter case gained me as well as reflecting on the lessons learned from his most recent DEI refresher seminar. A man in touch with the times, Connor Gantry. Not!

"Parker, trust me," Gantry says in a tone smooth enough to run for Congress. "You'll want this one. It's a doozy. Bigger and sexier than Splinter. Besides, this isn't me imposing on your personal day. I got a call from the director's office in DC, asking specifically for you to be assigned to the case."

I'm stumped for a comeback.

It isn't every day that the *director of the FBI* asks for a specific agent to be assigned to a case.

In fact, I've never heard of it happening before.

Hearing my pause, Gantry answers my unvoiced question: "A heavy hitter called in a favor with the director."

"Who, sir?" I ask, genuinely curious.

By 'heavy hitter' I guess he means someone of influence. But who on earth would call the director of the FBI and ask that a particular SAC be put in charge of a case? That isn't the way the Bureau works.

"Sujit Chopra," Gantry says. "Parker, this one's a ticking timebomb and a potential PR nightmare. Get up there, stat. Your team's already en route. And Parker?"

"Yes, sir?"

"Be careful with this one. Be very, very careful."

He hangs up, leaving me wondering what the heck just hit me.

I made the turn onto Arroyo Canyon Road while talking and am now driving aimlessly along. Naved's Camry has pulled ahead and is a couple hundred meters up the road. I pull over to the side and dial his cell.

"Gantry just called," I say when he picks up. "I have to go."

A slight pause then he comes back: "I understand."

"Let's pick this up later," I say. "I'm definitely intrigued by what you guys have, but I have to prioritize an active investigation."

"Susan, I get it, you don't have to explain."

"Okay, so I'm turning around and heading out. I'll talk to you later?"

"Of course."

I still feel oddly guilty as I make a U-turn and head back to Soledad.

Maybe it's because I feel I owe Naved and because Urduja seems like a bright, enthusiastic young woman.

Maybe she reminds me of me eleven or twelve years ago?

Back during those years after I graduated high school and was working three part-time jobs as well as putting myself through community college and trying to figure out the rest of my life.

Before the FBI.

Before Amit and Natalie.

Back when I was just me.

I glance in the rearview mirror and even though I can't see myself, I see young Susan way back there, still waiting for the light to change so she can start her life, with absolutely no idea of what lies ahead: all those years, all that freedom, all those life choices and life events, the good, the incredible, and the unbearable.

"I see you," I say softly.

And then I focus my attention on the road ahead.

SIX

The north end of SCV overlaps with the southern tip of the Angeles National Forest. A few miles further north-west is Castillo Lake and not far from there you'll find Miracle Mountain and the Seven Flags Amusement Park—all three count as our biggest and only real tourist attractions.

The particular stretch of the woods I'm headed to is off the beaten path. It's not an area I'm familiar with. Then again, the Angeles National Forest is over one thousand square miles and except for a few treks with Amit and Lata back in the day, and one memorable family outing at Castillo Lake, I've barely visited.

I slow down at the sight of an LA County sheriff's vehicle parked on the side of the road, near what looks like a dirt trail through the woods. A deputy holds up his hand to stop me, peeks in as I introduce myself, then waves me on.

"Straight up about a mile, then turn right at the top. Go slow or you'll miss the turn—it's a tough one. Keep going down that trail till you see the big gate, you can't miss that," he says.

I thank him and drive up a steadily rising dirt road. I vaguely remember someone talking about it once at a local bar and hangout, The Easy Dog. They were saying something about it being a good place to hunt and fish with the family.

Despite the deputy's caution, I almost miss the turn. I pass it then stop and reverse a few meters. It's just a wider gap between trees and unless someone knows it's there, it's impossible to spot. I can't imagine navigating this trail at night. There's no sign of any lights or human presence.

Just before I turn, I sense something or someone watching me. I stare out of the passenger side window. It takes me a long minute to see the tips of the ears of a gray rabbit twitch. As soon as I make eye contact, he bobs and bebops into the bush and is gone, poof, as if he was never there.

Yet the feeling of being watched persists.

I shut my eyes and sit still for a long moment, then open them and take in my surroundings without focusing on any one spot in particular, simply scanning the whole area. There's a faint sense of something flickering deep in the woods. Was that someone watching me through field glasses? Or through the telescopic sight of a rifle? Is hunting permitted in these parts? I wait another minute, but all is still.

Whatever or whoever it was, they're either gone or lying low now. I'm not about to go wandering through the woods on my own, not when I have a crime scene to get to urgently. This is easy country to disappear into. Easy country to commit murder and get away with it.

I let it go and drive on.

The dirt trail devolves to a mud track between trees, going downhill all the way. I glimpse water in the distance, and guess that that must be the pond the local hunters were talking about at the bar that night. "Watering hole," they called it. Seems a lot bigger than a hole but this is California where everything is ten times as big, including the sky, so people understate rather than exaggerate.

The woods thicken, shutting out most of the bright SoCal

sunshine. Strands of sunlight find the gaps in the leaf canopy, catching flecks of mica and quartz on the track and sending dazzling highlights into my eyes. Bird sounds echo in the forest. The rattling hum of my aging Prius sounds out of place in these surroundings, an alien intrusion into this unspoiled wilderness.

I feel the crunch of what sounds like gravel under my tires just before I spot the gate. It's huge, ornate, and looks startlingly out of place, like a gateway in some science fiction story, a portal to a parallel world. No nameplate or mailbox, but there's a sign that warns that trespassers will be prosecuted, among other things. The gate itself looks electrified. It's the first indication that any human habitation exists out here.

On its own, the gate starts to slide open on metal tracks, smoothly and efficiently. I spot the blinking red eye of a camera on a gatepost.

After what seems like a long, winding mile at least, the forest yields suddenly to reveal a large clearing and the back end of a log cabin beyond it, overlooking the body of water below.

Several law enforcement and first responder vehicles are parked haphazardly around the clearing. Uniforms mill around, looking like they're waiting for something or someone. Heads turn to look at me and I recognize several local cops as well as Chief McDougall.

My team is clustered around the large white panel van we typically use as an off-site HQ. I park the Prius beside the van and get out of the car.

"About time you showed up, jefe," Ramon says, standing up to greet me with a grin. His tattooed torso ripples beneath his tight tee shirt, the ink running up the side of his neck all the way to his left earlobe. Some of those are gang tats.

I frown. "I only just got the call twenty minutes ago. How long have you guys been out here?"

"We just got here," Kayla says. "Diaz is just pulling your chain."

Ramon winks at me, and I wag my finger at him in mock-warning.

David nods almost shyly, his bulk belying his introvert personality. "Cabin belongs to a Callum Chen. It's the only private property around."

"How's it possible for a citizen to own private property in a national forest?" I ask.

David holds his phone but barely looks at it, thanks to his phenomenal memory. "Because said private citizen was the one who donated this entire stretch of land to the county, back in the late 1880s, and lobbied for the creation of a national preserve. This and other similarly donated parcels made it possible to create the Angeles National Forest in 1892. Callum Chen was a very rich man. To retain the private ownership carve-out, the house is now owned by a living trust endowed by Callum Chen with his current heirs as beneficiaries."

"I'm guessing this Callum Chen isn't the one whose body we're here to see? Unless he's a couple of centuries old," I say.

David says, "As far as I can tell, there are only two Chens left. Margaret Chen, who is in her mid-nineties. And her son, Derek Chen. Both billionaires, by the way. Derek Chen is no spring chicken himself—he turned seventy earlier this year. I'm guessing our victim is one of them."

I look around at all the uniforms and detectives in the parking lot. Chief McDougall finishes a call and says something to his guys, as he glances toward me. I can hear the crunching of gravel under his boots all the way across the lot as he walks to me with a heavy stride.

"Parker, I don't know how you pulled this one, but it's getting to be a habit with you, stepping on my turf," the chief says, his nostrils flared over pinking cheeks. "This is SCVPD jurisdiction, and you damn well know it."

"Is it really?" Brine asks, surprising me. "I thought it's outside city limits." I'm surprised because Brine is the baby of my team, barely out of training and still learning the ropes. But I know he doesn't like McDougall, and only partly because the chief is notoriously homophobic.

McDougall glares at Brine.

I intervene before he can say something offensive.

"Technically, the Angeles National Forest comes under the LA County Sheriff's Department. But I'm sure you know, Brine, that Chief McDougall is a deputy sheriff of LA County as well as the chief of police of the Santa Carina Valley Police Department."

I turn to McDougall.

"Chief," I say calmly. "I'm just following orders. Take it up with my boss if you don't like it."

McDougall glares at me now. "Don't go getting all high and mighty just because you hit pay dirt with the Splinter thing. This is my town, Parker. McDougalls were sheriffs around these parts long before your people even dreamed of stepping out of South Asia."

Kayla bristles at that.

"No disrespect, chief," I say. "And I'll be happy to coordinate with SCVPD once I'm up to speed. I'll probably need local resources and a base. This doesn't have to be a contest. We worked together on Splinter. We can do it again. Why don't you assign a detective to partner with me and he or she can liaise between the Bureau and PD? We'll share everything we find."

McDougall looks surprised but takes the proffered olive branch. "Okay then," he says. "I'll hold you to that."

"About forensics," Brine says, "Mancini and her team are on the way. ETA twelve minutes."

Marisol Mancini is our chief investigative officer and arguably one of the best crime scene investigators in the Bureau.

If this is important enough for the director of the FBI to get involved, then it's good to know they've called in the A-team.

"Let me know when they arrive, Brine," I say, walking toward the cabin. "Now, let's get moving. We have a crime scene to view."

SEVEN

Cabin is the wrong word for the place. As we go down the stone-paved pathway I begin to see more of the log structure. It's like an enormous tree house built by a master architect. Every detail is sculpted, planned, designed. The overall effect is quite astonishing. It's a beautiful work of art. Even the area around the porch is carpeted by a plush, immaculately manicured lawn. From the familiar odor of chlorophyll, I assume that the grass has been recently cut, maybe just the day before.

"Is this a—?" I start to ask but as usual, my team's ahead of me.

"A classic Frank Lloyd Wright house?" David says. "Not officially but it does have his classic look, doesn't it?"

The front door is opened as we approach, revealing a fortyish woman in chic casual attire. She's polite, formal but genial.

"Hello and welcome, I am Fiona Worthing, executive assistant to Mrs. Margaret Chen. We have been expecting you, Special Agent in Charge Susan Parker."

"Thank you, Fiona," I say. "I'm going to need my team with

me, and my forensics investigators will be here soon, they'll need to examine the crime scene, too."

"Of course," she says. "I will take you now to view the body, after which Mrs. Chen would appreciate a word."

"Sure," I say. "Lead the way."

I exchange a glance with the others. So at least we know now that the victim is the son, not the mother.

As we walk, I note the signet ring with the alligator symbol on Worthing's left hand. "When did you graduate from Yale Law School?" I ask.

Fiona holds up the ring. "In 2005. I'm a licensed member of the bar here in California but I don't practice anymore."

Kayla raises her eyebrows to compliment me on my catch, but really, it's an easy one. No one wears an alligator unless they're a Yale alumnus. Well, except maybe for middle-aged men in polo shirts.

Worthing leads us through a sprawling living room with a gorgeous view of the lake and forest and a central fireplace ringed by seating for probably two dozen people. Past an enormous kitchen with every modern appliance imaginable. The entire cabin—or at least this floor—is designed with a fluid, open plan, one area flowing organically into the next. All the gizmos and appliances are state of the art, the hardwood floors gleaming and looking brand new. It's hard to believe the house is almost a hundred and fifty years old but then, I guess people with great wealth can afford to maintain their mansions.

Also state of the art are the small, discreet cameras everywhere that I know Ramon has already spotted and can probably identify down to the manufacturer's code—tech is his thing. They suggest a cutting-edge security system which befits this fabulous manse and its owners, but raises some interesting questions about how the killer got in and out without being recorded. Unless, that is, he was recorded, which would be a major break.

I glance at Ramon who nods, acknowledging that he's on the same page.

"It's hard to believe this house was built almost a hundred and fifty years ago," I say aloud. "Clearly, the Chens spend a great deal on its upkeep."

Worthing glances over her shoulder at me. "It's a matter of pride, SAC Parker. Their family history is tied into this house."

She stops, indicating something ahead.

The angled roof disappears abruptly to reveal a massive open deck overlooking the lake. It's a breathtaking view but I'm not interested in admiring it right now.

My attention is fixed on the body lying on the deck chair.

I approach it slowly, careful not to step on any forensic evidence although the floor of the deck appears to be pristine.

The body is of an elderly white male, dressed in loafers, pastel green tweed pants, a matching cashmere sweater and silk scarf. He appears to have been wearing a cashmere skull cap on his head, but the cap has slipped off and fallen to the deck just below the raised end of the deck chair. His hair is all gray, cropped short with a large bald spot on the top. The body lies face down, gray eyes wide open and bulging, as if shocked at how he could possibly have ended up like this in his own historic house.

The scarf is wrapped tightly around his throat—too tightly.

I suspect it might be the murder weapon.

The body has all the classic signs of a strangulation.

As I squat beside the deck chair and examine the corpse, I become aware of a peculiar odor. I turn my head and sniff, trying to identify it.

Fiona Worthing calls out from the French doors where she is still standing.

"It's a proprietary sunscreen made by a biopharma company Mr. Derek owns." She corrects herself: "*Owned.*"

I look at Kayla. "Find the sunscreen for Mancini, she's going to want it."

Brine has been recording our passage through the house on his phone, since Worthing opened the front door. I stand up now and indicate to him what I want covered. He gets coverage of the corpse from every possible angle, taking care not to step too close and contaminate any microscopic evidence.

While he works, I walk to the end of the deck and look out.

It's a beautiful Southern California afternoon.

Brilliant blue sky, that crisp cerulean blue that looks deeper and richer than any sky anywhere else. The only sight visible as far as the eye can see is forest.

I peer over the wooden railing.

About fifty feet below, the "Watering Hole" lies placid and calm, ranging out for perhaps a hundred meters in a rough oblong. It seems so peaceful here—I can picture Derek Chen lying on his deck chair, soaking in some rays and enjoying the quiet.

I watch a raptor bird with a reddish body and regular white-and-black markings on its wings swoop low, gliding over the water effortlessly. With only the gentlest of ripples, it plucks something out of the mirrored surface and takes to the air again. I'm fairly certain it's a red-shouldered hawk, native to the state.

It passes over the Chen cabin, and I look up to follow its progress.

I glimpse the gold and red stripes of the golden trout in its beak before it flashes away over the roof. I imagine it perching on a high branch somewhere, its razor-sharp beak ripping open the belly of the fish and eating greedily.

Even this billionaire's residence, despite its luxury and high-end security system, was breached, and its owner killed just as ruthlessly as that hawk will rip open that fish.

The question is who did it, and why?

EIGHT

Margaret Chen is impressive for her age.

It's hard to imagine the life this woman has lived. The old saying goes, time takes your jump shot. For most people, it takes everything else, too. I would consider myself lucky if I can still see straight, talk straight, and have my wits about me if I live to be her age. But this old lady can not only see and talk straight and seems to have her wits about her, she can even walk unaided.

Well, except for the decorative cane, which she holds before her now, both palms resting on its top, like a queen with her scepter.

"I know who's responsible for my son's murder," Margaret Chen says.

They are the first words she's uttered within a second of my walking in, even before Worthing has had a chance to introduce us formally.

Her voice is clear and carries the weight of authority, the voice of a woman accustomed to being obeyed but ready to press the point if not. The only sign of her mortality is a rhythmic shake in her head and upper shoulders. Like she's bopping along to a beat only she can hear.

"I'm saying this so you don't have to bother with all the foolishness of an investigation," she says. "I want you to find the man and bring him to justice."

I look at Fiona Worthing to see her reaction.

Worthing doesn't return the look. Her face is composed in a neutral expression, staring ahead at nothing in particular, eyes neither focused nor unfocused. She gives the impression of stoic loyalty.

I return my attention to the matriarch of the house.

"Mrs. Chen, I'm so sorry for your loss," I say in a soft tone. I mean it sincerely.

Chen makes a gesture like she's swatting away flies. "Pshaw! I don't want your damn sympathy, I want you to do your job!"

"That's exactly what we're doing, ma'am," I say.

"Then don't just stand around here. Go and arrest the man responsible!" she all but yells.

Kayla and I exchange glances. "Ma'am, let me try to understand what you're saying here. You know your son's murderer?"

"Goddamn it, woman, are you hard of hearing? I never said anything about the murderer. He doesn't matter. I said I know the man responsible!"

"I'm going to have to ask you to explain that, if you please," I say, keeping my voice calm despite her rising temper and voice. "Who is it you believe is responsible?"

"Trevor goddamn Blackburn, that's who! And it's not a question of belief, it's as plain as the nose on my face."

All of us take a moment to process that, exchanging looks and raised brows.

"Mrs. Chen," I continue, still keeping my voice gentle despite her increasingly shrill tone. "Trevor Blackburn is one of the richest men in the world right now, as I recall. Why is it you believe he would have anything to do with your son's murder?"

"Isn't it obvious? Because of his obsession!" Margaret Chen yells.

"What obsession would that be?" I ask patiently.

"Serial killers, of course!"

"You're saying Trevor Blackburn is obsessed with serial killers?" I ask.

"They were all obsessed," she says. "The whole dang lot."

"Which lot would that be, ma'am?" Kayla asks.

"Let's see now," Margaret Chen says, squinting. "There was Trevor Blackburn, Cara Brin, Riley Walling, Jake Perkins, and Zeus Hamilton. Those are the ones I know about at least. Did I get them all, Fi?"

Worthing confirms that she did.

I look at Kayla whose face mirrors my own reaction. She nods.

"Those are all billionaires in the Forbes Top 100, are they not, Mrs. Chen?" I say. "Some of the richest men and women in the country, and the world, if I'm not mistaken."

"Of course!" she snorts, as if it should be obvious.

"And you're saying they are all obsessed with... serial killers?" I ask skeptically.

"Yes!" Margaret Chen says. "Derek even used to joke about it. He called it the Billionaires Murder Club!"

"And this somehow led to Derek's murder?" I ask.

Margaret Chen makes a scoffing sound. "You mess with the bull, you get the horns. What did they think was going to happen when they stalked a serial killer? That he would bask in their applause and continue about his business pretty as you please? Fools! Nincompoops! You can't follow a tiger and expect him to simply ignore you. He turned on them, of course. And my poor Derek paid the price. But it's all Trevor Blackburn's fault. He's the one who needs to be held responsible for my son's murder. When are you going to arrest him, I want to know!"

NINE

He lifts the rifle as he sees the FBI agent emerge from the Chen house.

He follows her through the scope of the long gun, the precision-crafted Zeiss lens bringing her brunette ponytail and heart-shaped face into close, sharp focus as she turns to speak to her team.

Close enough to kiss—or kill.

She speaks quickly, assertively, giving each person instructions.

From their body language and responses, he can see that they all respect and like her.

That's unusual.

He's used to observing the local PD, watching them go about their business, interacting with each other. They fit the more typical image of small-town law enforcement, rambunctious, aggressive, testosterone driven. They're as apt to butt heads with each other, even get rough at times during an altercation, and seem to be driven more by their brute strength and force of will rather than their minds.

This FBI agent is different, in a way he can't quite make sense of.

She intrigues him.

He watches as she says something that makes the other four agents laugh spontaneously, joining in with a muted, quiet smile of her own that makes her relatively plain features light up with a certain attractive quality.

She's not gorgeous, but something about her says she could be, if she took the effort to doll up and dress right.

On the other hand, she doesn't give him the vibe of a woman who would go to such lengths just for a man, unless maybe it's a man she's really attracted to. She looks too self-confident, assertive, and accustomed to being in charge to doll up for any guy.

He hopes she isn't one of those radical feminists. He met one of those during a speed-dating meet and even five minutes was too long to spend in that woman's company. This FBI agent doesn't strike him as that type, but you can never really be sure these days.

He frowns, checking himself.

The hell is he doing, thinking such thoughts?

She's not a dating prospect.

She's the adversary!

Her job is to hunt and bring him to justice, using the full weight of her organization to track him down, corner him like a hunted beast, and put him in an iron cage.

He's pretty sure that if push comes to shove, she won't hesitate to shoot him down where he stands. He's heard that FBI agents are trained to shoot when in doubt.

There was a moment earlier, when he was watching her in her car at the turnoff, he thought she might have sensed him in the woods. Even though there was no way she could have spotted him, he still found his finger tightening on the trigger.

For all her friendly, efficient manner, she's a trained killer and he would be just another type of prey to her, no different from the way he would view a rabbit or deer when he's hunting.

She's not some girl on a dating app he can swipe right on, so why the hell is he even thinking of her in those terms?

Get your fucking head in the game, he tells himself.

Of course, it comes out in his father's voice.

It always does.

Twenty years gone, and he still hears his father's voice.

Fuck that motherfucker.

He continues watching the FBI agent as she and her team move across the lot.

TEN

"He is careful, this one."

Marisol Mancini indicates the sparse number of tagged plastic bags containing all the evidence collected from the Chen house.

We're in Mancini's sanctum, the clinical, all-white mobile laboratory that's the envy of other West Coast forensics teams. Only I'm in here, with the rest of my team waiting outside. She always says it's because the lab is a sterile environment, but I suspect the real reason is that Mancini is very cautious about whom she trusts. I'm lucky to be on her very short list.

Almost all FBI forensics work—evidence investigation as it's called internally—is conducted at the Bureau's laboratory in Quantico, Virginia. It's considered the finest in the country and is probably the largest crime lab in the world. What Mancini's Lab, as it's unofficially known, lacks in size, staff, and sheer volume of processing, it more than makes up for in cutting-edge tech. Besides, it saves loads of time shipping evidence back to Quantico or even to the local LA field office and enables her to process it on-site within hours. Since the first forty-eight hours are crucial for a murder investigation, that makes Mancini's Lab the equivalent of a superpower.

Mancini is independently wealthy and used her own money to fund this mobile lab. She's also disabled and wheel-chair bound for life, the consequence of a violent encounter with an unsub, an unidentified subject as we call them, who attacked her when she returned to a crime scene for a follow-up visit. She believes in the importance of experiencing the crime scene with her own senses, and built this mobile lab to enable herself to process evidence at the scene, speeding up our turn-around time considerably. She's a charismatic character, a very attractive, stylish, chain-smoking paraplegic and I treasure her friendship and insights.

I'm lucky to be one of the few people she trusts—I happened to arrive on the scene just in time to shoot dead the man who was about to finish off the job by killing her—and having her on my team is one reason we have one of the highest and fastest closure rates in the Bureau.

"He wears the gloves, of course," Marisol says, indicating a flatscreen that displays a chemical analysis. The file heading says *Glove Print Identification*. "Nitrile gloves."

I peer at the list of chemicals and percentages. "Nitrile. Not latex?"

She uses her hands to form a gesture of surprise. "It is unusual, no? Latex is better for fine work. But I think maybe he is not needing, how you say?"

She wiggles her fingers in a gesture.

"Surgical precision? Dexterity?" I offer.

She snaps her fingers. "So. He uses nitrile. Is bulky. Thick. But very effective to block the collection of fingerprints."

"What about hair? Sweat? Blood? Any bodily fluids?" I ask.

She shakes her head. "From trace elements I find at scene, I think he use this."

She taps a tab at the top of the screen to show me a

webpage. It shows a man dressed in white coveralls that encase his entire body, leaving only his face visible. The brand name says Tyvek Breathable Coveralls.

"Does it come in black?" I ask.

She smiles and points at me. "Great women think alike. Yes, black. Man in white suit stand out at night. Black suit, not so much."

She taps the screen again. "Many brands have such suits available in black. Not made by Dupont Tyvek but have similar properties. Same like suits we use for crime scenes."

"Please tell me these suits are only sold through medical suppliers," I say without much hope.

She indicates the website selling the suits. "Amazon. Walmart. Available anywhere. Anyone can buy online."

She taps the right-hand corner of the screen. "Some brands available for only $9.99. Also possible he just steal from somewhere."

"It's still a lot of trouble to go to, isn't it?" I ask. "I don't remember ever seeing an unsub who goes to such lengths to avoid leaving physical evidence."

Marisol nods. "Is unusual yes, but very effective. I think maybe he not wish to leave his DNA."

A serial killer who doesn't want to leave genetic evidence isn't that unusual. All serial killers are careful. They also usually possess above average intelligence, are careful, methodical planners, and have mastered the art of blending in. Almost all of us come into contact with one or more serial killers in the course of our daily lives—it could be a neighbor, a fellow shopper at a supermarket, a client, a customer, or even a social acquaintance—without ever having the slightest suspicion. For the most part, they live perfectly normal lives, only turning into deadly predators on certain carefully planned occasions, operating in the shadows or under cover of night. Very often, when a serial killer is finally apprehended, their spouse is the most shocked, having lived decades with the killer with no idea that they were capable of such horrific violence.

But using full-body hazmat-style suits is an unusual MO. It has to mean something.

I say, thinking aloud, "According to Margaret Chen, this group was stalking a serial killer and actually surveiling him while he committed murders. She believes that same serial killer tracked down Derek Chen and killed him."

"Yes, this is making sense," Mancini says. "It is foolish game, to stalk predator. Predator always end up stalking you!"

"That makes me wonder—serial killers usually stick to the same MO once it works for them. It's possible he's used these same objects in his previous kills. The nitrile gloves and biosuit. You said you were able to determine that from trace evidence. Would you be able to find it if it was present at other crime scenes?"

She shrugs. "Depends on how evidence collected in those scenes."

"But in theory, it's possible?" I ask, pressing the point.

She nods. "Possible."

"Okay," I say. "I've asked David to search the databases to call up all unsolved homicides in the state to start with. We can check them against the MO here, but there's probably still going to be a ton of them. We need a differentiator to help sift through the data. Marisol, can you give me anything specific to look for? Something that would connect all his kills forensically? A common chemical factor maybe?"

Marisol looks at her screen then at the evidence on the table, thinking. Her gaze drifts to her microscope. It's a multi-focus vortex microscope. She added it to her arsenal only a few weeks ago, proudly showing its ability to show every part of the image in sharp, high-resolution focus. Before, a photograph taken through a microscope showed only one point in focus, leaving the rest as a blur. Mancini's new toy definitely ups the game.

She nods finally, coming to a decision, and works the scope for a few minutes.

While I wait, I feel the phone in my jacket pocket vibrate but ignore it.

When she's ready, she wheels back a couple of feet to allow me access and points to the 'scope. "Look."

As I'm about to lean over the microscope to peer through the lens, she stops me and points to the tablet beside the instrument.

"It's 4k digital output," she says. "Remember?"

"Of course," I say, examining the image displayed on the tablet, trying to make sense of it.

It wouldn't look out of place at the Museum of Contemporary Art in Los Angeles.

Finally, I give up.

"What is it?" I ask.

Mancini laughs a tinkling laugh. "Sorry, I cannot resist! It is blow-up of a cross-section of a small sample of C_3H_6."

I look at her. "Assume I flunked chemistry."

She winks at me, enjoying herself. "It is plain old thermoplastic. Polypropylene or PP."

"Where did you find it?"

She wags a finger to indicate that I just asked the right question. "Embedded in strand of scarf."

I frown, holding up the bag containing the chief piece of physical evidence that we found on site. The silk scarf that was wound tightly around Derek Chen's neck.

"You're saying you found a trace of polypropylene in this silk scarf? How did it get there?"

"Most likely, I am thinking, transfer."

Transfer evidence happens routinely. A murderer touches another object or person after committing a crime, leaving traces of blood, semen, sweat, or DNA of some kind or other. Or they've just eaten lunch and leave traces of oil, bread, beef, etc. from the burger and fries they ate earlier. By analyzing these traces, we can sometimes track the unsub's movements back to a specific burger chain or restaurant, helping pin down their movements, and if we get lucky, their identity.

"So you're thinking Derek Chen's scarf had contact with some kind of plastic?"

Mancini shakes her head, an enigmatic smile playing on her pretty face. "Much better, Susan. I think the killer, he use something to strangle victim to death. Something strong and more better to grip and exert pressure than silk scarf."

She shows me the pictures of the body in situ, using her fingers to expand the digital images and zoom in on an exploded view of the scarf at the place where it makes contact with Derek Chen's throat. She shows me the tiny, regular ridge pattern that's embedded in the victim's tissue. In death, it's imprinted on the skin of the victim.

"That was not cause by silk scarf," she says confidently.

I stare at the expanded image, my mind visualizing a figure in a black hazmat suit entering the Chen house in the late evening, finding his way to the deck where Derek Chen lies on a deck chair reading a Kindle.

From my interviews with Margaret Chen and Fiona Worthing, I know that they were out last evening, the old lady enjoying a rare outing to attend a performance of *The Barber of Seville* at the Los Angeles Music Center.

I brush aside the question of how the killer bypassed or disabled the security system and cameras, and imagine him coming up on Derek Chen from behind, slipping the nylon rope over his scarf, then tightening it with strong, muscular hands, until he heard the sound of the hyoid bone snapping.

"He used a rope of some kind," I say slowly. "Where did he get it?"

"Something he find in house perhaps?" Marisol suggests.

I recall the clinical sterility of the Chen house. "No, he had to have brought it with him. What kind of rope, Marisol? Can you tell specifics from that trace sample?"

She smiles and taps the tablet, her long, tapering fingers dancing across the touchscreen like a virtuoso pianist performing a masterpiece. She holds up the results for me to see. It's another long string of chemical gibberish to my unschooled eyes.

"Clothesline," she says with another smile, knowing when not to prolong the suspense. "Braided nylon clothesline, I am thinking, from way the strands are twist around each other. It is common item. Easily available. But..." She pauses for emphasis. "If he is using same or similar nitrile gloves each time with same or similar clothesline, then combination of both will match other killings. Find this combination, you will find your killer, Susan."

I feel myself breaking out in a grin. "Braided nylon clothesline. Got it. Thank you, Marisol. That's beautiful! Amazing work. You're a freaking genius."

Marisol shrugs matter-of-factly. "I know this."

ELEVEN

Walking from Mancini's mobile lab to the van, I feel my phone buzzing again in my pocket.

Sujit Chopra calling.

It's the third time he's called.

This time, he's doing it via FaceTime, challenging me to take the call and show my face so he can judge me.

I'm tempted to ignore it as I did the first two times, but he'll probably just keep calling. He's one of those men who just doesn't know when to back off.

I slide my thumb over the screen to accept, while tapping the camera icon. Now, I'll be able to see him, but he can only hear my voice.

"Special Agent in Charge Susan Parker," I say, giving him the full formal treatment.

Sujit Chopra appears onscreen, dressed in a charcoal-gray business suit. He's seated on a couch with his back to a floor-to-ceiling glass wall that affords a view of downtown San Francisco. The red arches of the Golden Gate Bridge are visible in the background, seen from a high floor of an office building.

"Susan bete," he says. "How are you doing, my girl? Why don't you enable your camera so I can see you?"

'Bete' is the colloquial Hindi term for a woman young enough to be your daughter. Is he for real? Putting on the desi uncle act is rich coming from the likes of Sujit Chopra. This is a man who's more notorious than Leonardo DiCaprio for having an age limit for his girlfriends.

"Mr. Chopra, I'm working right now," I say. "I can't let a citizen into a crime scene."

"Yes, yes, of course," he says. "I heard about Chen and called my buddy Tom. I told him that you did such good work on the Splinter case, you would be the perfect agent for this one."

My buddy Tom is, of course, the director of the FBI, Thomas Ross.

If Sujit's trying to impress me with name-dropping, he's already failed.

I don't need anyone calling in any favors on my behalf.

Especially not Sujit Chopra.

He may be my late husband's uncle, but that still doesn't give him the right to take me for granted.

"What can I do for you, Mr. Chopra?" I say curtly, deliberately adopting a formal tone.

"Arrey, what is this 'Mr. Chopra' nonsense?" he says. "It's Sujit! Just Sujit. We are family, Sue."

"I'm a little busy right now. Can we get to the point?" I ask.

A slight pause.

His smile dims.

He's correctly interpreted my brusqueness as hostility.

Good. What was he expecting? That I would thank him profusely for having put in a word with the head of the FBI to toss me this case? To wax eloquent about his influence and reach? Shower insincere praises on him as I dutifully pander to his male ego?

Actually, that's probably exactly what he expected.

Well, screw him.

"Susan, Susan," he says in a placating tone, "I think maybe you're having a bad day."

That one almost makes me want to hang up. "Having a bad day" is often used as code by men implying that a woman coworker must be on her period. It takes an effort to stay on the line.

"I am trying to help you out here," he says. "You are a brilliantly talented young woman. A rising star in the FBI. You can go places. Sky's the limit. I only want the best for you. Because we are family, right?"

I let silence speak for me.

The truth is, I've worked hard to build my career up from scratch, coming from nothing, and it's taken me over a decade of grueling hard work, impossible hours, and life-threatening risks to get here.

Along the way, there's been a never-ending series of men, usually older, powerful men, who've seemed to take a perverse delight in placing obstacles in my path, talking down to me, impugning my talent and ability, making life so much harder than it had to be, mainly because I'm a woman, but also because I'm a person of color, because I have no godfathers or influential connections, and most of all because I don't play the corporate games and politics that seem to be de rigueur to get ahead in any large organization.

Worse men than Sujit Chopra have placed themselves in my way and done their best to impede my progress.

Several have tried to do much worse.

More than a few have even tried to harm or kill me or my family.

The serial killer the world knows as Splinter was only the latest.

I survived them all and I'm still standing.

So it's going to take a lot more than fake avuncular charm and Silicon Valley smooth talking to make me change my attitude now.

All this is in the silence I let hang between us while Sujit waits several seconds for a response. I see his expression change. When he finally figures out that none is forthcoming, his uncle act slips away, and he slides easily into tech tycoon mode.

He rises from the couch, the view of SF altering as he walks across the spacious office.

"Listen to me, Susan. We can help each other," he says in a more businesslike tone, his face tight. "This is my world. I know these people. I have access. It's a closed circle. You're an outsider, a babe in the woods. They won't let you in unless you have something they want, which right now you don't."

"Which world is that?" I ask, though I already know.

He means the world of the uber rich, the generationally wealthy, the influential, the powerful. Billionaires and those aspiring to be billionaires. The One Percenters who make up a tiny, tiny fraction of the world, yet own practically the whole world, and still want more. Always, they want more.

"Look," he says with sudden brusqueness, now reverting to the smug, superior tone that I'm familiar with. "You're in over your head on this one, Susan. You're going to run into a wall. Maybe you don't believe that now, but you will. There are places and people where even your FBI shield isn't going to work. That's my world. So, when you come to your senses and are ready to admit that you need help, give me a call. Just don't take too long. I have shit to do, too."

His thumb appears, hovers over the screen, then without so much as a ta-ta-bye-bye, he's gone.

I smile to myself, pleased that I didn't give an inch. Pleased

—and amused—that he sounded so abrupt, almost irritated at the very end.

I got under his skin.

Good.

So much for the Sujit Chopras of this world.

Although I feel the smile fade as quickly as it appeared.

I hate to admit it. I really do.

But he just might be right.

The rich, powerful men of this world often are. Not because they're smarter, but because the game is rigged and they're the ones who rigged it.

After spending hours in the Chen house talking to the curmudgeonly old lady and her brisk, lawyerly associate, and then being talked down to by Sujit Chopra, it feels like such a relief to climb into the van and hear the voices and see the faces of my team.

They all pause and look at me, instantly sensing my tension.

"Everything okay?" Kayla asks, looking at me.

"How are we doing on those calls?" I ask her, not exactly ignoring the question but answering it with a question of my own. "We need to talk to the other members of this Billionaires Murder Club, like, right now."

"Are we really calling them that?" Brine asks. "It's creepy."

"Sure," I say. "This whole thing is creepy, but it's what we were handed. So, tell me, guys, where are we on those interview requests?"

Their faces tell me the answer even before they speak.

"That bad, huh?"

"They've all lawyered up," David says. "I'm guessing they're going to go blue in the face denying any connection with Derek Chen."

"They're afraid of getting a bad look in the press, boss," Ramon says. "Can't really blame them."

I think about it for a minute.

If they want, the other billionaires could stonewall us through lawyers long enough that speaking to them becomes a moot point.

If Margaret Chen is even half right, and this is a serial killer striking back at this group in retaliation for spying on his kills, then this won't end with Derek Chen.

I need to get to these people right now, to know what they know, and I can't afford to sit around waiting for the lawyers to work out agreeable terms and conditions for interviews.

Under the circumstances, I have only one option. I have to ask someone for help, someone with more clout and reach.

I really, really hate asking him for help, but I need to do my job, and if that's what it takes, I can swallow my pride and bite the bullet.

I pick up my phone and dial.

Gantry picks up on the first ring.

"Sir, I need your help."

TWELVE

We're on a soundstage in a part of SCV I rarely visit. The film/TV production hub.

The thing about interviewing a billionaire is that you get to see the way they live. Or in this case, work. Not the full gold ticket tour, of course, but a glimpse at least.

It's like looking through a window into a fantasy world. At least that's how a former lower-middle-class (translation: dirt poor) orphan like myself views them.

The downside? They're not very nice people. They put on a good show of being nice, even too nice, but all that show only makes you doubt them even more.

As Kayla sums it up perfectly: major cringe.

SCV has a history of filling in as a location for countless Hollywood productions dating back to the silent film era when a local ranch hand parlayed his horse-riding, wrangling and lassoing skills into a role in a silent black and white western. He went on to become a major star of the silent era and his son followed in his footsteps, never reaching his father's dizzying heights but doing well enough in talkies and the early color movies. They both died relatively young, the son unmarried and childless, and in his will, he donated the bulk of their property and assets to the then newly incorporated city of Santa Carina Valley.

The city decided to use the land and money to build sound-stages and a production hub to attract Hollywood productions that found Los Angeles too expensive and bureaucratic (the licenses). The city fathers had an ambitious plan to make Santa Carina the New Hollywood. Their grandiose dream was never quite realized but enough Hollywood productions use the facilities to keep a steady flow of income pumping into the lifeblood of the local economy and keeping SCV's homegrown talent afloat.

The soundstage is currently transformed into a massive set for a reality dance series. Pretty much what you'd expect: glitzy dance floors, ersatz props, backdrops paying homage to classic movie musicals, shimmering outfits, all the bling and glam imaginable.

Our first billionaire subject, Cara Brin, is a judge on the show. Why on earth would a billionaire spend her days under hot lights that make you feel like your retinas are burning out?

Her dressing room has a gold star with her name on the outside. Apparently, it isn't enough that she owns the company that produces the show, she has to be the star on set, too. Talk about a billion-dollar ego.

"All the contestants and coaches on the show, they think they're really competing for the million dollar prize and a national showcase. But it's all just an act," Cara Brin says, sipping from a small plastic bottle filled with some kind of pressed fruit-vegetable concoction.

There are several bottles on a tray nearby, which Kayla and I politely declined. The pressed drinks are from Cara's brand of health foods. All the outfits worn on the show by the judges, hosts, and contestants are from her fashion line. The makeup and hair are, you guessed it, from her makeup line. Kayla and I are probably the only two things in this green room that aren't branded.

"An act?" I ask.

Cara's heavily mascaraed lashes curl over her sleepy-sexy eyes. "The whole contest, the entire show they're part of, is actually staged."

I can practically hear Kayla echoing my thought: Aren't *all* TV shows staged?

With the alert sensitivity of a showbiz celeb, Cara senses our confusion.

"Have you seen *Jury Duty*?" she asks.

"That's the show about a trial where a real juror thinks he's actually serving on a jury for a real murder trial, but in fact everyone else on the show is an actor playing a part," Kayla explains for my benefit.

She knows I never watch grown-up TV. Any spare leisure time I have—hah, what leisure time?—is spent with Natalie watching kiddie shows and movies. I almost always fall sleep midway, both of us curled up together, issuing mother-daughter versions of the same soft snore.

Cara snaps her fingers at Kayla. "Nailed it. So, *Murder on the Dance Floor* is basically *Jury Duty* meets *So You Think You Can Dance*. But with a murder thrown in, too. A fake murder, of course," she giggles. "Don't arrest me!"

"Who's the sucker?" I ask, trying to be polite and not tell her to shut the heck up and let us ask our questions.

"That's just it," Cara says excitedly. "They're *all* suckers. Even the live studio audience. Only the judges and the host are in the know, but we're also all producers on the show, so we're contractually committed to not disclose the truth until the last episode has aired and it's all been revealed."

"Does the TV audience get to know before they start watching?" I ask.

She rolls her eyes in impatience and shakes a tapered fingernail that looks more lethal than some hunting knives I've seen. "Nope! The whole thing is being staged for the benefit of the TV audience. We need the real-time reactions of the studio audience, the crew, and the other contestants to be natural. It's those reactions that really sell the concept!"

Kayla and I are both silent for a moment, which Cara clearly doesn't like.

"Don't you see it?" she asks with a tone of petulance. "All these people dancing for their lives to win the prize, and then all these strange things start happening! And *then* one of the dancers drops dead! Pandemonium! Chaos! There's a whole investigation and everything! Even the *FBI* gets involved! Well, fake FBI, of course." She adds the last bit after she remembers who she's pitching to, almost as an afterthought.

She looks at me speculatively. "Maybe we can get you both to do a walk-on?! It would be fun having real FBI agents on! Diverse rep is so important, don't you think? Women of color need to see more women with agency like yourselves! It sends a powerful positive message about law enforcement!"

I can't believe I'm being hustled to appear on a reality TV show by a person of interest in a murder investigation. Some days, this job really can be crazy.

"Let's talk about Derek Chen," I say. "We need to get some facts straight."

At the mention of Chen, a change comes over Cara Brin instantly. Her face loses its animated glow and seems to harden. She leans back and pulls herself in, visibly withdrawing. "My lawyer told your office already, I know nothing about that. As far as I know, none of my organizations had any association with Chen. I mean, I knew him socially, of course, and our paths might have crossed once or twice in the course of business, but not as a friend or anything like that."

I glance at Kayla. I know how much she loves to put privileged people in their place.

"You were on his contacts list," Kayla says. "His personal cellphone records showed that you and he had exchanged several dozen texts and calls over the past three weeks alone. And then there were emails..."

She stops because Cara is glaring at her with a look of such pure hatred that it instinctively makes my hand slide down toward my hip holster. Cara Brin, beauty line billionaire and self-branded celebrity, looks like she would like to strangle Special Agent Kayla Givens right here and now in her dressing room.

"That's private and confidential information!" Cara says. "You can't be allowed to see that!"

Kayla remains calm; she's used to outbursts like this one. We all are. It goes with the job. Oddly enough, it's always the rich and privileged who rage when confronted with evidence of their own mischief. Even hardened criminals off the street will usually respond with sullen hostility while the innocent poor or middle class will be bewildered, confused, angry, or a combination of all those. But the rich and powerful always rage. They take any attempt to pin blame at their doorstep so personally, like how dare we even *think* that they would ever do such a thing? The outrage dials up higher when they're guilty.

"The dead have no rights," Kayla replies. "But we have written authorization and signed waivers from Margaret Chen."

Cara glares at Kayla but is smart enough to say nothing.

"Tell us about your serial killer Murder Club," I say. "Margaret Chen has already told us about it, and we've accessed her son's computer and devices, so I'd appreciate it if you don't try to deny its existence. We know that you, Derek Chen, Trevor Blackburn, Riley Walling, Jake Perkins, and Zeus Hamilton were engaged in the illegal stalking of a person you believed was a serial killer. Derek told her that your group had somehow managed to identify this individual and were able to stalk him by hacking into his own camera network. You somehow were able to watch him committing actual crimes in this way. Murder."

I sense Kayla eyeing me.

She's heard the sharpness in my tone. Her ears have pricked up.

Since the incident that got me suspended from the Bureau, my team keeps a close watch on my temper. I've always had a short fuse—what I like to think of as the Irish in me, an idea I believe my maternal grandmother, my nana, put into my head during those early, fuzzy years when I was in Goa under her care. As an adult, before and after joining the FBI, I underwent extensive anger management and therapy to learn to manage my tendency to lose my cool under certain circumstances—the triggers are oddly similar in almost every case. I was doing great until Amit's death hit me like a freight train, knocking me completely off balance.

My unresolved rage and confusion over his death led me to an episode of total breakdown when I attacked a suspect in the Splinter case with what he later described as 'barbaric brutality'. He wasn't wrong: It took four LAPD uniformed cops to pull me off him. I'm well past that and closing out the Splinter case really helped me rein in my rage, but because my team loves and cares about me, they're always concerned that it could happen again.

They're damn right. It can and probably will, but when and where, even I can't say. I just know that *that* part of me, the Susan capable of transforming into a vengeful force of justice meting out barbaric brutality, still lives within me. Sooner or later, she will surface, given the right provocation.

But that isn't going to be today. I give Kayla a glance that reassures her. Cara is an egotistical, self-absorbed woman bloated on her own wealth, fame, and privilege, but that's just her brand. I don't believe she's a killer. What I do believe is that she's a possible victim which is why I'm pushing her buttons now.

When she starts to bluster about lawyers and tries to deny it all, I cut her off again.

"Cara, imagine what would happen if that information leaked online," I say. "It wouldn't be a very good look for you, would it?"

She stares at me, horrified. "You wouldn't... wouldn't leak that! You can't do that! You're the federal government! That would be... unethical!"

I lean back, dialing down my tone and intensity, playing it cool now that I've got her worried. "Of course, we wouldn't have anything to do with such a thing. But you know how it is. These things happen. Sometimes, they're impossible to trace back. And in any case, that wouldn't help you after the fact. How do you think your ten million followers would react if they knew your secret hobby was stalking serial killers and watching them murder innocent victims? Would they still love you and follow you? How about your partner brands? Your company's stock price? Your business relationships with Hollywood studios, fashion designers, chain stores, consumers? Do you think they'll find that palatable? That Cara Brin gets her rocks off by watching serial killers offing people?"

She half-rises from her chair in outrage, her heavily glossed lips quivering. "It's 172 million followers! Not *ten* million? How dare you insult me that way! I'm not going to be intimidated by your petty threats."

Kayla makes a placating gesture, jumping in to play good cop to my bad. "Miss Brin, Susan is concerned for your welfare. It seems very likely that this killer you and your friends were stalking came after Derek Chen and killed him. You could well be next on his list. It's in your own interest to cooperate."

After some more huffing and puffing, a brief interlude by each of her assistants in turn, followed by her talent manager, then her agent, then her *business* manager, and her image consultant, all of which she disposes of with astonishing efficiency in just a few seconds apiece, Cara finally considers us with a little less panic, but not much less hostility.

"What kind of cooperation?" she asks, with the shrewd suspicion of a born negotiator.

That's my cue.

"Complete access to your data cloud," I say at once.

Cara laughs aloud. "Dream on! Not in a million years."

"We can come back with a warrant," I say. "It would look better for you if you just volunteer."

Cara shakes her head. "We're done here."

She calls out to her personal assistant, who shows us the way out.

I'm tempted to ask her if this means we won't be on the show, but decide against it. Quips and murder investigations only go together on TV shows.

But it still leaves us with a major problem.

THIRTEEN

"That could have gone better," Kayla says when we're outside again in the Southern California sunshine.

"It would have gone the same no matter what we said or did," I say as we move toward the parking lot. "Her mind was made up before we even walked in there. Let's hope the next one is willing to play ball. What are David and Brine saying? I saw their updates but haven't had a chance to read through yet."

Because of the close timing of the interviews and their far-flung locations, Agents David Moskovitch and Brine Thomas are handling two other interviews today: Riley Walling and Zeus Hamilton.

"They struck out with Riley Walling, same as us," she says. "Plenty of blah blah about her business and success, but the minute they tried to pin her down on the Murder Club and asked for access to her data cloud, she sent them packing."

"And Zeus Hamilton?"

"That's quite a story, Brine says. Zeus turned it into a race thing, sending two government agents to interview a Black man, the federal government yadda yadda yadda."

"So he came at them, put them on the defensive. Smart

tactic." I think for a moment. "This is getting us nowhere. It's been three days since Derek Chen was killed. We need something to break, and fast. Let's head to Jake Perkins and hope we do better."

Kayla heads off to her car.

While I'm unlocking my Prius, I sense someone watching me.

When you grow up in the foster care system, especially if you've lived in group homes, as I have, or been to juvie, as I also have, then you learn early on to have eyes in the back of your head. As prey, we've been conditioned over millennia to be aware of predators stalking us.

That's how it feels when you have a group of older girls who resent you because of your skin color, or your intelligence, or just about anything that rationalizes their ripping you to shreds like a plastic doll. The feeling I'm getting right now is very much like that.

I look around but see only the usual studio people heading in and out of the lot. A bespectacled guy in a checked shirt sitting behind the wheel of a Ford truck and making notes on a clipboard, a stunning blonde getting out of her pink convertible, a grizzled older guy in a tank top standing by an Audi SUV and talking on his Bluetooth ear pod... Nobody's actually staring at me right this second.

I shrug it off as nerves and get into my car.

FOURTEEN

Jake Perkins is the next interview on our schedule.

I hate being beholden to Gantry for a favor but have to admit that he did come through. Getting this level of access so quickly would have taken weeks at the very least if we'd gone through the lawyers. Instead, we're getting to cover them in days.

Jake Perkins turns out to be a short, balding, middle-aged man built like a fire plug with a penchant for cowboy hats. He's asked us to meet him at Theatria, which is the fancy name the city uses for the auditorium in the downtown building which serves as the local convention center. When Kayla and I enter the empty auditorium, there are workers setting up a stage for what looks like a talk about finance. A guy carries a life-size cutout of Perkins past us as we go down the aisle.

Jake Perkins is comfortably seated in the front row of the auditorium, chatting with an attractive redhead in her mid-forties whose face looks vaguely familiar.

I feel like I've seen it on a front lawn somewhere. An election signboard? One of those 'So and so for such and such position' boards, maybe?

The mystery is solved when she introduces herself as Stacy Schwimmer, realtor, and hands me one of her business cards. That's when it clicks. I've seen her on those For Sale boards that realtors put on front lawns. Her card is a replica of the boards.

Most recently, I saw one of her boards on the house next door to the one that Naved was showing me the other day, the one where the woman was killed. That reminds me that I haven't spoken to Naved since I brushed him off that morning.

That makes me feel a little guilty.

Usually, I would have been doing these interviews with him, in the interests of inter-agency cooperation as I promised Chief McDougall.

Instead, McDougall chose to assign another detective to liaise with us. Detective Carlton. I know the guy well enough to not want him anywhere near these ultra-sensitive subjects.

Brine worked his magic and got him off my back, sticking him in the command center to handle paperwork and background searches. It's an under-utilization of his detective skills, and I bet he's probably already complaining to the chief and that will trigger an indignant call from Chief McDougall to me at any minute. Which is exactly what I want.

Jake Perkins saw us coming but has continued talking to the realtor as if we aren't here. Now, Kayla and I watch as Stacy leans over Jake Perkins' chair, her long red hair trailing down to mask her face as well as his, and whispers something to him. When she straightens up, he has a twinkly smile on his face.

She leaves us, going up the carpeted aisle on her high heels with a contented smile. I admire her arches and muscled calves. My ex-Marine sislaw Lata works out regularly and has the best toned legs I've seen around, but a contest with Ms. Schwimmer would be a close one. I wonder if Jake Perkins' interest in her involves more than just real estate.

Jake's expression changes the instant we're alone. He's

sitting in a front row seat, legs crossed, while Kayla and I stand at the foot of the stage, facing him. He shakes his head at us.

"It ain't going down like that," he says. "No way, no how."

"What exactly are we talking about here, Mr. Perkins?" I ask.

Jake adjusts the tip of his cowboy hat, moving it just a tad lower on his forehead to almost conceal his eyes. "You people want access to my cloud data, you're going to have to go through my lawyers. And in case you're not sure what that means either, lady, I'll spell it out for you. It means, it'll be a cold day in hell before you pry it out of my cold, dead hands."

"I'm not trying to violate your second amendment rights, sir," I say. "I just want to track down Derek Chen's killer."

"Go on, then, track him down," Perkins says. "Don't go digging into my stuff."

"Why the hostility, Mr. Perkins?" Kayla asks in a less confrontational tone. "We're just trying to do our job here. As a business associate of Derek Chen's and presumably a friend, don't you want us to apprehend his killer? Without your cooperation, that's going to be awfully difficult."

"Oh, no," he says with a short laugh. "You're not playing that mind game with me. You can't guilt me into giving you what you want. You want to catch the bastard who killed Derek, you follow the evidence."

"That's just it, Mr. Perkins," I say. "There isn't any. The killer was very methodical, almost clinical in the way he committed this murder. He left virtually no useful forensic evidence that we would usually expect to find."

Jake Perkins frowns and starts to say something then stops himself. "You're telling me the FBI can't solve one simple murder? I thought you guys were supposed to be the best of the best!"

"We are," I say, "and we *will* solve this murder, one way or another, rest assured. The question is, are you going to help us or obstruct us? Because as you are no doubt aware, obstruction of justice in a federal case is a federal crime."

He comes upright at once, pushing the hat back off his eggshell-smooth head. "Now hold your horses. Who said anything about obstruction? I'm talking to you, ain't I? Against my lawyer's advice, but I'm talking."

"You're not saying much," Kayla says.

"You're not saying *anything*, at least so far," I add, "except to deny us your cooperation. In my book, that's a hair's breadth away from obstruction of justice."

Jake Perkins starts to say something then cuts himself off again, thinking better of it. He regroups visibly. "Look, this guy, the killer. He had to have left something you can use. I know you guys have the most advanced crime lab in the world. You'll come up with something that'll lead you to him. You don't need me."

Something in his tone makes me perk up.

"What makes you so sure?" I ask.

"Huh?" He stares at me.

"What makes you so sure the killer left something we can use?" I ask.

He shrugs. "Killers get sloppy. They're not the brightest minds, otherwise they wouldn't be criminals in the first place, right? They'd be billionaires!"

"The difference is arguable," Kayla murmurs.

"*What?*" Jake Perkins asks, squinting at her.

"I'm not sure what kind of criminals you're referring to, Mr. Perkins," I say, "but I've had the opportunity to investigate a fair number of serial offenders over my career with the Bureau. I can assure you that many of them display high IQ levels and some are possessed of exceptional intelligence."

Perkins leans back, sloping his face to look up at me even though I'm several inches taller. "But not this guy, right?" he says. "This guy isn't any kind of genius. I mean, he can't be."

"What makes you think that?" I ask.

Perkins shrugs. "Just a hunch."

"A *hunch*?" Kayla says.

I study him.

Whether Jake Perkins' "aw shucks, I'm just a good ole country boy" act is genuine or just a persona he's chosen to don, like so many rich and privileged people who find it simpler to *perform* rather than *be*, especially given today's minefield of social sensitivities, he's still Jake Perkins, and I get the sense that he's not trying to be boorish or stupid. He's revealed something he didn't mean to and now he can't walk it back. I need to press harder on this.

"You're basing your assumptions on the times you watched him make his previous kills, aren't you?" I say with sudden insight. "You're convinced that Derek Chen's killer must be sloppy and careless because that's how he was when your Murder Club watched him go about his kills. That's it, isn't it?"

He backs away, palms up. "Hey, hey. I said no such thing. Don't go putting words in my mouth now, woman."

"Look, Mr. Perkins. Jake," I say, dialing down my tone and playing it softer. I'm taking my cue from the way Stacy Schwimmer was around him. He strikes me as a guy who would respond better to polite courtesy rather than aggressive attack. "We're on the same side here. We're the good guys. White hats all around. We need to find this guy and lock him up before he comes after you or one of your other friends. That's all we're trying to do here, keep you and your friends safe. Why don't you just cooperate with us and help yourself out?"

He looks at me in a way that tells me that the softer approach hit home.

He doesn't look like a cornered deer in the headlights now. He looks like just another middle-aged, worn down, blue-collar guy who sweated over every dollar until, whiz bang, one fine day, he woke up filthy rich. That's what the whole cowboy act and persona are about: keeping it simple, playing down the billionaire part so he can stay in touch with his small-town roots.

"Look, I'd like to help you. Honest, I would. But my hands are tied. That's all I can say. I really hope you catch the bastard who took out Chen. But I can't help you any further. I only took this meeting because, well, you never know what life brings us next, and I believe in hedging my bets rather than betting it all on one horse. Sujit Chopra is a shakedown artist, I know that. Hell, everybody knows that, but he's got the clout here in this town, and so I agreed to this meeting. But this is as far as I go, okay? Y'all have a blessed day."

He turns to walk up the aisle.

Kayla shakes her head in frustration.

I call out after him.

"You said your hands are tied. By whom?"

He keeps walking without turning back or answering.

"Great," Kayla says as we're walking out of the auditorium, "another washout. At this rate, we might as well have gone through the lawyers."

Her words trigger a thought. Before I can articulate it to Kayla, my phone rings.

Chief McD calling.

"Chief," I say. "What's up?"

FIFTEEN

Theatria is around the corner from our command center. For the Splinter case, we were given use of the old sheriff's station in the SCV courthouse complex. It's right in the city center. It's also several minutes away from the new sheriff's station, which suits me just fine.

I'm pleased to see Naved's Camry already parked in the lot when I pull in.

"Do you have a minute?" he asks.

"Sure," I say. "Just give me a sec to catch up with my guys. You should sit in. You're on the Murder Club case too now, *pardner!*"

The last is an inside joke between us: we were partners on the Splinter case, both people of color, which made our pairing up highly unlikely, statistically speaking. So we play it up by satirizing the western 'pardner' from the old cowboy movies, this valley being one of the birthplaces of the genre.

It's one of the reasons Chief McD deliberately assigned Carlton, an old-school head-bashing White male detective, to me instead of Naved. He resented the amount of press that Naved and I—and especially I—got on the Splinter case, partly also because it drew attention to how few non-White non-male officers he has on his force.

The backlash was quick and fierce. The fact that two of the handful of cops of color working in this town happened to be lauded nationally and internationally—the Splinter case was big news—while a couple of hundred mostly White cops have been working their butts off for decades without so much as an inch of newsprint to their name caused a lot of resentment.

I can only imagine what Naved must go through working in that environment. At least I get to call my own shots, for the most part, and get the freedom to run my own investigations with my hand-picked team.

"Okay, guys," I say, "let's review what we have so far."

We go over the four interviews with Cara Brin, Jake Perkins, Riley Walling, and Zeus Hamilton.

"So we basically have nada," I say when we're done. "None of them will even acknowledge the existence of the Murder Club, and it's a nope, no way to the request for data cloud access."

"That pretty much sums it up, chief," says David.

"What about Blackburn?" Naved asks.

"Trevor Blackburn is strictly off limits," I say. "That's a direct quote from Deputy Director Gantry. He says that there are certain forces at play here that are way above my pay grade and that Blackburn will not be able to help us at this time. We're free to pursue him through his lawyers, of course, but we all know how that's likely to go."

"Not all that different from the four bills you interviewed, jefe," Ramon says.

I nod. "Right. Now that we've actually wasted three days tracking down and speaking to them, it looks like they only agreed to meet with us to get it on the record. This way, they can say they cooperated fully with the authorities."

"Yeah, right!" Brine says, looking disgusted.

David pats Brine's shoulder. "Briney boy here's mad about Hamilton."

"Why'd he have to get nasty?" Brine grumbles. "We were perfectly polite. We'd barely walked in when he started slinging accusations at us. In a raised voice. In front of his assistants and other staff."

"Embarrassment only hurts your ego, Brine," I say. "When a person of interest shoots you from five feet away, that's when you should get mad."

I'm speaking from personal experience: A person of interest in a case once shot me without warning, before I'd had a chance to utter a single word. It was a clean shot, through and through, only—and I emphasize that *only*—taking a chunk of my flesh with it, without hitting any major organs or bone, but damn, it hurt like hell because of the shock. What made it worse was that I had to shoot the shooter before they shot me again, and that's a whole other story.

"Get over it, bruh," Ramon says. "You oughta hear the things I've had to take."

Brine nods. He's a good kid. Still green behind the ears, but he's learning every day, and I expect him to be an outstanding agent in time.

"Let's review it one more time," I start.

It's depressingly little.

"Are we sure there was even a serial killer at all?" Kayla asks, raising the question that we've all probably been thinking, including myself. "I mean, all we have is Margaret Chen's claim that Derek told her about it."

"We have all the emails and texts between the bills," Ramon says. As our resident tech guru, he focuses on the forensic technical evidence.

He's chosen to shorten 'billionaires' to 'bills' which works for me. I've even used the shortform on the whiteboard.

"Yes, but none of them actually mention any Murder Club,

serial killer, or murders. It's all pretty innocuous. Nothing we can use in court."

I make a note of that: David is a lawyer and forensic accountant and is our go-to when we need to determine whether the FBI has a case that's ready to take to the state attorney's office.

"Okay," I say, "let's focus on this alleged serial killer. Let's take Margaret Chen's word for it for the time being. I know, David," I add as he starts to raise a hand. "I know it's hearsay and we can't use her in court to make a case. But before we can even *get* to court, we have to have a perp. And to get the perp, we need to have suspects, which we're woefully lacking right now. So let's change our approach. Forget the Murder Club bills."

I pick up one of the many crime scene pictures from a stack of printouts, turn it over to the blank side, and stick it on the whiteboard beneath the six pictures of the Murder Club, centered in the space. I take the red marker and draw a question mark on the white glossy paper.

"*He's* the guy we should be thinking about. Derek Chen's killer. And since we're buying the Murder Club story, he's an active serial killer. He's out there right now," I say. "Scouting out his next victim. Planning his next kill. It's him we need to focus on. We get him, we break this whole case wide open."

SIXTEEN

"How are we going to do that, jefe?" Ramon asks. "We don't know a thing about the dude!"

I tap the white marker on the box where I've added the screenshot of the chemical analysis of the polypropylene traces Mancini found on the silk scarf. It's not the first time we've gone over this ground in the past few days but it's all we have.

"We have this at least. It's not much, I admit, but it's something. Forensics tells us that he most likely used a rope over the scarf to strangle Derek Chen. Almost certainly a braided nylon clothesline. Now that's an unusual item. I mean, why a clothesline? Why not a wire, or a regular rope, or just about anything else? Why something as specific as a clothesline?"

I look around. Nobody has an immediate answer, which is rare for my team. Usually everyone's falling over themselves to shoot off multiple plausible explanations. But this isolated forensic detail, detached from any other connections, offers no viable investigation pathway. It's a blind trail leading down an unknown path. Still, it's all we have.

"Come on, people," I say. "Let's earn our paychecks. Give me something, anything. No one? All right, I'll go first. Maybe he's in a line of work that requires him to handle this kind of material."

"A line of work like what?" Ramon asks doubtfully, then adds with a mischievous twinkle, "Housewife?"

"Laundry employee?" Brine offers, just as doubtfully.

"Do laundries even use clotheslines? Don't they use industrial dryers?" David says.

"Home Depot employee!" Kayla suggests. "One of those guys who move a lot of stock around. Maybe he cuts off lengths of nylon rope for customers, and that's how it got onto his gloves?"

"He wouldn't have reused the same gloves," I say. "At work, he'd have been using the standard yellow rubber gloves. Those are made of latex. Mancini said this guy used nitrile gloves. And if he does work at a store, he'd be handling way more items than just nylon ropes. There were no other significant trace amounts of other substances. Just the polypropylene rope."

We shoot a few more suggestions around but get nowhere.

Finally, we admit defeat for the moment at least.

"We need something else to go on, jefe, we can't make a whole case on just clothesline," Ramon points out.

He has a point. Sure, there have been murderers convicted on just forensic evidence, but this is much too thin to stand up in court.

Time to pivot. "Okay, moving on," I say. "What about the actual murders that this serial killer committed?" I circle that item on the board. "If he was local and operating in SCV, there would have to be active files on those cases. Right?"

My last question is directed to Naved.

"That's what I came to speak to you about," Naved says.

He looks around at the others. "But maybe we should discuss it privately before sharing with the group?"

I shrug. "We're all on the same team here, Naved."

"Yes, yes," he says, "I know. But—"

He breaks off when a young woman in a blue and red checked uniform and *Top Dog* cap with a logo of a dog with its oversized tongue hanging out comes into the command center, carrying two large pizza boxes and a cardboard tray of sodas.

"Urduja," Naved says, "perfect timing!"

Everyone makes noises of approval as Urduja sets down the food and drinks. Even I'll admit, the cheese and roasted meat smells are mouth-wateringly welcome.

"Thanks, U," Brine says, taking care of the payment and adding a generous tip.

Urduja smiles.

"Guys, you all know Urduja," Naved says.

"'Sup, sis." Kayla raises a fist which Urduja duly bumps. The others all greet her as well.

"Urduja here has a theory that I'd like her to share with all of you," Naved says. "If that's okay with you, Susan."

I frown. "Is this about the podcast case?"

"Yes and no."

"I'm not sure what that means," I say, "but I need us to focus here on the Murder Club case. That's an active investigation and I'm under a lot of pressure here. We're already past the first seventy-two hours without anything to show for it. Gantry's breathing down my neck and the director is breathing down *his* neck, so we really need to crack this one. Maybe after we're done, we can circle back to the podcast thing and brainstorm on it?"

"I get that," Naved says. "And I don't mean to press the point, Susan, but trust me on this. I really think Urduja has something here and you should hear her out."

"I have my scrapbook with me!" Urduja says, a little too excitedly. She reaches into her backpack and pulls out a large scrapbook, the kind we used back in school.

The entire team is looking at me now. I'm on the spot. I'm a little irritated by Naved pushing this here in front of everyone, instead of waiting to speak in private, but at the same time, I don't want to seem rude. Besides, he did offer to explain it to me privately, and I was the one who told him to go ahead. In the end, my stomach makes the decision.

"Hey," I say, shrugging, "we're gonna take a break for dinner anyway, right? Let's eat while Urduja tells her story. Floor's all yours, Urduja."

I pluck a slice and soda and glance over at Naved. I give him a look that's meant to convey: *This better be worth our while.*

He nods once, conveying back: *It is.*

Then I sit back to see what Urduja has to say.

"Hi everyone," she says, giving us all a little wave. "I'm Urduja as I guess you all know by now. I go to community college here in Santa Carina Valley, and my ambition is to join the FBI someday and be an agent like you guys."

She gives me an adoring, reverential look. "Especially Susan. She's my idol."

I almost choke on my soda.

I recover and raise my slice by way of acknowledgment. "Thanks." I'm not sure what to say to a compliment that massive.

Kayla gives me the double raised eyebrow and a silent slow clap. *My idol,* she mouths silently.

I roll my eyes at her. I'm sure I'll be hearing about that forever now.

"I have a true crime podcast," Urduja says, "which I do with two of my friends. They actually wanted to be here today, too, but I wasn't sure if that would be okay with you guys since I know that all your work is supposed to be confidential and all. Anyway, we do this podcast together and it's all about this one case right here in SCV. When I say one case, I actually mean a bunch of cases, but they're all local, I mean. That is, they're all different cases, but they're all really just one big case. That's what we believe. My podcast partners and I."

I'm starting to really question my judgment now.

What was I thinking, giving Urduja the floor and letting her ramble on about her amateur sleuthing?

My team is listening to her while they chew their dinner, but that's probably out of politeness.

I bet they're all wondering the same thing I am: We're FBI agents working a major case and pressed for time. Why the hell are we listening to a nineteen-year-old droning on about true crime?

Then Urduja does something I wasn't expecting and changes the narrative.

She opens the first page of her scrapbook and shows us a large heading written out with black chisel marker.

It reads: *The Clothesline Killer*.

SEVENTEEN

Dinner is done.

Pizza crusts and assorted debris lie around, forgotten. Soda cans lie opened on desktops. The team—and I—have switched to coffee now. It's time to get really serious.

Ramon has rolled up his sleeves, which puts his muscled forearms and tattoos on display, and is typing away furiously on both his laptops in turn, deep-researching references, dates, following every single rabbit of a fact that Urduja has hauled out of her treasure trove down the labyrinthine rabbit holes of the internet. David has filled pages of his yellow legal pad with notes. Kayla is asking questions constantly, clarifying details, names, dates, as much as Urduja is able to give her. Brine is the only one still working on his dinner, packing an entire twelve-inch stuffed crust double cheese pepperoni pizza and a whole two-liter bottle of Coke Zero into his beanpole thin body. Where it all goes, I can't imagine, but he's giving his undivided attention to Urduja's presentation, just like the rest of us.

Whatever we were expecting, it wasn't this. This is not amateur hour. This is an investigative report that would make most agents proud. Sure, it isn't perfect, it's full of holes and inconsistencies, and there are a ton of vital facts and evidence missing, but as an overview, which is what it is right now, it's compelling, credible, and very convincing.

"It first started as a buzz around foster homes. Kids talking about this kid they'd heard of whose mom was strangled to death in the middle of the night by a guy wearing a boogeyman mask," Urduja is saying. "Some of them called him that at first, the Boogeyman. But all the stories also talked about how he used a length of clothesline, and that's what stuck him the name —Clothesline Killer. Because, like, anyone can be the Boogeyman, but a guy who uses clothesline to strangle? That was so weirdly *specific*."

Brine is the most enthusiastic, apologetically raising a hand to ask questions. He asks now, "So this is all just kids talking?"

Urduja nods. "Pretty much. Though some of us began picking up other details, too. Stuff someone had actually seen themselves at the scene, or overheard officers talking about. Like the cereal."

David frowns. "Cereal?"

"The Clothesline Killer would strangle a mom in her bed," Urduja explains. "Then go to the kitchen, pour himself a bowl of milk and cereal. Didn't matter which brand, which type. He'd eat it right there in the kitchen, in the house where he'd just committed murder, while the kids slept on."

Kayla and Ramon both look at me.

I nod grimly. "DNA off the cereal bowls, the spoons."

Urduja takes a deep breath. "There's something else."

She takes a minute, staring down at the floor blankly for a second before continuing, "I saw him."

I sit upright. Brine stops rocking his chair and puts his boots on the ground.

"At least, I think I did," she says uncertainly. "You have to remember, I was just a kid. I was thirsty. I didn't go to Mom because I'd learned a long time ago that she would just keep snoring or growl at me to 'go geddit yourself whydontcha'. I walked into the kitchen. There was a little moonlight, just enough to see a shape at the kitchen table, the reflection off the spoon as he lifted it to his mouth. He froze when I walked in."

"What did you do?" Kayla asks, hand poised before her mouth, even though Urduja's very presence right now testifies to the fact that she quite obviously survived that encounter. My heart is in my mouth, thinking of Natalie, imagining her finding a monster sitting at a kitchen table and him looking at her.

"I was dopey," Urduja says, a tiny tear trickling down from one eye. "Pretty out of it. I guess I took him for one of Mom's boyfriends. She had a few. I just ignored him, went over to the sink, drew a cup of water, drank it down. I remember spilling some on my nightie and dabbing at it. Then I turned and went back to bed."

"This pendejo say anything, do anything?" Ramon asks.

Urduja shakes her head, wiping the tear away with a practiced motion. "He just sat there, still as a statue, until I walked away. I think I heard the sound of the spoon in the bowl again when I was in the hallway, so he probably just kept on eating."

"Stone cold son of a bitch," Kayla says.

Urduja continues in this vein for a while, until finally she wraps it up with a summary of all that the Clothesline Killer's orphaned victims have pieced together over the years.

I look over at Naved. He's staring at Urduja with a rapt expression. I've seen that look before—on Amit's face. It's the look of a proud dad when his daughter does good. Naved isn't Urduja's dad, of course, but clearly he's like a father figure to her, and right now, he's basking in the glow of paternal pride.

He senses me looking at him and gives me a quizzical look. *What do you think?*

I shrug, nodding slowly, eyebrows raised. *What can I say? I'm impressed!*

He smiles. *Told ya, pardner!*

"Urduja," I say, trying to find the words to express what I want to say.

"All my friends just call me U," she says.

"U," I say, "this is awesome work. Brilliant. I can't believe you did all this yourself."

She blushes brightly, her brown cheeks flushing with a pink tinge. "It's not all me! Shalini and Minsk did a lot of the work. I just put it all together."

Her humility is appealing. *I just put it all together*.

"Well, Urduja, your friends and you did a terrific job. This is solid investigative work. Some very good information here."

Naved has joined us. "I went back with U to her trailer and looked it all over," he says. "I know there's a lot of gaps and holes but there's definitely something here."

"Absolutely," I say. "There's no question that this is the work of a serial killer targeting women of a certain social class and demographic profile over the years. So the first case you found dates back how many years?"

Urduja turns the pages of the scrapbook. "About eight years. We think there might have been more, even earlier than that. But we couldn't find anything worth putting in the book."

I look at her, thinking that through. Eight years ago, she would have been barely eleven years old.

"Urduja, what was your motivation for starting on this when you were that young?" I ask. "What triggered it? Something you saw on TV? A documentary? The news?"

A peculiar expression comes over her face. Her bright, shining eyes grow dull all of a sudden. She looks away, lowering her head. An attitude of shame is expressed in her body language. I've obviously touched a very personal nerve.

"I'm sorry if that was too intrusive," I say. "I'm just trying to understand."

Urduja looks up at me and suddenly, I can see the eleven-year-old she would have been when her interest was first sparked. A scared, nervous eleven-year-old.

"The first one happened to us."

I stare at her, unsure if I misheard the words, or am misinterpreting their meaning.

"By 'us', you mean...?" I leave the question unfinished.

She withdraws a little further into herself. Her voice lowers even more until I can only just hear her.

"My family. My siblings. My... my mom."

I look at Naved. From the look on his face, I see that even he didn't know.

Urduja is trembling slightly, her head lowered. She looks like she might faint at any minute.

I take her by the elbow and gently guide her to the nearest chair and sit her down.

I pull up another chair and sit beside her.

Naved does the same but gives us space.

The rest of the team pauses what they're doing to look at us. I hear Kayla whispering something to Brine.

"Your mother was the first victim?" I ask in a low voice that only Urduja and at the most Naved can hear.

Her head bobs once. Her chin is practically resting on her chest now.

"May I put my arm around you?" I ask.

After a brief pause, she nods again.

I sit with my arm around her for several minutes.

With my free hand and mouthing words silently, I sign and ask Naved to get her some water and something to drink. He does so at once, returning with a small, white cardboard cup from the dispenser and a cup of chai in the other hand.

Urduja takes the water and then the chai gratefully, leaning her head against my shoulder. I keep my arm around her, smelling her shampoo and something else, a delicate aroma that I'm pretty sure is shea butter.

I can't help but think of my sweet Natalie in this moment.

Urduja seems to have channeled her emotions into her hobby. And in doing so, she's opened a doorway that lets in light on our case as well.

Because, based on what she's shown us and told us, I'm already convinced that the Clothesline Killer she and her friends have been tracking for all these years is the same serial killer that the billionaire Murder Club members were stalking online.

Now, all I have to do is track down the bastard and nail him before he strikes again.

EIGHTEEN

After she's recovered sufficiently, I ask Naved to take Urduja home.

She protests, saying she's fine really and she can continue, but I know better.

I'm over the moon to have caught this very lucky break in my case, and still have a ton of questions for her, but I'm not going to keep working her tonight at the expense of her mental health.

Besides, she's already gifted us the break we needed.

After Naved leaves, I look at the rest of my team.

I don't even have to ask the question.

"That's heavy stuff, jefe," Ramon says.

"Can't imagine how that young woman could keep working on the case all these years," David says, "after all the trauma she suffered as a child."

"I think she *needed* to keep working it," Kayla says. "It's probably what kept her going, gave her a concrete goal. Catching the killer who destroyed her family and bringing him to justice."

"I agree," I say. "It's no coincidence that her life ambition is to become an FBI agent."

"I joined up because my best friend was taken by a stranger when I was five," Brine says unexpectedly.

We all look at him. Brine never talks about his past or his personal life. We know he's bisexual and at times he's dropped a mention of a current boyfriend or girlfriend, and once he got teased about a hickey on his neck that stayed for days, but this is news to us.

"We were on our bikes on the sidewalk outside our houses when it happened," Brine says. "We were next-door neighbors. This car pulled up to the curb, a man was driving. I remember he had a 'stache and I thought that was funny because his hair was blond under his hat, but the 'stache was black, and that made me giggle. I was five, remember. Anyway, he said something to Delano and me, I think he was asking us for directions to someplace very close by, on the same street, and Delano answered. He pointed and said it's right there, mister. The guy asked Delano if he would hop in and show him. Delano said sure and got in the car. The guy asked me to come too, but I didn't like him because of his hair and 'stache being different colors, so I didn't say anything. He drove off. And I never saw Delano again."

We're all silent after this astonishing monologue.

"Jeez, Brine," Ramon says. "That's mad terrible. So the guy just abducted your buddy and disappeared him?"

Brine nods. "Pretty much. It's still an unsolved case in the Bureau's files. I have a copy at home. I look at it from time to time and try to figure it out but there's literally nothing else. I was the only witness, and it was almost two decades ago now."

We all take a minute to process that.

"I'm really sorry about what happened to you, Brine," I say. "I can't imagine what it must have done to you, seeing your best friend abducted in front of you when you were that young."

Brine crushes a brown paper bag until it's the size of a ping pong ball and flings it at the waste bin twenty feet away. It goes in without so much as touching the rim or sides of the bin. He was a state-level basketball player back in high school. He gave up a potentially very lucrative career to join the Bureau. I've always wondered why. Now I know.

"It made me feel like I was somehow responsible," he mutters. "Even though I fucking know I wasn't, and everyone from my parents to my therapist have told me a thousand times that it wasn't my fault. Deep down, five-year-old me still thinks that I could have done something to stop it, that I could have stopped my friend from being taken."

"You couldn't," I say softly. I reach out and touch his arm. "We've all faced some loss, some trauma. Things we couldn't stop, or prevent, or do anything about after it happened. But we're not doing nothing. We're FBI agents. We put our lives on the line to make sure that the same shit doesn't happen to other people. And when it does, we haul ass to nail the bastards who do those things. That's why we're all here. That's why Urduja came to us. We owe it to her, to all those victims the Clothesline Killer strangled in their beds while their kids slept beside them, to all those kids who lost their moms to this monster. And that's how we're going to make it right. For Brine. For Urduja. For Derek Chen. For everyone who's been the victim of a monster like this guy. So let's get to work now, let's take what that amazing, brave, brilliant young woman has given us, and figure out who this guy is and nail him."

Naved returns several hours later.

"How is she?" I ask.

"She's good," he says. "Just needs a good night's sleep is all, she said. I made sure her roomies were at home before I dropped her off. I think it did her a lot of good, telling us about it. Now, she knows it's not just going to stay a podcast, it's connected to a real case. She has a huge amount of respect for you. She idolizes you, Susan. She's thrilled that you're going to look into the Clothesline Killer. It's the break she's been praying for all these years. She just got overwhelmed when she realized how long it's taken to get to this point and that it was all worth it because the FBI is taking it up; she knows that the FBI has the best track record of any law enforcement department. She kept thanking me over and over again, and she says she needs to thank you, too, for listening to her."

"That we do," I say. "And we are taking it very seriously. But hey, she's the one we should be thanking. She brought us a break we really needed, on a platter! She's a very special young woman and she's going to go far. Tell me, her roomies, are they the same two girls she mentioned she's doing the podcast with?"

He nods. "Shalini and Minsk. They're victims of the Clothesline Killer too, just like her. That's how they know each other. They run a support group of sorts, for kids who've lost their parents to violence or addiction, or need help, or a place to stay; it's pretty informal and a bit chaotic at times, but they're good kids doing good work. And they're all hustling night and day just to stay afloat."

"What about the authorities? Local? Civic? They must offer these victims some help, too? I mean, it's standard for SCVPD to offer counseling, social workers, outreach, community support in such cases, isn't it?"

Naved sighs and hefts the pile of SCVPD case folders he's brought back with him. They're the ones he was able to dig up on the Clothesline Killer murders, except of course they're not tagged as such in SCVPD records. They're just individual cases, not interlinked as a serial killer's victims, which is why they were never brought to the Bureau's attention. It's only thanks to Urduja's meticulous groundwork that we were even able to piece together a timeline and tentative locations, which in turn enabled Naved to pull files on murders that corresponded with those dates and addresses.

"Not really. A little, sure. But nowhere near what they really need. These kids have basically survived by relying on each other. It's not uncommon, you know. I've seen it before in the foster care system, too. Kids form strong bonds with each other because they've all seen some kind of adult misbehavior, be it addiction, domestic abuse, violence, and they learn early on that it's better to trust other kids like themselves than adults. They're too vulnerable to adults, and there are a lot of people out there who prey on kids like these in one way or another."

"Tell me about it," I say.

Naved looks surprised. "You were in the system?"

"Only most of my childhood," I say. "But enough about me. Tell me about these cases. Our suspect's got to be in here, right?"

"Okay," Naved says, "but prepare to be disappointed. Very."

That doesn't sound very promising, but I know Naved has a tendency to downplay things.

"There are five files here," he says. "Two open, three shut. These are the three closed files."

I take the binders from him and start flipping through. "They got the unsub on three of these? How is that possible? We know he was free just three days ago when he killed Derek Chen. Did he make bail? I don't get it."

"In one case, the one you're looking at, they set one of the ex-husbands for the murder. He was very free with his fists, had a history of domestic abuse with his other girlfriends. Half a dozen TROs in the past, history of alcohol and drug abuse. Multiple offenses, complaints. It's a long list. They have his semen inside her, evidence of sexual intercourse the same night, and he was seen leaving the scene by witnesses. He pulled a gun on them when they tried to arrest him, so they got him on a third strike. He agreed to a plea in exchange for a reduced sentence. They filed manslaughter charges and he's doing time in county, his fourth year, sixteen more to go."

I flip through the pages. "This can't be our guy. Our unsub's still active."

"Let me finish. The other two closed cases are much the same. Different doers, one a vagrant who was seen hanging around the area, petty thief, small-time fraud. They suspected him of breaking in to steal something, the woman catches him in the act, he strangles her to death."

I flip through the second file. "In her own bed? While her children slept through the whole thing in the next room? That doesn't even fit! If she caught him stealing, there would be evidence of a struggle, a fight."

"Hear me out. The vagrant died in prison last year, got into a fight in the yard, had his head bashed in with a dumbbell."

"So that door's shut? Now we can't even confirm or deny the facts?"

"Exactly. Now we come to the third case. That one they pinned on a teenage son who had moved out but still visited from time to time."

I slap the top of the binders. "This is all BS, Naved. These aren't our guy. They screwed up."

"You want to tell McDougall that? These are cases they prosecuted and closed. One guy's in county, another's dead, the third is in juvie. He gets out in four months when he's eighteen."

"He can't be our unsub either," I say. "We know that the earliest murder was at least eight years ago. Possibly even before that, if Urduja's mom wasn't the first victim. This kid would have been, what, nine or ten back then? Unless he was built like a full-grown man in his late twenties or early thirties, which I doubt, it obviously wasn't him, so they screwed up royally. They caught the wrong guys."

"In three separate cases?" Naved asks.

"Don't tell me you believe this?" I ask.

"It's not about what I believe, Susan. It's what they believe. McDougall and the SCVPD. And the SCV attorney's office. According to them, these are done deals. Case closed."

I stare at the files. "So nobody's looking for the real killer? The Clothesline Killer? They don't even know they have a serial on their hands?"

"Exactly," he says.

I sit back and run my fingers through my hair. They feel greasy to my touch. I need a shower, and not just the quick two-minute rush job I had to make do with this morning.

"We have to tell McD, show him what we have, convince him. He can't ignore the evidence."

"Which evidence is that? Urduja's scrapbook? Her and the other kids' memories of the Boogeyman they grew up hearing about? These case files? He'll toss us out on our butts faster than you can say don't waste my time."

"What about the two open cases?" I ask.

Naved shakes his head. "More of the same. They tried to pin it on persons known to the victims."

"What about forensic evidence which would corroborate what we're looking for—the nitrile and polypropylene traces?"

Another shake of his head. "The forensics on these cases was pretty sloppy. Just fingerprinting and DNA mostly. They only looked for what they wanted, nothing else."

"We can re-look at the evidence, get Mancini to test it. If our chemical combo is present, she'll find it."

"Another no-go. The forensic evidence collected was stored off-site. SCVPD uses a storage locker for closed cases. The locker facility had a small electrical fire last year. Most of the files and evidence were destroyed or damaged. Even if the forensics on these cases is still there, it would be contaminated."

"Damn it."

I've seen this before, especially with local PDs in small towns. They find the evidence they need to fit their theory of the crime, rather than the other way about. It's true that most violent crimes against women are committed by men known to them. But by exclusively gathering evidence to fit that theory, the investigators fail to spread a wider net, overlooking other less likely suspects. That's what happened in these cases.

It seems like whichever way I turn, there's a wall. Only a few hours ago, I was on top of the world. I thought we were going to crack this case wide open. Instead, we're not much better off than where we were.

"Okay, okay," I say, breathing and trying to collect myself. "Let me think for a minute."

My phone buzzes in my pocket. I ignore it.

"We'll start over," I say finally. "Do this from scratch."

Naved looks at me. "Do what from scratch?"

"Investigate these eight murders. Clean slate. Look at them as if they've never been investigated before. Pound the pavement, knock on doors, question witnesses, gather evidence, the whole nine yards. It's the only way. We open fresh files, not with SCVPD, just with the task force. We run the whole show ourselves, so we avoid clashing with McD and his bulls. We track it down, identify the unsub, and nail him."

Naves stares down at the folders. "I don't know, Susan. In theory, that could work. But these women are all dead, nobody saw or heard anything that was of real value. Most of the kids were too small, they were asleep when it happened, and the older ones, like Urduja and her pals, they didn't see anything we can use. Only one kid across all these cases said he saw the killer and he apparently wore a mask. That's in the scrapbook, as you know, even though it's not in these files. In fact, what isn't in these files would fill a whole case file in itself! So even that lone witness statement doesn't help us at all. The kid was four and he actually said he saw the Boogeyman, but we assume it was a man wearing a Boogeyman mask. The detectives dismissed it as a night terror in their notes, and never followed up."

"What about the scenes?"

He shakes his head. "The original crime scenes are now occupied by new residents. The evidence destroyed or contaminated. It could be a whole lot of work with nothing left to show for it."

"We have to do *something*," I say. "We can't just sit on our hands. There's a killer out there!"

He leans back and spreads his hands. "Tell me what we do then, because I'm out of ideas. That's why I ambushed you today and got you to hear Urduja out. I worked on this for the past three days while you guys were on the Murder Club murder, and I've gone over it forwards and backwards a hundred times. I can tell you this much, there's nothing here that's going to help us nail this bastard. We need to find new evidence."

NINETEEN

There she is.

He was starting to think she might be pulling an all-nighter. Like she did the first night of the Derek Chen investigation. He glances at the time on his smartphone screen. It's early morning, only an hour or two to dawn. But it looks like she and her people are all getting into their cars and heading home for the night.

He watches the FBI agent in charge.

My favorite fed, he thinks with amusement, watching his quarry as she says something to the others who wave back at her, before walking over to her own little hybrid.

Susan Parker should look exhausted and drained after the past three days. She's been working nonstop on this case—*his* case—and even when she's gotten home, she's spent very little of the time actually resting or sleeping.

He knows this because he's wired up her house.

Little cameras everywhere, even in her daughter's bedroom.

Two in *her* bedroom.

He's enjoyed watching Susan change, and shower. People

never think to look up at their shower head. The idea that there could be a camera in the shower head seems impossible.

The surveillance cameras he uses are all-weather proof. They're military grade, so they need to be able to function even in the harshest weather conditions and remain undetectable.

The only one in the house he was slightly concerned might notice them is the sister-in-law, but so far, they've passed muster even with her.

She's an ex-Marine, he looked her up. Decorated veteran, no less. Semper Fi. Nice. He's pretty sure that if he were to meet her under the right circumstances, they would find they had a lot in common. As best as he could figure it, they had even been deployed to the 'stan around the same time. Who knows? Maybe they even knew a couple of jarheads in common.

So he's been watching Susan Parker twenty-four-seven, even scrubbing back the timeline on his recordings in the mornings when he wakes up to pause and replay the good parts. Like shower time. He loves shower time.

Susan Parker is quite a dish.

He's *into* her now, for sure.

How could he not be when they've shared such intimate moments together?

He knows he's promised himself he won't let this become about *that*, but he can hardly help it.

Even now, as the others all pull out of the parking lot and she finally gets in her Prius, he admires how good she looks.

He waits till she pulls out, turns into the street, and travels about a hundred meters before he follows.

SCV is a sleepy 'burb and there's almost no traffic at this hour, but almost isn't none, and his truck blends right in.

She's home in less than three minutes at this hour. He keeps going past her lane, which is so quiet and deserted at this hour she would definitely notice him if he drove past. He pulls over in a cul de sac next to the public park, taps on his tablet, and watches her enter the house on the multiple split screens. She takes off her shoes as she enters, goes up the stairs, pausing on the second but topmost one which creaks, then continues into her daughter's bedroom.

He watches her watching her daughter sleep, that sweet, perfect sleep of the truly innocent.

He can't see Susan's face but from her body language, he can tell that she's in her feelings.

She makes a small move as if she wants so badly to put her arms around the kid and hug her tightly.

But that would wake her up.

She settles for wrapping her arms around herself, watches for another minute or two, then goes to her bedroom.

Her sister-in-law's room is dark. The Marine is sleeping for once, though he knows she was awake just a couple hours ago.

He watches Susan sink down on the edge of her bed, shoes still in one hand, and stare down at the carpet, lost in deep thought.

After several minutes, she lets herself fall back onto her bed.

She's forgotten to put the shoes down, they're still in her hand, now lying on the bedcover.

She lies there, not moving for several minutes.

He sees her breathing change from the rhythm of her chest rising and falling.

She's falling asleep.

He starts the car.

He might as well head back home.

She'll get an early start, he knows, and he needs to get one, too.

He has plans for tomorrow. Big plans.

He's turning the truck around when sudden movement on his screen attracts his attention. He stops in the middle of the street.

She's sitting upright again.

As he watches with interest, she gets up from the bed, goes downstairs again, enters the playroom, shutting the door.

Takes out her cellphone and makes a call.

From the way she walks constantly, talking with an urgent attitude, he guesses the call is important.

She looks wide awake again, and excited.

Even in the darkness, he can see the flash of her eyes caught by the cameras as she looks up, walking and talking constantly.

She's up to something.

Not for the first—or the last—time, he wishes he had audio so he could hear what she's saying.

Whatever it is, it's obviously super urgent.

And almost surely about him.

He grins and puts the truck back into gear, resuming the drive back to his place.

TWENTY

I'm up before the crows this morning.

Except crows sleep at night. And I haven't so much as closed my eyes for five minutes.

Okay, so the only thing I have in common with the crows is the crow's feet under my eyes.

I've been busy.

I'm sitting at the kitchen table downstairs, watching and tracking as the machinery I set into motion earlier this morning goes to work.

I'm going after the Murder Club.

Yesterday's interviews made it clear that they've closed ranks. Even if they agreed to further interviews, we could expect them to be as non-productive as the first ones.

Besides, the top dog in the pack, Trevor Blackburn, hasn't even agreed to a *first* interview yet.

Even if we went through lawyers and knocked heads for months, there's little chance we would get their permission to access their data clouds. And without access to their data, we aren't likely to get anywhere anytime soon.

Derek Chen might be his most recent victim, but he wasn't the only one. And while I gave a damn whether or not the killer went after the rest of the Murder Club next, I do care about doing my job and seeing justice delivered for the mothers he's killed over the years and the children whose lives he had ruined.

The Murder Club sure as hell don't care about those dead moms and their kids. To them, their wealth and power is paramount. They're willing to do anything to keep their ivory towers barred and barricaded against me. And they have the money and clout to do that.

But they've underestimated me.

I might not have deep pockets and high-level contacts, but I have something none of them do. Something more powerful than all five of them combined.

The power of the federal government.

Late last night, or rather, early this morning, I got a federal judge out of bed, one whom I had interacted with on more than one occasion before and who trusted my good judgment well enough to issue bench warrants authorizing my team to seize all electronic devices and search them for incriminating evidence. It took some convincing but the signed witness statement I had collected from Margaret Chen about the Murder Club proved to be the tipping point that sold her on it. She signed off on the warrants barely two hours ago, just in time for Kayla and David to get it out to agents who had been told to stand by.

At 6.24 a.m. this morning, Trevor Blackburn leaves his palatial residence overlooking the Pacific Ocean, climbs into his Mediterranean blue $28 million Rolls-Royce, and drives the half mile to his front gate.

The instant he exits his property and sets foot—sets wheel, actually—on the public road, he finds his way blocked by black SUVs.

Federal agents in dark suits appear, flashing badges and a

federal bench warrant authorizing them to seize all his devices and personal computer. The devices and computer of his executive assistant are being simultaneously seized by agents at her condo several miles away, in a carefully coordinated operation.

Within minutes, the agents have climbed back into their vehicles and driven away, leaving the world's seventh richest man to fume and rant.

Similar warrants have been served simultaneously on the other four billionaires and their assistants, and their devices and computers seized as well. The federal warrants include the passcodes and draw patterns required to unlock the devices; where biometrics are required, the furious owners are legally compelled to unlock the devices on the spot.

As Blackburn fumes and rants, the FBI agents from the San Francisco field office upload the contents of his and his EA's devices, as well as those of the rest of the Murder Club, to the Bureau's secure data cloud.

Minutes after they do, my associate Agent Ramon Diaz has access to all the data and unleashes Carlotta on the haul. Carlotta, in case I haven't mentioned this before, is Ramon's pet project, a ChatGPT-based AI deep-search bot using Personalized Natural Language Processing, P-NLP or Penelope as it's known.

Sitting at the kitchen table, sipping a giant mug of Lata's delicious, aromatic chicory coffee, I watch my phone light up as Carlotta unearths one gem after another and tosses them at me on our team's private group chat.

"There you are," Lata says, tying her robe sash as she comes in yawning. "Did you grab some shut-eye?"

I answer the question with a smile and a "Good morning, sislaw."

"I'll take that as a no," she says, looking disappointed. "You gotta get your zees, Suse. You can't keep up this pace forever."

"Maybe just till I'm forty?" I say.

She sighs. "It's too early for your wisecracks. Listen, you must be bushed. I can take Nats to school," she offers, pouring herself a big mug of chicory coffee.

"It's cool, I've got it," I say.

I drop off Natalie in the mornings as often as I can, since I'm almost never around at pick-up time.

Lata takes a seat across from me. Our place is small. Cozy is the word we use to describe it. The kitchen table is barely big enough to accommodate two people and we could both pick up each other's mugs without even reaching out. That puts Lata right in my face.

"So," she says, "any more dead billionaires?"

I reluctantly take my eyes off my screen and look at my sislaw. "Hope not. The live ones are trouble enough. You're growing out your hair?" I say.

"You just noticed?" she says with a small laugh. "It's almost three inches. Been growing it for weeks."

Lata usually keeps her hair short and tight, not quite the crew cut required by the Corps on active duty, but close. She's been a Marine ever since Amit and I started dating and kept the hair even after she mustered out, so I don't think I've ever seen her with her hair grown, except maybe in old photographs.

"It looks nice," I say. "Really nice. You should grow it out more."

"That's the plan," she says. "I'm hoping it'll soften my sharp edges."

I make a face. "Forget that!"

She's referring to her last serious girlfriend Ariana's comment just before they broke up. Something about Lata having too many sharp edges. I told Lata that was BS at the time, and I meant it.

"You're one of the kindest, sweetest, most generous, giving people I know," I say to her, reaching out to take her hand.

Her palms are callused and hard from her regular workouts,

but her fingernails are medium length and beautifully painted, with her own special paisleys done in deep orange.

I hold them up.

"And you're an awesome artist. Look at these! Freida's Nail Salon doesn't do them half as well."

She clasps her hand around mine with a sisterly grip, smiling. "Thanks, Suse, you're awesome too, but it still doesn't change the fact."

"What fact is that?" I ask.

"That every time I'm in a relationship that's turning serious, I get dumped. And it's always me who's the problem."

I make a sound of disgust and dismissal. "Bakwas! That's on them. It's not your fault if those women didn't appreciate the best thing that had ever happened to them. Their loss."

She starts to say something else, but I shake my head. "No, listen to me. You're awesome and the woman you fall in love with is the luckiest person in the world. That's the plain truth and I'll swear to it in federal court if I have to. So don't let anyone tell you different, okay?"

She smiles and pulls me closer in a tight clasp, kissing the back of my hand. "Thanks, Suse. I needed that."

"Your only problem, and to me it's not even a problem, it's just a facet of your personality, is that you're really, totally self-aware. If someone criticizes you, you go, yeah, she has a point. But it's not on you, Lata. You're awesome, and it's only a matter of time before you find the person who sees that and appreciates you for what you are."

She sighs heavily. "I guess. But it's hard, it's really hard. Modern dating. I mean, I don't know about guys but it's tough as nails for women these days."

She looks at me with a question in her eyes but doesn't say anything.

I raise my eyebrow. "What?"

She shakes her head. "Never mind."

"Hey. No secrets, remember?" I say.

She bites her lower lip. "Well, it's been way more than a year now. Coming up on a year and a half in a few weeks."

Uh-oh. I know what's coming.

"A year since what?" I ask, though I know exactly what she's talking about.

She tilts her head. "You know. Since... Amit."

I swallow. Even the mention of his name sets something to work in my guts, like a machine that never truly shuts down, just dials down into sleep mode from time to time, but is always there, always churning, always seeking, never finding.

She reaches out and takes hold of my hands again, looking deep into my eyes. "It's okay to move on, Suse. You're entitled."

I fight the urge to yank my hands away and walk out of the kitchen. I love my sislaw but I don't want to have this conversation. Not right now. Maybe never.

"I'm not ready," I say.

"That's okay, too," she says gently. "But you deserve to live your life. To want. To need. To desire. It's okay to feel all those things."

My eyes prickle with tears. I force them back.

"Okay," I say.

"I'm not saying you should get on Tinder right now. Or whatever app straight girls are into right now. I'm just saying if you happen to meet someone, you don't have to, you know, hold back."

I laugh a small, bitter laugh.

She frowns a question.

I shake my head. "I'm just thinking that I basically meet three kinds of men in my line of work: criminals, suspects, and law enforcement. Those are the only ones I'm likely to meet, so, you know. It's pretty much a bust across the board."

She points at my phone. "You never know. There could be a tall, dark, eminently eligible billionaire in your immediate future."

I mime putting my fingers down my throat and making gagging noises.

"Mom? Bua?" Natalie demands, storming into the kitchen like a pocket tornado. "I can't find my LOL water bottle. The one Taylor gave me as a return gift on her birthday."

She's practically in tears but notices me frozen in the act of pretending to puke.

"Ew! Are you throwing up?" she signs. "What did you have? Was it Lata-bua's coffee?"

"Hey. Mind it," Lata signs, then adds, "We're just kidding around. You know, I seem to remember someone telling me to get that bottle outta their sight, they didn't want to see it anymore. They were on their way to toss it in the trash but someone, a very forward-thinking auntie, retrieved the item in question and stowed it away safely."

Natalie stares at Lata with a frown. "You mean you kept it? In real life?"

Lata goes to the hallway closet, opens it, and takes out a clear plastic water bottle with stickers and bling all over, every available inch decorated with marker-drawn heart emojis and smiley faces with shades on. "Would this refresh your memory?"

Natalie makes a squealing sound, takes the water bottle, gives it a great big hug, and does her elbow dance around the kitchen.

I look at Lata. "I guess 'the worst enemies ever' made up after their big fight and are BFFs again."

She nods. "Until the next time!"

"Okay," I say, standing up. "Let's get you to school, young lady." I touch Lata's shoulder. "Thanks for the pep talk."

"Likewise!" she shoots back. "And remember! Billionaires are people, too!"

She gives me a wink.

I give her an eyeroll and head out with Natalie.

TWENTY-ONE

Naved calls just as I'm reminding Natalie to please eat her veggies at lunch and not swap them with friends for nuggets.

She sticks out her tongue at me in defiance but balances it out by giving me a flying kiss.

I take the call as I watch my daughter run up the sidewalk, ponytail bouncing, to meet up with a smartly turned out blonde girl getting out of a Lexus. Taylor hugs Natalie, both girls squealing and jumping up and down as the river of kids streams around them.

Yup. Looks like the big breakup is done and dusted. The BFFs are back together again.

"Hi, Naved," I say as I navigate the endless line of parents heading to work after dropping their kids off.

"Well, someone's having a great morning," Naved says.

"Just dropped Natalie off," I say, pulling out of the school lot and rejoining morning traffic on Golden Valley Road.

"You must have been up all night setting this thing up! It's quite a coup."

He's talking about the warrant servings. "It was worth it. We got a ton of stuff."

"Including?" he asks.

"Including the emails and group chats on the Murder Club. We got it all."

"Excellent. Where are you now?"

"On my way in. ETA four minutes."

"Great. I'm here already. See you in a few."

Just as I disconnect, my phone lights up with another incoming.

Sujit Chopra calling.

"Go suck a Faberge egg," I say to myself as I reject the call.

I'm pulling into the parking lot of the old sheriff's station when I get yet another call.

Connor Gantry calling.

That's another one I'd love to blow off, but I can't.

I park and slide the green button.

"Parker, there's an order to the universe and it's there for a reason," Gantry says without preliminary.

Neil DeGrasse Tyson you're not. "Sir?"

"You should have checked with me before issuing those bench warrants," he says. "You ruffled a lot of feathers."

Birds of a kind. "Sir, it was the only way. They were stonewalling us."

"You're too young and brash to understand this now, Parker, so I'm letting you off with a warning this time, but in future, when in doubt, consult your betters."

"Sir," I say unemotionally.

I was prepared for that the minute I decided to call Judge Carter at three this morning to request the bench warrants. It's a small price to pay.

Ramon is at his workstation, working two laptops, a tablet,

and three phones all at once. He raises his hand while he continues to type one-handed. I can never figure out how he's able to do that!

"Diaz, you better be ready to dazzle!" I sing out. "Tell me we got something."

"Got some, jefe?" he sings back. "We frickin' hit the motherlode! Gimme me two more minutes, I'll give you da world!"

David waves a hundred-dollar bill. "He's hacking the encrypted directory hidden deep inside all their hard drives. I have a hundred here that says he can't do it."

I look at Brine. He shakes his head.

"That's an AES-256 bit encryption," Brine says. "Level four. The highest standard of data protection in existence. Even the NSA can't crack it. Too rich for my taste."

"I'll take that bet," Kayla says, fishing a hundred-dollar note from her wallet, "I gotta Benjamin says my brown bruh breaks that badass wide open."

"Well," I say, "nothing like a little healthy competition. Where's Naved?"

Brine jerks his head.

Naved comes up with a fresh cup of coffee in each hand. He offers one to me.

"Thanks," I say.

Ramon lets out a triumphant whistle, loud and piercing enough to double as a factory whistle announcing the start of a shift. "Ramon da man strikes again! I got da muscle *and* I got da muscle! Come and take a look, jefe, we struck gold!"

It takes me a minute to get him to explain what he's found.

When I get it, I'm ready to whistle in delight, too.

Shriek and shout, dance and stomp!

We really did hit the motherlode.

It's not every day that we have actual video coverage of a serial killer committing his crimes.

But that's what it appears the Murder Club had on their

devices, or rather, on the cloud to which they backed up their devices, and which Special Agent Ramon Diaz has miraculously been able to extract and download.

Naved, David, Brine, Kayla, and I are gathered around Ramon's workstation.

Ramon is very full of himself for pulling off the impossible and is crowing about how he cracked an AES-256 bit encryption. "I used a related-key attack to break it. Turns out these dudes were using their stock prices on a specific day as the base key. Once I figured that out, Carlotta ran a deep search trying out multiple related keys based on the stock prices of their six companies on certain days when the stock market hit record highs until I found one where the numbers fit."

He talks about symmetric encryption algorithms using 256-bit keys, converting data and text into a cipher code by using 4x4 blocks of sixteen bytes each, then using multiple round keys using Rijndael's key schedule, and—

I stop him there. "Whoa. Whoa there, digital cowboy. We get it. You're a wizard. All hail the great and mighty Oz. Now, can we take a peek at the actual goodies?"

Ramon grins and taps out a series of commands. "Bring a big bucket, jefe. You gonna get more candy than you can handle!"

He points at his laptop screen. "These files here look like video. I figure they'll be the best place to start. Agreed?"

"Agreed. Let's try that one. That is a date sequence, right?" I point to one of the files. They all have numbers in lieu of names.

Ramon nods. "Yup. System's set to store files by date and time down to the second, in chronological order. That one's the first, dates back quite a few years. Hang on, let me just do a quick preview scrub."

He hits play on one, uses the keyboard to run it through at several times normal viewing speed, stops suddenly, shuts it down, and moves on to the next. I blink and look away after a few seconds, unable to focus. It's all jerky movements and changing camera angles jumbled together in a mishmash. Only Ramon is able to make sense of it, I don't know how. Practice, I guess. Or maybe he just processes visual information differently. After similar brief scans of three or four files in that manner, he sits back and looks up at me.

"Some heavy stuff on them, Susan. You sure you're ready to view?"

He doesn't usually use my name so when he does, I know he's being serious.

I nod grimly. "Hit me."

I don't bother to check with the rest of my team. We're all on the job here, and that job involves viewing some of the worst things human beings are capable of doing to each other. There's no place for squeamish.

"Okay," Ramon says. "These look like they're all captured on surveillance cameras in real time, as they happened. The cameras are probably motion-activated, so the feed switches from camera to camera as the unsub moves through the scene, following him."

By him, he means the killer.

I exchange glances with the others. They're all equally somber, preparing themselves for what's probably going to be a harrowing watch. I do the same. Naved nods. This is something we have to do.

"Okay," I tell Ramon. "Play it."

He taps the space bar, and a video begins to play on his laptop screen.

TWENTY-TWO

I'm expecting grainy images, like the surveillance camera footage they show in movies and TV shows.

But this is nothing like that.

It's almost black and white, like the color has been bleached out of the recording, leaving only a few hints here and there. But the image is sharp enough to make out details of features and even read signs and numbers.

Brine asks a question and David answers with the opinion that it looks like a full color recording that someone used a filter on to turn into a quasi-black-and-white image. He points out hints of red in the recording and mentions a film. *Schindler's List*. I haven't seen the film, but the comparison David is making is not to the movie itself but to its use of color.

In that film, David says, Steven Spielberg chose to film in color but later at the post-production stage, he bleached out all the colors from the footage except for red.

The person who set up these recordings seems to have taken his cue from the master. Apart from objects which are red, everything else is black and white, though the filter gives the entire scene a faint reddish hue. It's a tint that lends everything a malevolent feel, like the world viewed through a devilish blood-tinted lens.

Appropriate, given the subject matter.

We start with a view of the entrance to a subdevelopment named Greenberry Estates.

I feel a small frisson.

I know that place.

It's a trailer park in Canyon Country, only a quarter mile or so from the go-kart track and Indian restaurant that Lata, Natalie and I visited a few days ago. We drove past that very sign coming and going.

"That's in Canyon Country about ten minutes' drive from here," I say to the others.

Except for Naved, none of them actually live in SCV and he only moved here a few months ago. But they all nod, taking my word for it.

A red pickup truck drives into Greenberry Estates. It appears to be very late at night, from the darkness and absence of other vehicles or people.

Something about that truck stirs a faint memory. I follow it around my head, but it leads me nowhere. I swat it down. It's a pickup truck. They're as common here as dirt. I've probably seen a thousand if I've seen one. I focus on watching the video.

The view shifts to the red truck again as it comes around a corner and parks near a trailer.

Most of Greenberry Estates consists of a trailer park where a couple hundred RVs are parked more or less permanently, a few meters from each other on grassy patches. People rent out the parking space and are billed extra for amenities like water, gas, electricity, trash. Some of the residents are so poor they can't afford even those basic amenities and just stay there in their immobile mobile homes.

The rest of the subdevelopment consists of manufactured homes on tiny handkerchief-sized lots, some single wide, others double wide trailers set on cinder blocks and given the trappings of a regular house.

That's the section we're visiting in the video.

The red truck's driver-side door opens and a man gets out.

He appears to be of average height and weight, dressed in coveralls and with a red baseball cap set low on his face, concealing all but the tip of his nose, his mouth, and chin. He walks slowly but with a light step that suggests he's in good shape physically.

I'd estimate his age at early thirties, same as my own.

"Are these cameras on the lot already?" Kayla asks with a speculative tone. "They can't be, right?"

Ramon shakes his head. "Unsub must have set them up."

The view switches to another camera inside the house. The man with the red cap enters the house and stands still for a moment, listening.

After a moment, he moves through the house.

Manufactured homes are pretty much like regular houses, except that instead of brick and concrete or wood, they consist mainly of a metal storage container that's cut open at the top and bottom to accommodate an A-frame roof and a concrete or wooden floor. Spaces for windows and doors are cut out and frames installed. Once you paint them and furnish them and fit them out with plumbing, lights, etc, they look pretty much like regular houses on the inside, but are much cheaper to put up.

The unsub moves through the house until he comes to the first of two bedrooms.

This one has two small children asleep in their beds.

For one heart-stopping moment, I think he's going to go in and kill the children.

But after a few minutes watching them sleep, he moves on.

The second bedroom has what he's here for.

The woman sleeping on the bed wears what appears to be a nurse's scrubs. She's dead to the world. From the way her mouth is wide open and her throat seems to vibrate on screen, I get the sense that she might be snoring. It's impossible to tell for sure because there's no sound on the video.

The unsub unties something at his waist, like he's unbuckling a belt.

Kayla makes a small sound and I know she's thinking the same thing: the bastard is going to assault her.

But instead of a belt, he unties a rope from around his waist.

It's difficult to be certain because of how dark the room is, even with the high-definition clarity of the video, but I'd be willing to bet a hundred dollars that it's a double-braided nylon rope, like the one used to kill Derek Chen.

He holds it up, turning it around his hands to get a firm grip.

Then he looks up at the camera, placed overhead on the low ceiling. I'm guessing it's hidden in the light fixture.

He stares directly at us, as if he actually *sees* us through the lens of the camera.

As if he knows we're watching him, from years in the future, and is *aware* of our presence.

As if he knew we, or someone like us, would find this footage and watch him.

We all curse at the absence of a face.

"Of course he's wearing a mask," Kayla says. "He isn't stupid."

The mask is grotesque, a mass of deformities and warts and protruding lumps that add up to a monstrous whole. I can't place it from any horror film franchise but then again, I don't get much time to catch up on the latest releases.

"Anyone recognize what character that is?" I ask.

"That's no movie bad guy, jefe," Ramon says. "It's one of those monster masks they sell at Halloween."

"Looks like the Boogeyman," Brine says.

The unsub stares up at the camera for a few more seconds, as if making sure we're paying attention.

He raises the clothesline, showing it to us, to the camera.

The gesture has an element of demonstrativeness. As if he's proud of what he's about to do and is showing us how we can also do the same.

Watch me now, watch how I do this.

My skin prickles and an icy rod presses against my spine.

The unsub bends over the sleeping woman—the sleeping mother—and in a single, quick move, wraps the clothesline around her throat and tightens it with muscular force.

The corded muscles in his forearms, shoulders, and back work as he puts his strength into it.

The mother never has a chance.

If there's any struggle on her part, it's only a brief, instinctive thrashing of her legs and lower body, which is easily subdued by the killer. He's literally sitting on her.

Her face and the trauma inflicted on her throat are mercifully concealed from our view by his own upper body and the back of his head.

But I can still imagine it and from the silence of the others, I know they're imagining it, too.

It's horrible.

My gut churns with a sick sensation.

I won't actually be sick, I don't think, because I've had enough experience with bastards like this one over the last decade, but I'm glad I haven't had a full breakfast this morning.

The killer's elbows stick out as he pulls the ends of the rope tight.

I can almost *feel* the moment when he snaps her spinal cord, ending her life.

Done, he remains crouched over her for a moment.

Listening perhaps?

Alert to sounds from the other room?

From outside?

After what seems like an eternity, he climbs off her, sits on the side of the bed, and then he does something wholly unexpected.

He has a moment of what looks very much like genuine remorse.

He lowers his face to his hands, bends over his knees, and his body shudders, spasming.

"Is the fucker actually... crying?" Kayla asks with a tone of disbelief.

Nobody answers but my instinct says *yes, he is*.

After venting himself, he gathers himself up, then goes out of the bedroom, checks briefly on the kids in their room—still asleep, mercifully, I think. For all the horrors that I witness in my line of work, the one thing that always threatens to break me is the violence done to young children. Still, my nerves remain on edge for every second that he watches those two kids sleeping.

I just strangled your mother to death. What should I do with you? I imagine him thinking.

It's a relief when he finally moves on to the kitchen.

He opens the refrigerator door and looks in.

For a half second, I start to hope that he'll take off his mask, and the light from the fridge will illuminate his face so we can get an ID, but no such luck.

He takes out a cardboard container of milk and finds a half-eaten pack of Oreos on the counter.

He sits at the tiny kitchen table, eats the Oreos, and drinks the milk, lifting just the bottom of the mask to expose his mouth. The top angle of the camera makes it impossible to even make out his chin and mouth clearly. He eats with the eagerness of a kid after a hard sports game.

"Fucking unbelievable!" Kayla says.

Brine makes a sound. "He's a ghoul."

David points to the screen. "He set up the cameras himself, like Ramon said. Had to have. It's the only explanation."

"That means he likes to record himself committing his crimes," Naved says. "To rewatch later maybe? To relive the pleasure?"

"Or because he wants to be seen," I say.

They all look at me.

"We live in an age of social media and the internet, where oversharing is a part of our culture," I say. "Maybe he wanted these videos to be viewed by people so that he could feel seen."

"Validation," Kayla says. "Yeah, that makes sense."

"It could also mean that he knew they would end up in the hands of law enforcement sooner or later," David says.

"So... he wants to get caught?" Brine asks.

"Exactly," David replies. "Most serial killers want an audience. They enjoy attention, especially public fame. And for the smartest ones, the investigators hunting them are the only ones capable of fully understanding, and appreciating, the sheer effort and intelligence involved in getting away with their crimes."

"Mutual respect," Brine suggests.

David nods. "If a tree falls in the forest and no one sees it, did it really fall?"

"That's some heavy Schrödinger's cat sci-fi analysis," Ramon points out. "I like Susan's theory better."

"The way he looks up at the camera at crucial points—he's playing to his audience. It's like a well-rehearsed script he's enacting," I say.

"Or re-enacting?" Brine asks.

I look at him.

"I did a lot of theater in school and college," he says defensively. "The way he moves, the way he holds himself—"

"Like he's posing," Kayla says.

"Yes, as if he's blocked out his movements in advance, like we do on stage, and is working off a script, but also as if he's recreating the whole thing from memory. In theater, my acting teacher taught us that all real art has to come from real emotion. The only way for an actor to come across as believable in a performance is to put something from his own life into it. Maybe this guy is re-enacting something that actually happened in his own life once."

"Reliving the original crime over and over again," I say slowly. "I like it, Brine."

Brine looks pleased. As the baby of the team, he's very accepting of his position, content to carry and fetch, and work in a supportive capacity. It's not that he isn't ambitious, the word is baked into the DNA of every FBI hire, but simply that he wants to learn and knows that the best way to do that is to shut up and listen. Still, he often comes up with small insights that I find very valuable.

"Okay," I tell Ramon. "Let's look at the others."

There are seven more videos in the folder. It takes us the better part of two hours to go through them all, stopping after each one to discuss and compare notes with the previous videos.

They are all very, very similar.

Too similar to be a coincidence.

The houses change.

The women change, slightly.

Some have only one child, one has four kids, the others two or three.

But they're all mothers of small children below the age of puberty.

They're all fairly poor, even the one who lives in a relatively decent condo in the Svenson Ranch neighborhood. The condo was her settlement in the divorce, we learn later, from a husband who ended up a homeless drug addict and OD'd on the street.

He records himself on multiple cameras in every instance.

Always driving the same beat-up old red pickup truck. An ancient Ford, we all agree by the time we're done viewing the videos, though the license plate is consistently blurry. Mud on the plates, most likely, an old trick.

He always checks on the children each time. Watching them sleep before and after he commits the killings.

It's not a murderous gaze, I believe.

He doesn't look like he wants to kill them.

It's like he feels for them.

In every video, he uses the same method to kill the women.

In only one case, a woman starts to fight back—rousing out of sleep just at the moment that he starts to put the clothesline around her throat—but her struggle is short-lived. He's too strong, too determined, and even though she's much larger than him, and probably heavier, too, he prevails in the end. They end up on the floor, but it's carpeted, and the three children in the next room sleep through it.

When it's over, he hauls her off the carpet and places her back onto the bed.

He then rearranges her corpse so that she's once again lying on her stomach, face turned away. From the care with which he does this, and the way he adjusts her hair and the angle of her head, it's clear that this is important to him.

Staging is a crucial part of many serial killers' crime scenes. Almost always because they're trying to recreate the original crime, something that they committed years or even decades earlier. That's the fountainhead, the original wellspring from which all these other crimes spring.

After we're done viewing the videos, we discuss these details at length, tossing around theories.

Naved excuses himself to take a call before returning a few minutes later, not looking happy.

Whatever it is, it will have to wait.

We've got a big break on the case, and I'm keen to keep the momentum going.

"Okay, so now we know this is our guy. It has to be. Naved,

I need you to press SCVPD. These are all local crimes, they happened right here in Santa Carina Valley. There have to be files on each of them. Maybe McDougall or one of his bulls already knew they had a serial killer operating locally. We need them to hand over all those files and materials. For all we know, they might already have the killer on a list of suspects they've been looking at already. With this video evidence and the additional details, it should be possible to make a definite ID and nab the guy. We could close this case out today."

Naved nods as he hears me out, then shakes his head slowly and says, "That's not going to happen, Susan. I just got a call. We have a problem. A very big one."

TWENTY-THREE

The brand new sheriff's station of Santa Carina Valley is situated on an overlook, with a sweeping view of the entire valley. On three sides is a steep fall. The imposing entrance is just off Whitey Canyon Road.

The two-story building is all brick and glass and looks like a part of the landscape now, but it was only completed less than six months ago, heavily over budget and almost a year late. The project was among the most hotly debated items during the last municipal elections, the chief bone of contention being that McDougall's family-owned realty development firm was in business with the Texas-based company that secured the contract for the construction of the new station, as well as a much more lucrative contract for the new central mall scheduled to be built on the site of the old town mall, starting a year and a half from now.

The McDougalls were an old family, one of the founders of the city, and it would take a lot more than allegations of corruption to dent their ironclad reputation.

McDougall's office reflects that power and untouchability. As does the fact that he remains seated as Naved and I enter.

Behind him, the glass walls of his spacious office boast a spectacular view of the valley but I'm not here to sightsee. I'm pissed
off and spoiling for a fight.

"SAC Parker," says Chief McDougall. "Glad you could
make it."

"You didn't give me much choice, chief," I say.

He gives me an amused look. "Well, since this is a joint
investigation, it's only natural that we should meet and
exchange notes, don't you think?"

"The joint investigation is being run out of the old sheriff's
station," I say, working hard to keep my tone civil. "You're
welcome to drop by anytime. Besides, you've assigned Detective
Seth to liaise with the Bureau on behalf of SCVPD and he was
right there beside me, working the case."

"Liaise is the right word, SAC Parker," McDougall says.
"Detective Seth works for me. I'm the one in charge."

I bite back a response and say, "That's why I'm here, chief.
So, what can I do for you?"

He smiles, pleased at my conceding the first round to him.
"Tell me, SAC Parker, where are you with the Derek Chen
murder?"

He still hasn't asked us to sit, but I'm not about to remain
standing before him like a schoolgirl summoned to the princi-
pal's office. I take a seat and make myself comfortable, taking my
time about it.

Naved follows my cue.

After a suitable pause, I speak casually. "We've caught a
major break in the investigation. We now believe there are at
least eight other related murders, possibly more. We're investigating this as a serial killer case."

McDougall raises his bushy eyebrows. They could do with a
trim. So could the copious growth sprouting from his ears and
nostrils.

"Let's not jump to conclusions, Parker," he says. "This is a joint investigation and the Derek Chen murder occurred in my jurisdiction. As of now, it's a single murder and that makes it SCVPD's case. You may have pulled some strings to get yourself this case, but if you think you're going to turn it into another media circus to boost your career, you've got another think coming. We don't just decide randomly to call single murders a serial killing unless we actually have hard evidence linking it to other murders. Or didn't they teach you that at Quantico?"

Naved speaks up. "Sir, what SAC Parker means is that we've found new evidence that shows irrefutably that the same killer committed other murders."

McDougall frowns at Naved, as if disappointed that he even presumed to speak out of turn. "Before we go any further, let me ask: Was any of this so-called new evidence the product of the FBI's recent search warrants served on several friends of Derek Chen?"

Naved looks at me.

"Yes," I say.

McDougall nods. "Thought so. In that case, we're not going to discuss that any further." He jabs a finger at me. "You need to hand over those devices and any product of your searches to SCVPD right now. All of it."

Now it's my turn to look at Naved before turning back to McDougall.

"Why the hell would I do that? The devices were obtained as a result of federal warrants. That makes all the contents the Bureau's property. Besides, it's material evidence of multiple homicides."

McDougall leans forward, his eyes cold and lips tight. "What it is, is illegally obtained private and confidential information belonging to private citizens whose rights were violated. You need to hand over all of it to me immediately."

I frown. What the hell is this? I feel like I've been sandbagged. "The warrants were perfectly legal. I spoke to the deputy director this morning about them, and he had no issues. They're signed by federal judge Alicia Carter and are based on a sworn affidavit by Margaret Chen."

McDougall smiles as if he's enjoying having to break the news to me: "Margaret Chen suffered a stroke around 9 a.m. this morning. She's in a coma, and because of her age and condition, isn't expected to recover."

That comes as a bit of a shock, but it doesn't deter me. "Doesn't change a thing. The affidavit is still valid, so is the warrant."

McDougall shakes his head, still grinning. "Her executive assistant Fiona Worthing was present as a witness when you had Chen sign the affidavit, right?"

"Right." I have a sinking feeling I know what he's going to say next.

"Right, so Worthing says that Chen wasn't in her right mind when she agreed to your request. She claims that her employer was stricken by grief and mentally incompetent to make any major legal decisions."

"Even so, chief, the warrant was valid at the time of service. The devices and the data obtained off the cloud is legally admissible as evidence."

McDougall looks at Naved. "Detective Seth, what time did your task force begin downloading the data?"

Naved looks at me. I shrug. He might as well tell the truth. The exact time down to the nearest micro-second will be stamped on the digital files anyway; there's no point lying about it.

"I don't recall the exact time, but it was probably around nine-thirty or so," Naved says.

McDougall looks at me. "Chen was in a coma by then. The affidavit was no longer valid. The warrants weren't worth the paper they were printed on. Anything you got off those cloud servers was inadmissible."

"Now, hold on a minute, chief," I say, starting to feel my face growing hot. "That's not how it works. If you really want to go down this path, let's get some lawyers in here and let them thrash it out. But until someone with authority over me tells me to cease and desist, I'm going to keep using that data as evidence."

McDougall points to my phone. "I think your phone's ringing."

I look at my phone. It is in fact ringing. I've kept it on silent and because I was caught up, didn't notice the vibration.

Connor Gantry calling.

"SAC Parker," says the deputy director in my ear. "There's a serious issue with those bench warrants you signed today. I've just been informed that—"

"Sir," I say, interrupting my boss who hates anyone interrupting him, "we have solid evidence of the killer. It's a serial killer and he's killed a number of women. We can nail him on that evidence alone."

"Parker," Gantry says when he resumes, in a colder tone, "you are to hand over all data files obtained as a result of those unlawful search warrants to Chief McDougall right away. Any evidence you found is now tainted and will be inadmissible in a court of law. Do you understand me?"

"Sir, we can get this guy. Once we do, there's sure to be ample evidence to link him to the murders. Even if we aren't able to use these files, we'll still have him. We can take a killer off the streets."

"I'll say this once more for the last time," Gantry says sharply. "Hand over all evidence to McDougall. That's a direct order."

And before I can say anything else, he's hung up.

McDougall grins at me knowingly. "Got your hat handed to you, did you?"

"Chief, don't do this. You can claim the arrest, if you like. I just want to stop him from killing more women."

McDougall ignores me. He snags his landline phone off the cradle and holds it out. "Call your team and ask them to bring the devices and files over to me right away."

I shake my head slowly. "I'm not going to do that, chief."

His eyes narrow. "Either you do what I ask, or I'll have you arrested for obstruction of justice."

"You'll arrest *me* for obstruction of justice?" I repeat, hardly able to believe my ears.

"You heard me."

I stand up abruptly, knocking my chair over. It hits the floor behind me with a clatter but I'm already off to the races, talking furiously: "Listen, chief, I don't know what bug bit you on your ass today, but that's BS. I'm heading up this task force, investigating a series of brutal homicides committed by a psychopathic serial killer operating right here in Santa Carina Valley. I have hard evidence linking Derek Chen's murder to at least eight earlier killings. That makes a total of nine murders. There are possibly more that we don't know about yet. This is a guy who takes great pleasure in committing vicious, violent homicides, and it looks like he's been getting away with it for years. That's not going to look too good for you and SCVPD once the whole story comes out."

"Are you threatening me?" McDougall bellows, the veins in his neck standing out.

"I'm trying to make you see sense. You work with me on this and I'm happy to share the spotlight with you. Hell, for all I care, you can hog the whole spotlight. I'm only interested in putting this psycho behind bars. In case you've forgotten, that's supposed to be your job, too."

McDougall glowers at me. "Parker. You've gone too far this time."

I hear the door open behind me.

McDougall must have jabbed an intercom button to summon in his flunkeys. I was too busy mouthing off to notice.

"Take SAC Parker into custody, book her, and charge her for obstruction of justice," McDougall barks to the two uniformed officers behind me.

They move forward without hesitation, removing their handcuffs and ordering me to put my hands behind my back.

I start to resist then see Naved shaking his head slowly, once. His eyes plead with me not to do anything to make this worse.

As I feel the cold steel on my wrists, I look at McDougall.

"Why are you doing this, chief?" I ask. "Did someone get to you? Is it Trevor Blackburn? Is he pressuring you to derail the investigation somehow? Are you in business with him?"

McDougall looks at me with disgust. "Take her away."

"Blackburn's not the subject of my investigation, chief," I call out as the two officers lead me to the door. "You don't have to do this. All I want is the killer."

There's no reply from McDougall.

I'm led out of his office, through the station, and down to the basement, where I'm shown to a holding cell.

As the heavy bars clang shut on me, my first thought is of my daughter Natalie.

TWENTY-FOUR

I'm left in the holding cell for several hours.

They've taken my phone and weapons—my primary as well as my backup gun. I've been put in the last cell in the row. The cell opposite me is empty, and to my right is a blank wall. The corridor on my left is too long for me to be able to see anything except the bars of the other cells. At the other end of that corridor is the door through which I was brought in, operated by a buzzer on the other side. Nobody has come in or gone out since I was put in here. From the occasional sounds of coughing, babbling, and the unmistakable sound (and smell) of flatulence, I know there's at least one or two other occupants down here, but I have no interest in talking to them.

For the first few hours, I keep expecting someone to come and bring me to booking. That never happens. Either McDougall's bulls are deliberately taking their own sweet time, or they've gotten busy with something else.

When Naved and I drove here, it was around noon, lunchtime, and we were just about to break to grab a bite before he told me about the call from the chief. By my estimate, it's either late afternoon or early evening now.

Natalie will have been home at least a couple of hours. In another hour or so, she and Lata will sit down to dinner. They're not really expecting me because they know how hectic the first few days of a new investigation can get, but Lata would have sent me a message just to check by now. When I don't respond, she'll assume I'm too caught up to answer and go ahead without me. She won't start to worry until later tonight when she puts Natalie to bed and sees that I still haven't replied or even called in to say goodnight to my daughter.

At that point, even Natalie will worry a little.

When I was abducted at gunpoint on my front doorstep by Splinter's accomplice last Christmas Eve, then held captive in his basement therapy room, or dungeon torture chamber, which is how I think of it, Natalie and Lata spent three harrowing days and nights.

I'm pacing the floor of my cell, burning up brain cells, when I hear the jarring buzz of the cell block door opening.

Footsteps coming down the corridor.

Stopping before my cell.

"Are you okay?" Naved asks.

I stare at him.

"Okay," he says, "stupid question. McDougall behaved like an AH. He shouldn't have done this to you."

"Oh," I say with mock sweetness. "Is that what happened? I thought that's just his personality."

His face is serious, but he manages to crack a hint of a smile. "You weren't exactly playing nice with him either, you know. He has a thing about women mouthing off to him. It brings out the ornery in him."

"Oh," I say, batting my eyelashes, "did poor big dumb sheriff feel emasculated because itty bitty little woman stood up to him?"

He laughs at that one. "Okay. I'm getting you outta here, so I need you to put the sarcasm on ice till we've left the station.

Right now, he's just grandstanding. Push him any harder and you'll make an enemy for life. And you don't want to do that."

I'm tempted to retort to that, too, but just then I hear the jangling of a keyring and decide to hold my tongue.

A uniformed cop appears, carrying the keyring in question, and looks at me intently. His nameplate says *Chris Suarez*.

"Boy, you must have really touched a nerve there to get Mac so mad at you, sister."

I stare back at Officer Suarez. "I'm not your sister."

He laughs and says, "Step back, please. Walk to the back of the cell and keep your hands where I can see them at all times."

I do as he says.

Officer Suarez unlocks the door and holds it open, stepping back.

"Hope you enjoyed your stay," he says. "Come back anytime!"

He laughs at his own wit.

I flip him the bird as I walk away, but do it in front of myself, so he can't see it.

Naved sighs and shoots me a look.

A few minutes later, Naved and I step out of the front door of the sheriff's station into a blood-red sunset.

A soft breeze down the hillside brings the sweet smell of orange blossoms to me. The aroma is sometimes mistaken for jasmine or night blossom but to me, it always smells like a beautiful spring evening. The sun is low on the horizon, about an hour from setting. I'm relieved that Lata and Natalie didn't have to worry why I hadn't texted or come home tonight.

I've got my phone back and start it up again. It instantly lights up with multiple notifications. I tap on the WhatsApp from Lata first. The timestamp says she sent it just a few minutes ago.

Home for dinner?

> Doesn't look like it. Might be a long night.

I don't expect a reply instantly but just as I switch over to the task force group chat, a notification buzzes.

It's Lata again:

> DPSS came by for a house visit. U know anything about it?

I frown at the message. DPSS stands for Department of Public Social Services. I can't think of any reason why they would visit my house.

> Nope. Everything ok?

> All fine. Talk when you get home. With N now.

That means she doesn't want to talk on the phone right now because Natalie would overhear—read Lata's lips—and that makes me even more anxious. I'm inclined to call anyway, but I'm only five minutes from home. I decide it's simpler to just drive over and stop there on my way back to the command center.

"Hey," I say to Naved, "I'm going to stop by my place for a minute if that's okay with you."

I start toward my car, but Naved remains standing.

"What?" I ask.

"He wants a word with you first," Naved says.

"To hell with that," I say indignantly. "I'm not talking to McD right now. He cost us almost a whole day. Let's get back to work."

"I don't mean McDougall," Naved says. "You know he's just the puppet. I'm talking about the guy who pulls his strings. He's the real reason McD let you out."

I frown at Naved across the top of my Prius. "Who are you talking about?"

Naved gestures with his chin.

I turn and look over my shoulder.

There's a car parked across the gravel lot. I barely glanced at it when I stepped out. Now I see that it's a long, low-slung, sleek, black machine that you could easily mistake for a Batmobile. Its supercar looks and impossibly deep black paint job proclaim it as high end uber-luxury. Definitely not the usual ride you see around SCV. And definitely not something I'd expect to see parked in the sheriff's station lot.

I look back at Naved questioningly.

"He just wants a few words. I can drive your car back to the command center if you like."

I shrug and toss him the keys.

He catches them one handed and adds, "See you in a few. Call me if there's anything."

As he gets into my Prius, I walk over to the black hypercar.

When I get closer, I see the embossed logo. It's an inverted E touching a B.

I'm no car freak but Amit was into them, and I recall him pointing one of these out to me once when we were dating and telling me that the letters stand for the company's founder. Ettore Bugatti.

The passenger side door opens as I approach.

I look inside.

The man behind the steering wheel is clad all in black, like his car. A black cardigan over a white tee shirt and black jeans.

He flashes a handsome grin at me. Impossibly white teeth in a lightly tanned face. Gray eyes bracketed by crinkles when he smiles. Mahogany hair threaded with silver. He carries his five decades very well.

"Good evening, Susan," Trevor Blackburn says. "May I request the pleasure of your company?"

TWENTY-FIVE

Sitting in Trevor Blackburn's Bugatti after spending most of the day in a police lock-up is surreal.

The interior of the car feels like the cockpit of a black spaceship hurtling through space. The illusion is heightened by the absence of streetlights or buildings. The only light visible outside the dark, tinted windows is starlight. To my left, rapidly falling behind us, is the reddish hue of the fading twilight. There's nothing but the powerful car carrying us across the dark starlit landscape, and the two of us in this luxurious enclosed space. It's a strange, dreamlike experience. Is this what it feels like to be a jetsetter?

We're driving across the Santa Carina Hills, north of the valley, en route to Agua Dulce. The setting sun is low on the horizon, visible only in the gaps between the mountains. I wonder if Blackburn has a residence in Agua Dulce. It is considered the millionaire's backyard of SCV. I don't recall ever hearing about it. Then again, we don't exactly move in the same circles.

"I'm sorry about the way Gerry behaved with you today," Blackburn says.

Gerald "Gerry" McDougall.

"The thing about pit bulls is they're only trying to please their owners. They're not really bad dogs, they're just bred and trained that way," I say.

I feel him turn his head to look at me once, then he bursts out laughing. It's a throaty, full-bodied laugh, uninhibited but with the natural reserve of the born wealthy upper crust.

"You live up to your reputation, I have to say, Susan Parker."

"Yeah, well, like the old saying goes, don't judge me by my enemies, judge me by my friends."

He throttles down, the expensive machine's rumble lowering its tone to a growl, then a tiny vibrating sound, felt rather than heard. He rolls to a halt on the shoulder.

He looks at me. "I want to show you something."

He gets out.

I take a moment. I'm still mad as hell at McDougall for ambushing me like he did, and knowing that he was only the puppet makes me want to vent my anger at this rich bastard who was pulling his strings.

But where's that going to get me? Back in a holding cell? Or worse?

I have to approach this differently, come at it from a new angle. Deal with Blackburn, get him to make McDougall cooperate with me so we can work together to catch the serial killer who's killing single moms in my town. Eight already on video, and who knows how many more that we don't know about.

I know Blackburn is here because of Derek Chen's murder and the Billionaires Murder Club. But this is about much more than six One Percenters now.

Right then and there I make a decision that if I have to make some kind of backdoor deal with Blackburn to get what I want, I'll make it.

I climb out of the Bugatti.

"How much does a jalopy like this go for these days?" I ask casually.

He laughs softly. "Nineteen million dollars. It's the only one in existence, by the way. Its name in French translates as 'The Black Car'."

I slam the door shut harder than it's meant to be shut. "I guess that's the color of the money you used to buy it."

He smiles at me. "Miss Parker, I get that you're mad at me."

I smile back, showing teeth. "Oh no, Mr. Blackburn. You've got me all wrong. I'm not mad at you. I just happen to hate your ilk."

"My... ilk?" he asks, the smile still lingering on his face.

"Your kind. Filthy rich, powerful men who believe the world is theirs for the taking."

He shrugs. The smile hasn't left his face. "Whose is it then?"

"Everybody's?" I say.

"Come on, Susan. May I call you Susan? I'm going to call you Susan. Susan, get real. I know you're not that naïve."

"Aren't I? Maybe you'd like to tell me what and who I am then?" I ask.

He gestures at a grassy valley bathed in the orange yellow light of sundown. "All this land out there. Waiting to be developed. It could be another Santa Carina. I intend to develop it and build a city here. Do you know what it takes to build a city, Susan?"

"Money? Power? Corruption?" I say.

"Sure. Make the world go round. But more than that, it takes chutzpah."

"Also, audacity. Self-confidence. Arrogance. Sounds like you." I look out at the valley below us. It's barely visible, just a few humps and clumps between the rolling hills. But I believe him when he says it's a good location for a city. He'd know.

"Sure," he says, undaunted. "Do you really think just

anyone can do it? Of course not. It takes a certain kind of man. I happen to be that kind of man. I understand that you dislike me for it. I get that a lot. But it doesn't change the fact. I can do things like this, build a city, that not everyone can."

"Trevor," I say, "it's been a long day. A long few days, in fact. I have a job to do. I've already lost most of today because of your pet pit bull. I'd really like to get back to it."

"I understand, Susan. I've already expressed my regret for how the chief handled that with you earlier today. He over-stepped. Putting you in the lock-up was unnecessary and excessive. He was just supposed to talk to you, get you to play ball."

I exhale. "It wouldn't have made a difference. You see, Trevor, my job is to catch killers like this one who's killing single mothers in their homes while their children are sleeping in the next room, sometimes in the same room itself. He likes to record these kills on high-definition video for posterity. But it doesn't change the fact that he's a dangerously sick murderer who's clearly addicted to it and will go on killing until he's stopped. And right now, I'm the only one who can stop him because I seem to be the only one who's looking for him."

He looks at me, his eyes glinting in the dusky light. The sun has gone down but there's more than enough illumination in the air to see the line of his jaw and his features.

"You're not the only one," he says. "We've been looking for him for some time now."

I try to decipher the expression in his eyes. It's difficult to get a read. I don't know Trevor Blackburn well enough to have a yardstick by which to judge his reactions and expressions.

"You and the rest of your Murder Club?" I ask.

His mouth twitches. "I like that. We *are* a Murder Club, aren't we?"

"What do you plan to do if and when you find him?" I ask.

He looks out into the distance, features limned by the magic glow of dusk. "Talk to him."

"About what? City planning and administration?"

"About what he does, why he does it."

I sigh. "Trevor. I hate to break it to you but you're not the first person to be fascinated by serial killers. None of you are. There's a whole subcommunity out there. Reddit groups. True crime junkies. A lot of them, not surprisingly, are women. There are studies published about why women, especially educated, relatively privileged young women, are obsessed with true crime, particularly serial killers. I don't know the psychopathology behind it. But there are experts you can talk to. You're richer than God. You don't have to go on YouTube. You can hire the best criminologists, talk to them, try to figure out the phenomenon. Get permission to visit the penitentiaries where convicted serial killers are serving out their term. Watch *Mindhunter*. Documentaries. There's tons of things you can do. But the one thing you *can't* seriously expect to do and survive doing, is talk to a real flesh-and-blood serial killer out in the wild. Derek Chen learned that the hard way. Let that be a lesson to you all."

"Derek Chen was weak," Blackburn says. "We knew he didn't fit in. But he kept coming back. Even after we told him no, he came back and pleaded—*pleaded*—with us to let him in. We tolerated him but we knew he didn't have the stomach for it. The first time we watched one of the kills, he threw up on himself. He couldn't even make it to the toilet or use a trash can. He just puked all over himself."

"Sounds like a natural, perfectly reasonable human reaction," I say. "Those videos are puke-worthy."

"I'm betting you didn't puke," he says, eyeing me. "You're a strong woman, Susan Parker."

"I'm a federal agent, Trevor, and right now, you seem to be in the way of my doing my job. Speaking of which, you've just admitted to watching the videos. We have hard evidence of the files on your data cloud. That's enough for me to arrest you and put you behind bars in a federal lock-up. You had evidence of capital crimes and did not report them. That makes you an accomplice to those crimes."

He shrugs without actually moving his shoulders. He's somehow able to convey what he wants to convey with minimal gestures, so when he does move, or look, or turn to look, it's with the full intensity of his personality.

"I know you have handcuffs right there, I can see them when your jacket rises. Put them on."

He offers me his wrists, held together. I'm already reaching for my handcuffs, unclipping them from the back of my belt, but my hand stays there, as I think it through.

When I hesitate, he says, "I see that you're weighing the consequences. You've already seen what happens when you come at me and my friends with federal bench warrants. Sure, you'll have the satisfaction of locking me up, maybe you'll lock all of us up for a few hours. But then you'll have to deal with the fallout. Are you prepared for that? I know you're a great detective. I've read your file. But how good are you at politics, media management, legal tactics? Do you really want to spend the next several months of your life, maybe even the next few years, tied up in knots? Or do you want to keep doing what you do best? Putting killers away and saving innocent lives? Pick your battles carefully, Susan Parker, and pick your enemies even more carefully. Because every new enemy you make is a friend lost for life."

TWENTY-SIX

Trevor is still waiting, wrists held out.

I curse myself silently, but know I have no choice.

The instant I slip these cuffs on him, the game changes for good. There'll be no going back. Half of law enforcement is arresting bad guys. The other half—the more important half, some would say—is knowing who not to arrest and when and why not to arrest them. FBI agents often have to let a number of people walk in order to nab the actual criminals. You have to know when to cut your losses.

I bring my hands out front again, without the handcuffs.

Trevor nods once as if he was expecting it, shoots his cuffs, and lowers his wrists.

"You're a smart woman, Susan, but you tend to rush in where angels fear to tread. That stunt you pulled this morning, it cost me. I had an important deal I was about to close. A lot of vital data was on my phone. You made it impossible for me to close that deal in time."

"I find that hard to believe," I say. "All your data is backed up to the cloud. It wouldn't have been hard for you to download it in seconds."

"So I thought. Except your cyber cowboy changed all the passwords and shut me out."

I shrug. "Routine precaution to prevent you from going back in and deleting files. We were actually done with your devices by noon. You would have had them back by the end of the day, with your original passcodes restored, but I got shanghaied by your pet pit bull."

"How the hell did your people break into it? Even the NSA can't crack 256-bit encryption. Wait, don't tell me. Your cowboy figured out the key. That's it, isn't it? Smart man. He should come work for me."

"The cyber cowboy is a cyber vaquero, Trevor, and he doesn't work for the dark side. He lost his entire family to gang violence, back when he was a banger in East LA. He's dedicated the rest of his life to putting away bad guys. He's not for hire. Now, let's get back on point. Why did you really sic your pit bull on me?"

He looks out at the valley. "I want this guy as bad as you do, Susan. You may not believe that, but it's true."

This is unbelievable. "I know you're used to getting everything you want, Trevor. But some things even all the money in the world can't buy. What the hell do you want with a serial killer? What would you even do with him once you have him?"

He keeps his face averted, preventing me from seeing his eyes. "That's my business."

"No, actually, it's *my* business. I need to find him and arrest him and every minute I stand here talking to you is a minute wasted. For all we know, he could be out there, getting ready to kill another single mother tonight."

"That's not going to happen," Trevor says. "He won't be killing any more single moms. That part of his life is done. He won't get another chance."

"You can't possibly know that," I say.

Trevor turns to look at me directly. Even in the dusky

twilight, the force of his attention is a physical thing. I feel it like a hand on my chest.

"He's coming after us," Trevor says. "He killed Derek Chen. Now he wants to kill the rest of us, one by one."

"And you're sure of this how?" I ask skeptically. "He send you a postcard? An email? Text message? A DM on social media?"

"He told us," Trevor says after a very long pause. "It's on the last video, right at the end. There's no audio but he mouths it to the camera. Ask your daughter."

"My daughter?" I say, startled.

"She reads lips, doesn't she?" he says matter-of-factly.

I blink, caught off guard. "Yes. But I'm not going to show *her* the videos!"

"Then show it to someone at the Bureau who lip reads. Or SCVPD. You'll see it. He clearly says, 'you're next' at the end of that last video."

"And that means he's coming for you? The Murder Club?"

Trevor nods.

I think about it.

"Okay, let's say I check the video and agree with your conclusion. He's coming after the Murder Club now. He's done Derek Chen, now he wants the rest of you. All the more reason why you should want me to stop him. Unless your idea of a good time is getting stalked and slaughtered by a serial killer."

"If you think I have a death wish, you're wrong," he says quietly. "I can't vouch for the others. Especially Riley. That man is certifiable. I wouldn't put it past him. And Cara has her own weird fixation. They all have sick, twisted ideas about this whole thing."

This is getting curiouser and curiouser, as the cat said. "Sounds like you're not a fan of your fellow Murder Club members, Trevor."

"What can I say? The rich are different, the very rich are weird," he says with a straight face.

I wait for the punch line. It never comes. "And you exclude yourself?" I say.

"I wasn't born rich, Susan. I know you think I was, so does everyone else. But it's all a façade, an act. I covered up my tracks really well. It helps to have almost unlimited resources to do it. I took speech coaches, movement coaches, acting lessons, the works. I changed the way I talked, walked, behaved. I became a different person, one more in line with the image I wanted to project of a born rich guy. Trevor Blackburn is a performance."

I laugh at the audacity. "And you're not really a billionaire? All that market cap and net asset value is just part of the script? Where's the camera?"

"You're missing the point. I assumed a persona that matched the wealth and power. I buried the real Trevor so far down, nobody will ever find it. Not even you and your cyber vaquero."

"Okay, so you covered up your past. It's been done before. Hell, it's almost a part of the American story. Rags to riches, changes name, identity, family history, the works. What does that have to do with catching a serial killer?"

He pauses for another long moment before answering, making his response seem more important for my having waited for it. "I'm not interested in him for the same reasons as the others," he says. "What I want from him is something you wouldn't understand."

"You'd be surprised. Try me."

"No," he says. "That's the one thing I can't talk about. But here's the deal I'm offering you, Susan."

Here it comes. The moment I've been waiting for. *Get ready, Suse. Be prepared to sell your soul.* If that's the only way to get a killer off the streets, then so be it.

"Find him," Trevor says. "You and your team are exceptionally good at what you do. I know that. I had you guys checked out very thoroughly. If you go after this guy, you will find him. I want you to do that."

"You do?" I say, surprised.

"All I ask is that when you have him in your custody, before you turn him over to the Bureau, or to SCVPD, whatever the hell the process is, before you put this guy behind bars to await trial, you give me a couple of hours with him."

I stare at him, speechless for a moment. "You're kidding, right?"

"I don't want to kill him, or hurt him, or torture him. Nothing physical. Nothing kinky. I just want to talk to him. You can wait outside the room. You can have him in chains if you like. Strap him up like Hannibal Lecter in that movie. I just want to be in the same room as him for a couple of hours, to talk."

"Talk about *what*?" I ask.

"That's my business," he says. "That's the part you can't ask me about. You also can't record any part of our conversation, or video it, or eavesdrop in any way. I have to be guaranteed total privacy with him. That's my one and only condition."

"No go," I say firmly. "I can't make that deal. I'll be in direct violation of federal law and multiple statutes covering chain of custody."

"You won't get into any trouble," he says with quiet confidence. "I give you my word."

I'm tempted to tell him his word's worth jackshit to me, but I bite my lip. "I can't do it, Trevor. I don't get why it's such a big deal but it's just not possible. There will be eyes on him the instant he's in custody. I can lie to you now but what would be the point? If that's your dealbreaker, then it's no deal."

His jaw tightens and he gets a hard, steely look in his eyes. "No is not an option, Susan. If you want the Clothesline Killer, you need to figure out a way to give me what I ask."

"Why?" I ask. "Why is it so important that you speak to him alone? What aren't you telling me? And how the hell do you know we're calling him the Clothesline Killer? Even McD doesn't know that! What's going on here, Trevor? What's your real interest in this guy?"

He looks away. "I have my reasons. Just an hour or two. Just talk. You're a brilliant young woman, Susan Parker. Make it happen."

I stare at him, my mind working furiously, trying to make sense of it all. "And then what? You come out and walk away?"

"I walk away."

"And that's it? That's all you want? Two hours with him alone?"

"And privacy. No cameras or listening devices. That's it."

I think about it for a long moment. "And if I do this, you'll stop throwing up hurdles in my way like today? You'll let me get on with my job? You'll get McDougall to back off? Call off your lawyers, who've been badgering the FBI Office of General Counsel all day threatening multiple billion-dollar lawsuits?"

He spreads his hands in a decisive gesture. "Everything. And I'll do you one better, Susan. I won't just back off completely. I'll put all the resources at my command at your disposal. Whatever you need, you just have to ask, and you'll have it. Private jets. Cars. Choppers. Drones. Satellites. You name it. I'll do everything in my power to help you catch this guy. You see, Susan, we really want the same thing. We both want to find him. We have common cause. What do you say? Do we have a deal?"

TWENTY-SEVEN

We drive back in darkness, the hills an alien landscape in the pitch blackness of a rural California night.

With no town or habitation for several miles around, and no streetlights and buildings on the way, we could be hurtling through a barren land to nowhere.

It's several minutes before we're close enough to regain cell-phone coverage. My phone alerts me by immediately buzzing with multiple text messages, emails, and missed call notifications.

Three of them are from Lata.

> Hey, where are you?

> If you're pulling an all-nighter, call me when you have a minute. Need to talk about the DPSS visit.

And from a few minutes ago—

> Hey. Change of plans. Heading out for dinner. In case you can get away for a bit, join us at Royal Indian Kitchen. N would be happy. You gotta eat, rite?

What is DPSS doing, visiting my house? There's something in that first text that tells me that whatever it is, it's important. I know my sislaw well enough to read her tone even in a text message.

I frown, looking out the window at the dark countryside rushing past. We're within sight of the lights of Santa Carina Valley now, only about fifteen miles from the city center. I look over at Trevor. He's focused on driving but he's aware of me looking and gives me a quick acknowledging glance.

"Ten minutes," he says quietly.

I nod as I feel my phone buzzing again.

It's Naved. "Everything all right?" he says in a conversational tone that tells me he's asking more than just that simple question.

"Copacetic," I say. "On my way back right now."

"Okay," he says, "listen, I should have mentioned this earlier. I took the liberty of telling the team to pack up and head home. I figured it's already pretty late and I wasn't sure—"

"It's cool," I say. "You did the right thing. I'm actually headed to dinner right now."

"Dinner?" he says.

I can hear him thinking but not voicing the obvious question. "It's a family thing. Lata and Natalie are grabbing dinner at Royal Indian Kitchen, and I'm joining them." A thought strikes me. "Why don't you join us? Do you know where it is?"

"Sure, but if it's a family dinner..."

"No, it's fine. I want to talk to you afterwards."

"Okay," he says. "I'll see you there."

Trevor nods when I look at him.

"Royal Indian Kitchen?" he says.

"If you don't mind?"

He gives me one of his minimalistic shrugs where he barely moves his shoulders yet there's no mistaking it. "I was about to ask you out to dinner. It's the least I can do after disrupting your evening. But I couldn't help overhearing that you're meeting family. And a coworker. So I'll leave you to it."

"Thanks."

I'm still mulling over the part about him asking me out to dinner several minutes later when he pulls into the driveway of the restaurant. It's a small lot, only large enough for about a dozen cars and one stands out immediately. It's a Bugatti too, black, sleek, low-slung and could also be a contender for a Batmobile.

"Isn't that—?" I say.

"No," Trevor says.

I stare at the car as he pulls over. "It looks exactly like this one to me."

Trevor smiles at me. "That's a Bugatti Mistral. Ninety-nine manufactured, all sold. Price tag $5 million. That's a fourth of what my La Voiture Noire cost."

"Which is one of a kind," I say. "Got it. Good to know. I'll keep that in mind if I'm looking to upgrade from my Prius!"

A family of diners exiting the restaurant reacts at the sight of Trevor's car. One of the teenagers points to the other Bugatti and says something excitedly to the rest.

"Thanks for the ride, Trevor. I'll be in touch," I say.

He gives me a look.

"What?" I ask as I try to feel for the door handle. Either there isn't one or I'm not sophisticated enough to find it.

"Family is complicated, I get it," he says as I continue my silent struggle.

I frown, not sure what he means. "I guess."

To my surprise, he gets out and walks around the front of the car. For a minute I think he's inviting himself to dinner with me, then I see that he's walking around to open the passenger side door for me. He holds it open.

Well, that's definitely better than flailing around in search of a door handle or button.

"I'll wait to hear back from you, Susan," Trevor says. "And remember, anything you need."

"Thanks, Trevor," I say.

Since he took the effort of getting out to open my door, I feel it's only polite for me to stand and wait as he gets back in and drives off.

I don't wave or anything, but I do feel a tiny thrill when the other diners all look at me curiously, trying to place me as a celebrity of some sort.

I should know better but I just can't resist confounding them.

"Boy, that was a really nice Uber! Five stars to the driver!" I say.

They stare at me as I go in.

I'm trying hard not to laugh.

Any amusement I'm feeling dies as soon as I spot Lata and Natalie at our favorite booth.

They're not alone.

TWENTY-EIGHT

"Susan, bete, so good to see you again," Sujit says from his seat.

Aishwarya, of course, doesn't even bother to greet me. If she had her way, I'd have been the one cremated sixteen months ago, not her only son. She considers most people unworthy of her attention and has no problem acting like they simply don't exist.

"Mom!"

Natalie practically jumps at me, wrapping her arms around my waist to give me a warm, loving hug.

She signs at me furiously, confident in the knowledge that neither her grandmother nor her great-uncle knows ASL.

Aishwarya alternates between pretending that Natalie's disability is curable—it isn't, she was born with it—or that her deafness means that she's also intellectually disabled, which she most definitely is not.

"Dadu isn't here," Natalie says. "I wish he could have come, too!"

"Where is Kundan?" I ask Lata.

"He's in New York," Lata says. "My mom flew down to LA to close out some kind of business deal with Sujit Uncle. They were in the neighborhood and dropped by. I was going to order in for them, but Aishwarya wanted to go out to dinner, and Natalie got excited about it, too, so here we are."

I find that hard to believe given the way Sujit has been pestering me the past couple of days.

"Have you guys ordered yet?" I ask, trying to get past the obvious. "I'm famished."

Natalie says, "Mom, can Taylor and I go to the water park on Saturday?"

I smile at her. "You mean, like a playdate?"

She starts to answer just as someone approaches our table.

It's the couple who were coming in just as I entered. A young man and woman a little younger than me. Their faces look flushed with probably more than just youth. I can smell the alcohol on them even from five feet away. The woman is holding up her phone to click a picture of me.

"Hey!" I say, raising my hand to block my face. "What do you think you're doing?"

"You're Trevor Blackburn's girlfriend!" she says excitedly in Hindi. "Could you sign your autograph, please?"

I stand up, keeping my hand in front of me to prevent her from taking a picture of my face. "Ma'am. You're mistaken. I'm not anyone's girlfriend. All that man did was drop me off and open a car door for me."

"Nobody does that, not even husbands!" she says insistently, looking at the young man beside her. "Have you ever opened a door for me, Ayushman?"

"Ma'am," I say, "I'm a federal agent. You're disturbing me and my family. Please return to your table and enjoy your dinner."

She looks at me, checking out my hair, my face, my clothes. "Federal agent?" She laughs.

"Okay," I say, "that's enough. Please leave now or I'll have to ask you to undergo a field sobriety test."

They stare at me.

"A drunk driving test," I say for their benefit. "One of you was driving that Audi I saw you park outside, right? You're both clearly intoxicated. How do you think you'll do if you're tested for your blood alcohol level?"

The husband mutters something in his wife's ear and tugs at her shoulder as he backs away. She shoots me a withering look.

Everyone in the restaurant is staring at me.

I sit down at the table and attempt a reassuring smile at Natalie, who's wide-eyed and very curious.

"Mom, who's Trevor Blackburn?" she asks me excitedly.

"Nobody, sweetie. Just someone I had to talk to for my case. Look, the food's here. Let's eat. You must be hungry!"

Lata props a menu open to shield her hands from Natalie, and signs: *What the hell was that?*

I sigh and shake my head, signing: *Nothing. Talk later.*

"So how is your business deal coming along, Aishwarya?" I ask as I scoop up some butter chicken with a piece of garlic naan.

"Sujit has been trying to get through to you for hours," Aishwarya says in a critical tone.

"I need to talk to you, Susie bete," he says. "You haven't been returning my calls and texts."

Lata looks a question at me. I shake my head again, indicating that I'll tell her about it later. She continues eating but her attention is on Sujit and me now.

"I've been a little busy, Sujit," I say, serving Natalie another malai kofta and some gravy. "I'm working a case."

"Doesn't sound like it," Aishwarya says unexpectedly. "Looks like you're busy gallivanting around with older men having a good time at the taxpayer's expense."

Both Lata and I look at her at the same time, with what I'd bet are identical stunned expressions.

"Mom!" Lata says. "What are you doing?"

Aishwarya sniffs and takes a sip of her wine, the most expensive label they serve here. She makes a show of picking at her kababs, barely eating a sliver of meat.

"I'm just pointing out the obvious, darling," Aishwarya says. "Women who throw themselves at a certain kind of man in public can't expect to be treated like goddesses or saints, can they?"

Lata looks at her mother furiously. "Stop it."

Aishwarya glances at her sideways. "I can't even talk to my own family?"

Lata jabs a finger at Aishwarya and makes a throat-slicing gesture.

Aishwarya rolls her eyes and sips her wine again as her other hand toys with her pearl necklace.

It's not the quiet family meal I had expected. And it's pretty obvious that Sujit had a lot to do with that. If he thinks because he called the director to get me put in charge of the case, that gives him full access, he's sadly mistaken.

It also makes me more than a little suspicious of his motives.

TWENTY-NINE

"We need to talk," Sujit says as we're leaving the restaurant.

I ignore him and tell Lata, "Give me the keys, I'll drive."

"Um, didn't make sense for us to take separate cars. Sujit said he'll drop us back after dinner." Lata looks at me apologetically. "Sorry."

"It's okay," I say. It's really not but that isn't Lata's fault.

Looks like I'm going to have to endure another ride in another Bugatti tonight. The irony makes me want to puke.

Sujit and Aishwarya walk across the parking lot while I take Natalie's hand and wait at the entrance.

"Mom, is everything okay?" Natalie asks me.

She's been really quiet all through dinner, which isn't like her. She's a smart girl. She feels the tension at these family get-togethers, and she knows Aishwarya well enough to know how bristly she can be. That's family. Can't hide them. Can't hide from them.

I reach down and pick her up.

She's too heavy to carry anymore and that makes me miss the little tyke I used to carry on my hip.

I kiss her on her cheek, marveling at its softness and smoothness.

"Everything's fine, honeycheeks," I say. "It was just a little misunderstanding, that's all."

She giggles. "Honeycheeks." Then she adds, "Dadi was in a bad mood."

"Yes, she was," I say, not sure how else to answer that. She's not wrong. Except that if that was a mood tonight, then Aishwarya is always in a mood.

"Dadi's always in a bad mood," Natalie says, as if reading my mind.

I touch the tip of her nose. "Remember what I always tell you. We can't control how other people feel and think, only how we feel and think."

"What did that lady want?" she asks.

She means the autograph-seeker.

"She was drunk," I say matter-of-factly.

Natalie looks at me intently. "If you have a boyfriend, you'll tell me, won't you, Mom?"

"I don't have a boyfriend, sweetie. No plans to get one either," I say.

"So Trevor Blackbird isn't your boyfriend?" she asks, as if confirming the fact.

"Blackburn. No. He's just someone I had to talk to for a case."

"Is Naved your boyfriend?" she asks.

I turn my head to stare at her. "Detective Seth? He's a coworker! Why would you even ask that?"

"Because he's been waiting for you for hours, Mom."

I turn my head to look where she's looking.

Naved is leaning against my Prius.

He sees me looking and waves.

Natalie waves at him.

Naved waves again at Natalie.

A deep low rumble makes me aware that the Bugatti has pulled up before us. Sujit is at the wheel, glaring up at me. I'm sure it's only because he's aware of American etiquette that he isn't hitting the horn. If this was Delhi, his home stomping ground, he'd be standing on that horn.

"Sweetie, Mom has to go to work now. Lata-bua will take you home, okay?"

I put Natalie down, but she clings to my neck.

"I want to come with you, Mom," she says. "In your car."

I look at Lata who shrugs.

"Wouldn't you rather ride in Sujit Uncle's fancy sports car?" I ask.

Natalie makes a face. "I don't like his car. It smells like Sujit Uncle."

I'm not sure what that means and I'm not inclined to ask. So I shrug and tell Lata that I have to collect my car from Naved anyway, so I'll take Natalie home. She reminds me it's a school night, then gets into the Bugatti with her mother and uncle.

Sujit guns the accelerator harder than needed, producing an irate growl, and zooms out of the parking lot.

Natalie and I walk across the lot to my Prius.

"Uncle Naved!" Natalie says, sounding happy to see him.

Naved knows ASL and signs back.

"Hi, Natalie, how are you, munchkin?"

"I'm good. Mom got called Trevor Blackbird's girlfriend by some drunk lady and Dadi was in a very bad mood because she's always in a bad mood."

Naved raises his eyebrows at me.

I shake my head: *Don't ask.*

I take the keys from him and we all climb into the Prius.

"I'm so sorry, I completely forgot you were coming. When did you get here?"

Natalie signs before he can answer. "Naved Uncle came while you were arguing with the drunk lady. He went out of the restaurant. Why didn't you have dinner with us, Naved Uncle?"

"Yes, why didn't you?" I ask then realize why. "Oh God. I didn't know Aishwarya and Sujit were going to be there as well. I thought it was just Lata and Natalie. I'm so sorry."

"That's all right," he says. "I needed a little time to make some calls to my family in New York anyway."

To Natalie he adds: "My wife and two sons are still back there in New York City. I'm sure they'd love to meet you sometime."

Natalie signs back enthusiastically to concur, then adds solemnly: "Trevor Blackburn is not Mommy's boyfriend. He's just a case she's working on."

I ask Naved to wait while I take Natalie into the house, get her changed into her nightsuit, and put her to bed.

The drive home, short as it was, was enough to lull her, and she's ready to sleep by the time she's done brushing her teeth. I promise her two bedtime stories tomorrow night to make it up to her and kiss her goodnight. She kisses me back and tells me she loves me.

I stand at her bedroom doorway for a moment, watching her as she drops off. I love her like crazy but when I watch her sleeping, I feel like my love is multiplied tenfold. It makes me remember what I'm working and fighting for, putting the predators away to help make the world a safer place for Natalie.

When she was a baby, Amit and I used a baby camera to watch her. I look up at the spot above her bed where the paint is still a little peeled, wondering if I should re-install one, just to be able to check in on her again on those long days and nights when I'm working cases.

I decide against it.

Natalie would consider it a violation of her privacy, and she's not wrong.

As I'm going down the stairs, a message vibrates my phone.

I'm at the Hyatt downtown. If you change your mind, I'd still like to chat. Won't take long.

Sujit just won't quit. Ass.

Lata waits for me at the foot of the stairs. "We really need to talk. Like right now."

THIRTY

Lata hands me a visiting card with a DCFS logo in the top left corner and a DPSS log in the top right corner.

Brook Wentworth, Senior Inspector

Department of Child and Family Services, Los Angeles County

The address lists the Santa Carina Valley office on Golden Valley Road.

"That's the guy who visited today," she says.

The name means absolutely nothing to me.

"What did he want?" I ask, turning the card over.

Lata glances up at the ceiling. We're standing in the kitchen, directly below Natalie's bedroom. "He said DCFS had received a complaint of child abuse."

I stare at her. "What? From who?"

"Policy is not to disclose complainant's identity, he said."

"It's an anonymous complaint? That's crazy. Who would lodge a complaint like that?"

She looks at me. Her arms are crossed across her chest. "I thought maybe you would know."

"I haven't a clue, Lata. Someone complained that Natalie might be abused? Abused by whom?"

"He wouldn't say. But the implication was that it was one or both of us." She gestures. "Who else is there?"

I try to think but nothing about this makes any sense at all. "What else did he say?"

"Not much. He was mostly asking a lot of questions. He wanted to see where Natalie slept, ate, played. He was making a lot of notes. For the file, he said."

There's a file investigating me and my sislaw for suspected child abuse? Of Natalie? My head reels.

"I don't understand. Where is this coming from? Who would file such a complaint?" I look around, trying to think of someone, anyone, with a motive. I come up blank.

"I don't know, Susan, but he scared the shit out of me. He was really serious, a very intense guy. He asked me all kinds of questions, very personal questions. Intimate stuff."

"Like what?"

"Like who I am sleeping with. My sexual preferences. My feelings about younger women. He said women but I think he was really asking about girls. I think he was implying—" She passes a hand across her face, overwhelmed. "It was horrible."

"What?" I can't believe my ears. "This is such bullshit. You don't have to answer all that. That's illegal. He can't ask you questions like that. He can't question your sexual preferences! That's discrimination."

"I didn't know what to do. When he told me there had been a complaint, I was so stunned. He said the questions were routine. I didn't want to seem evasive or avoid answering anything. I wanted to cooperate, so he would finish up and leave."

"Jesus, Lata. I'm so sorry you went through that. I wish I

had been here. I only saw your missed calls after six. My phone was off most of the day."

"How come?" she asks, wiping a tear from her cheek.

I don't want to have to explain to her about how I spent the day in the SCVPD lock-up. Because then I'd have to tell her everything. "It's a long story. I had a really tough day, but this is unbelievable. I can't believe someone would complain."

I walk around the kitchen, trying to think of how to handle this.

"Susan, Susan, listen to me," Lata says, clutching my sleeve. "He'll be coming back this weekend. He asked me when he would be able to interview both of us together, and he also wants to interview Natalie separately the same day. I told him Sunday would probably be good. I didn't want to tell him that when you're working a case, sometimes you don't get a break for days, so I just said Sunday."

"You did good. I'll make sure I'm here Sunday. We'll deal with this together. It's some kind of mistake. It has to be."

"I asked him what the usual procedure was for such a complaint," Lata says. "He said first he has to investigate the matter thoroughly, speak to all the parties concerned, maybe interview neighbors and work colleagues, superiors, bosses, friends, relatives, etc."

I imagine this guy Brook Wentworth talking to our next-door neighbors, Naved, my team, McDougall, Gantry, Sujit, Aishwarya... My head spins and suddenly the rich, heavy Indian curry and buttered naan sits in my belly like lead.

"And then what?" I ask, already knowing and dreading the answer. "What happens when he finishes the investigation?"

She shrugs glumly. "If he finds evidence, that's how he put it, if he finds evidence of abuse, then DCFS, with the support of the sheriff's department, removes the child from the unsafe environment. Those were his exact words. After that, the county decides whether to bring criminal charges."

Removes the child from the unsafe environment. With the help of the sheriff's department. Here in SCV, the LA County sheriff's deputies are the Santa Carina Valley Police Department. That means McDougall's people. Oh, wouldn't that bastard gloat!

They're talking about taking my daughter away from me and filing criminal charges against me—or us—for child abuse.

I thought I was having a lousy day until now. But it just managed to get even worse.

I look at the card again, memorizing the name: Brook Wentworth.

"I'm going to go up and see him tomorrow," I tell Lata. "This has to be some kind of misunderstanding. I'll handle it. You did good, Lata. Don't worry. I'll handle it."

I'm putting up a brave front for Lata, but inside, I'm jelly.

The thought of losing Natalie is unbearable.

If Amit's death made me have a meltdown, then God alone knows what would happen if I lost Natalie.

I can't let that happen, no matter what it takes.

THIRTY-ONE

Walking out of the house, the April air feels cool and crisp after the warmth of the house and the heat I'm feeling after talking to Lata. The car feels stuffy and close after the news I've just received.

"I'm sorry I kept you waiting," I tell Naved as I get back in the Prius. I start the car. "Let me drive you home. It's the least I can do for you bringing my car over."

Naved looks at me as I drive, seeing something in my face. "What happened?"

I shake my head, barely trusting myself to talk.

"What is it?" he asks, sounding alarmed now. "Is Natalie okay?"

At the mention of my daughter's name, I almost lose it. With difficulty, I keep a grip on my emotions. "It's something personal. I don't want to get into it right now."

I feel him staring at me for a long moment.

"All right," he says at last. "But I'm here for you if you want to talk about it."

"Thanks, Naved. This has really turned out to be a lousy day."

"I can only imagine, Susan." He pauses. "We can pick this up tomorrow if you like. We don't have to do this right now."

"No," I say, suddenly afraid of him leaving and me being left alone with all the terrible thoughts now swirling inside my head. "No, I want to do this. We've already lost enough time. I want to work on the case."

"You sure?" he asks as I turn onto Bouquet Canyon.

"I'm sure. Let's do this."

"All right," he says. "But don't jump to conclusions until you hear me out completely. Deal?"

"Okay," I say, more than a little distracted by thoughts of my life and career being upended by a false claim of child abuse. Not to mention Lata's life, too. Who the hell would complain about us? Someone with a grudge?

Naved goes on, "So, you know that I moved out here from NYC, while my wife and sons stayed back, right?"

"Yes," I say, only half listening as I turn onto Plum Canyon.

"I didn't get into details when I first met you because, well, we were kind of busy working the Splinter case."

"Sure."

"Okay, so there's more to it than that." He sucks in a breath. "My wife was actually related to Dr. Rao, Splinter's last victim. So, when he and his entire family were wiped out, she inherited his house."

I glance over at him. He's talking about the house where my husband Amit died. That cuts through the fog of anger and confusion over Lata's news.

"Okay," I say. "Go on."

"She didn't want anything to do with it. It's a murder house. She wanted to sell it. That's actually why I transferred here. To sell the house for her and also, well, so that we could take a break. We'd been having some ups and downs in our marriage."

"Okay," I say, going up Timothy Drive. The neighborhood is dead silent and deserted at this house.

I'm starting to pay a little more attention to Naved.

Maybe it's because I'm too mad about the DCFS complaint to deal with it right now and it's a relief to have something else to think about. Or maybe because the only thing that can really cut through my permanently intense focus is the possibility of learning something new about Amit's death.

I reach the cul de sac at the end of the street and park outside the house Naved is renting. I turn and look at him.

"So you came over here to put some distance between you and your wife and to sell the Rao house, which takes some time these days. Am I right so far?" I say.

So far it makes sense. I've never asked Naved about his personal life because our relationship is strictly professional, but now that he's revealing it, I'll also admit that it was pretty obvious he was estranged from his wife. Kayla mentioned it to me after she overheard him arguing with his wife on a long-distance call.

"Exactly. Which is why I transferred to SCVPD for the duration." Naved looks out the windshield. "There's something else. The house was under a mortgage. Dr. Rao died without having paid it off so technically, the mortgage reverts to the company because of this thing called a Mello-Roos. Boring technical stuff, don't need to get into it. Anyway, the point is that the company is actually owned by Sujit Chopra and Aishwarya Kapoor."

A prickle of unease starts somewhere at the back of my throat. Coincidences always make me suspicious. Maybe because in law enforcement, we know that there are no coincidences, only connections, and connections usually lead somewhere damning.

"My mother-in-law and her brother? That makes sense. I know they're big-time into real estate in the area," I say, willing to give it the benefit of the doubt—for now.

"Yes, but Sujit Chopra reached out and offered me a deal."

"Of course," I say. "That's his style. What kind of sleazy deal did he offer?"

"It was actually a pretty decent deal. They wanted nothing to do with a house in which so many people had died, the last one being his own sister's son. He offered to help me sell it and whatever we got from the sale, he would split it fifty-fifty, that being the amount that Rao had repaid before he died as well as his original down payment."

"Okay," I say. "I'm with you so far. You take a break from your wife. You come down here to SCV. You meet with Sujit Chopra. You make this deal. You put the house up for sale. You split the proceeds, maybe make your wife happy in the process, all's well that ends well. I get it. But why are you telling me all this?"

He takes a deep breath and releases it. I sense that he's about to get to the heart of it, and that it's going to be something unpleasant. I just know. It's been a lousy day, and it looks like it's not yet over.

"Because I am who I am," Naved says, "and because I promised you that I would keep digging into Amit's death until I found something, I checked out both of them."

"Both of whom?" I say. "You mean Sujit and Aishwarya? Wait. What do you mean, you *checked* them out?"

He looks at me. "I used the SCVPD system to track their GPS history."

I frown. "To map out their movements?"

It's routine for cops to look up a suspect's GPS history to see if their alibis hold up, or if they were in the vicinity of the crime when it occurred despite claiming they weren't. Most crimes these days are solved through GPS history. The vast majority of criminals don't realize that everywhere they go, they're being tracked by their own phones. With the GPS history, it's not difficult to then find surveillance cameras in the vicinity and find them on camera to corroborate. That double whammy is key evidence that puts away more lawbreakers than actual investigation these days.

But why would Naved have checked my mother-in-law and her brother's GPS history unless...

"You suspected something?" I say. "Something to do with Amit's death?"

Naved nods once. "It came up in conversation when Sujit and I talked about the house. There was something about the way he evaded a question or two that raised my antenna. I wanted to confirm a hunch."

"And? What did you find?" I ask.

I feel the skin on my forearms prickle as I anticipate his answer.

Naved looks at me with that sad look in his eyes that comes from having seen too much of the human capacity for evil.

"Sujit Chopra was at the house, the Rao house, at the exact same time as your husband Amit. Minutes before his death," he says.

THIRTY-TWO

I feel like a bomb has gone off in my chest.

I'm standing on the street outside my car, outside Naved's rental.

It's a chilly April night, temperatures still below fifty, but I feel like my heart is on fire.

I'm pacing the blacktop, feeling like putting my fist through the windshield of one of the cars parked nearby, picking up a rock and smashing it through a window, anything to express the rage I'm experiencing.

It's like an animal trapped inside me, furious to be released.

Naved gets out of the Prius, asking me if I'm all right, asking me if I want to come into the house and sit for a minute, take a drink of water.

I ignore him.

Too many things have gone too spectacularly wrong today.

He starts to say something, but I don't hear his words.

I hold up my hand, showing him my palm.

He cuts off in mid-sentence.

My hand opens the door of the Prius.

I get in.

The car feels unreasonably hot and stuffy.

I wind down all the windows, all four of them, breaking the driver's side window winder when I apply more pressure than the cheap plastic can endure.

I toss the jagged piece of plastic out. It clatters on the street.

Naved looks down at it, then at me.

I floor the accelerator, leaping away from him, down the street.

I take turns at hairpin speed, cut onto Plum Canyon too fast. If any other vehicle happens to be coming down at that exact second, we would meet in a devastating collision.

Luckily for me, no other car does come at that exact second.

I take the turn onto Bouquet Canyon like a maniac. A red pickup truck idling at the light is the only witness to my frenetic Steve McQueen recklessness. I barely glimpse the male driver behind the wheel as I fly past him, but I'm sure he's as shocked as anyone would be.

If he knew I was a cop, a federal agent at that, he would be doubly shocked.

The light at the next crossroad is orange.

I race toward it like my life depends on it.

It turns red a nanosecond before I reach the crossing.

I screech to a halt, peeling off rubber from my poor, much-abused tires. My Prius protests, trembling from my rough driving.

There are no other cars at the crossing. I could cut the red light and just go, nobody would know. But I can see a camera up there, its glass eye gleaming, and even though I'm mad as hell, I'm not inclined to break the law.

Not just yet anyway.

As I wait for the interminable light to change back, I text furiously.

> You still up?

Sujit's response comes almost at once:

Sure.

Coming to you, meet me in the lobby.

When the light changes, I drop the phone and blaze through the intersection.

Well, 'blaze' might be an overstatement. It's still just a beat-up old Prius. But I abuse the heck out of it.

I pull up at the entrance of the downtown Hyatt and am out of the car in an instant.

The valet looks at the Prius dubiously, then reacts as I toss the keys to him.

"Keep it close," I say as I hit the glass door of the lobby with the heel of my palm.

The lobby with its luxurious furnishings and pastel décor is a contrast to my overheated state. I do a full circle, scanning for my target. No sign of him.

The elevator to my right pings and Sujit steps out.

"Susan, bete," he says, "I'm so glad—"

"Let's go to your car," I say. "Let's take a drive."

"Okay," he says, not sounding entirely convinced, but playing along.

He glances at me several times as we wait for the valet to bring his Bugatti around. It's the same valet who just parked my Prius, but if he's wondering how I traded up this fast, he's not saying.

We get in the Bugatti, which feels cool and luxuriant after my beat-up old ride, but there's an odd lingering scent, something I can't quite place. Then I remember Natalie mentioning it. *It smells like Sujit Uncle.* I laugh softly. She nailed it.

Sujit eyes me doubtfully when I laugh.

I shake my head, straightening my face. "Drive," I say.

He drives us out of the Hyatt's exit gate.

When we're a couple hundred meters down Cinema Drive, he starts to say, "Where exactly are we going, Susan, bete? It's quite—"

I cut him off. "Pull over."

He frowns, looking around. There's nothing in sight except trees and to our left, the empty lot of McBain Transit Center, the bus terminus. It's deserted at this hour.

"Here?" he asks.

"Right here," I say, pointing.

He pulls over.

The instant the car's in neutral, I pull out my Glock Gen 5 and ram it into Sujit Chopra's side, pressing it into his lower ribs, digging the muzzle in hard enough to make him cry out in pain.

"You bastard," I say into his ear. "What did you do to Amit? Did you kill him?"

THIRTY-THREE

"What the fuck are you doing?" Sujit barks.

"I'm holding a Glock nine millimeter aimed at your heart. All I have to do is apply five and a half pounds of pressure to this trigger and a nine-millimeter lead jacketed bullet will shatter your ribs, puncture your lung and pierce your heart. You'll be dead before you hear the gunshot."

That gets his attention.

His eyes flicker downwards, then back at my face. His left arm, which was creeping up the steering wheel, the fist curling like he was winding up to punch me in the head, stops moving and the fingers uncurl.

"You can't shoot me!" he says. "We're family!"

"Amit was family, too. He was your nephew."

"What are you talking about?" he asks.

"I know you were there that day, at the Rao house when he died. Don't even think about lying to me."

He stares at me, licking his lips to wet them. I can see his mind trying to work out the angles. I don't intend to give him time to come up with a story so I press the muzzle of the Glock into his ribs. He squirms.

"That fucking hurts, Susan!"

"What were you doing there the day Amit died?" I ask.

His eyes flick sideways, the classic tell of a person who's lying. "I don't know what you're talking about."

I twist the muzzle, feeling it grind against bone.

He winces. "Mind it!"

"Don't lie to me. What were you doing in the Rao house that day?"

His eyes stare out the windshield at the street. He's still trying to deny his way through. "What house?"

"Sujit, stop bullshitting. You know what I'm talking about. Give me a straight answer."

Anger flares in his eyes again. "You're out of your mind, Susie. What is this behavior? This is how you treat people? Just because you're an FBI agent? You think you can brutalize anyone into telling you the truth?"

I hate being called Susie or Sue, and he knows it.

"Stop avoiding my question. Answer me!" I snarl.

"Or what? You will shoot me?" he challenges.

"Yes. I'll shoot you."

His eyes dart at me again, examining my face.

He smells of expensive perfume and expensive whisky. But under those, there's also the faint sour odor of cold sweat.

"Okay," he says, dialing down his male ego and righteous rage. "Okay, dammit. Back off. I'll answer your question. Just get that thing out of my ribs."

I stare at him intently, leaning closer, close enough to smell his aftershave.

"I don't need this gun to take you down. I could rip your throat out with my bare teeth if I want. All I'd have to do is say that you tried to sexually assault me and I fought back. Remember that in case you get the urge to try anything," I say.

He needs to be reminded, like all powerful men do when confronted by a woman.

The gun isn't the thing to fear.

I am.

He nods once, Adam's apple bobbing as he swallows. "Okay. Got it."

I remove the Glock from his ribs, releasing the pressure, but keep it down there, a few inches from him.

"Talk," I say.

He massages the spot where I pressed and twisted in the gun. "I think you tore a muscle or something. It hurts like mad."

"Take some Tylenol," I say, unsympathetically. "Now talk."

"Amit called me that day."

I feel my grip tighten on the Glock. More than a year later, and the mere mention of his name makes me clench up. "Go on."

"He asked to meet me there. He chose the place. He knew that it was my company that sold the house to Rao. He said he needed to show me something and to meet him there."

"What did he want to show you?" I ask, still suspicious.

"I don't know," Sujit says. "I never found out what it was. When I got there, he was already dead. It was... horrible."

I lean in, bringing in the Glock again.

He winces. "I'm telling the truth!"

"You weren't the one who reported his death to the police," I say. "A neighbor called it in. They said they heard gunshots. A patrol car checked it out, found the front door unlocked, went in and found Amit."

Sujit nods vigorously. "I started to dial 911. I was going to call it in. But then I thought of our family. I thought about how it was going to look. You know how the system works. They would have treated me like a suspect."

I grit my teeth. The small muscles in the hand with which I'm holding the Glock feel as tight as wires. "My husband was lying in a pool of his blood. Your nephew! For all you knew, he could have still been alive, maybe he could have been saved. And you couldn't even dial an ambulance?"

Sujit shakes his head emphatically. "Susan, he was dead. I am one hundred percent certain."

"So you're a doctor now? How could you have been certain?"

The thought of Amit lying there on the wooden floor, bleeding out, makes me so... I don't even have words to describe the emotion.

But he's right. I've read the medical examiner's report. Amit was killed instantly. Sujit calling 911 wouldn't have saved him. Still, I'm not willing to let Sujit off easy. He kept this information private for all this time instead of sharing it with the cops or FBI. That's a potential felony in itself.

"What did he say when he called you?" I ask.

Sujit spreads his palms in an Indian shrug. "He just said he wanted to meet me."

"That's it?" I ask.

He holds up his palms. "I swear I'm telling the truth, Susie. All Amit said was that he had found out something he wanted to share with me, ask my opinion about. I was curious. I asked him. He wouldn't share any details, wouldn't say anything. He just said to meet him there and we'd talk about it in person. It's important, tau. Those were his exact words. 'It's important, tau'. That was all."

"You must have had *some* inkling," I say.

He shakes his head. "No, I had no idea."

Something glimmers in his eye. He stares out the windshield at the dark stand of trees beside us.

I raise the Glock, forcing his attention back at me. "You just remembered something. What was it?"

He shakes his head but says, "I don't know for sure, but..."

"What?"

"At the time, I remember thinking that maybe it was something to do with the deal."

"What deal?"

"The same thing I've been trying to talk to you about the past few days."

I frown, trying to think back to the time I was in the parking lot of the Chen cabin, talking to Sujit on FaceTime when he called from his office in San Francisco. "You said you could help me with getting access to Derek Chen's friends, the ones in the private group he was in," I say. "Is that what you're referring to?"

"Yes, yes. Same thing. But mainly Trevor Blackburn. He's the ringleader. The others just go along with him."

"What's this deal you're talking about? What does Blackburn have to do with it?"

"Our company," he says, "the one Aishwarya and I own, we're in the process of securing a major deal right here in the valley. It's a huge deal. The biggest in the region. We've got everything on our side, the politicians, the local interest groups, the votes we need on the city board, all except for one thing."

A flash of insight strikes me. "Let me guess: McDougall."

Sujit looks surprised. "Yes. The chief is in bed with Blackburn. McDougall's family has interests in the region and Blackburn has been supporting their growth and expansion. He's got deep pockets, that son of a bitch. He's got his eye on Santa Carina Valley. He aims to make it a tech hub to rival Silicon Valley. It's already happening. Southern California is attracting a lot of tech companies. Our deal would pump a huge amount of money into local SCV infrastructure and redevelopment, create thousands of new jobs, bring investment flooding in. It would be like creating another Silicon Valley."

"And Blackburn wants the same thing?" I ask. He doesn't need to know that I already have Blackburn's take on it. I want to hear Sujit's version and compare notes.

"Not exactly. He's floated a rival project. He plans to set up a new satellite township just north of here, about fifteen miles up in the Santa Carina Hills. He's proposing to build a city out there from the ground up. He claims he'll hire local labor and talent, employ SCV citizens, and create a tech corridor."

"So it's kind of the same thing as what you're proposing except not in the existing SCV?" I ask. "Why not just do it here then?"

Sujit makes a face. "He claims that redeveloping downtown will overburden SCV's existing infrastructure and resources. The town isn't built for such a major expansion. He says that by building the satellite township out in the Santa Carina hills it will create new opportunities, housing, jobs for locals, while pumping revenue into SCV. He even has a name for it. Silicon Valley South!"

"Catchy," I say.

He gives me a sour look.

"What does all this have to do with Amit?" I ask.

"This deal has been in the works for the past two years. It's a huge deal. A total game changer. When Amit called me that day out of the blue, I thought maybe he had learned something about it and wanted to speak with me privately. I would have hired him in a heartbeat."

"Why meet at the Rao house then?" I ask, still doubtful. "Why not somewhere else private? A hotel room? Your office?"

He shrugs. "I asked him the same question. He didn't give me a reason, just asked me to be there."

"And you just went?"

"He was my nephew, he wanted to meet."

"And when you found him dead, what did you think? What was your first thought?"

"I don't know. I was just... shocked. It was the last thing I expected."

"You've had time to think about it since then. What's your

theory now?" I ask.

He looks at me. "Amit's death was a suicide."

"It was murder."

He looks genuinely startled. "What are you saying?"

I ignore the question. "Did Amit know something about the deal that could have damaged your chances?"

He stares at me. "Are you thinking I had something to do with his death? Bete, I told you already. I found him dead. I don't know anything else."

I hate to admit it, but it rings true. I can't think of a single reason why Sujit would have wanted to kill Amit, or a way that he could have done it, covered it up to make it look like suicide, and gotten away with it. He's a total crapola of a guy but that doesn't make him a killer. Still, my training has taught me to push even when it seems pointless. You can never tell where the tipping point is until you push past it.

"This deal," I say. "How much is it worth to you or Blackburn ultimately? How much do either of you stand to gain from your rival proposals?"

He shrugs. "Twelve, maybe as much as fourteen."

"Million?"

He makes a scoffing sound.

"Twelve to fourteen *billion*?" I say, astonished.

"Conservative estimate," he says.

"So what the hell do you want from me?" I ask, though I have a pretty good idea by now.

"With Derek Chen's death, the deal is in a precarious place. The six of them are all in bed financially on Silicon Valley South. They've invested a lot of resources, time, energy, money already to make sure they get it. Chen's loss means they have to fill that gap. We're talking tens of billions in financing here. Blackburn's under a lot of pressure. You're a thorn in his side, you and this investigation. It's the last thing he needs right now, when we're so close to the end. He is going to try to get to you.

He'll make life hard for you, maybe even threaten you, threaten your family. Don't be fooled by his looks and charisma. Bloody bastard's a goonda. A thug."

I'm tempted to ask him if he's talking about himself. "And what exactly is it you expect me to do?" I ask, although I have a pretty good idea about that as well.

He looks at me craftily. "Arrest Trevor Blackburn for being party to the serial killings and not reporting them to the authorities. That makes him as good as having been an accomplice, doesn't it? Arrest him for murder."

"Based on what evidence?" I ask.

"Find something, anything," he says, a little too vehemently. "Just arrest him! Put him away for a day, a week, a few hours, anything. All we need is to break the news that he's involved, leak the videos to the media, let public opinion do the rest. It doesn't even matter what happens in court."

I smile. "Your strategy is painfully obvious, Uncle Sujit." I use the avuncular term with a sarcastic tone. "All you really want is to remove your biggest obstacle so you can push ahead, force his partners to join up with you—they're used to playing both sides anyway—and ramrod your own deal through in the meantime. After that, it doesn't matter to you what happens to Trevor Blackburn, does it? Only that you've made your billions."

He gives me a dirty look. "We're family!"

"You should have remembered that when your nephew was lying there in his own blood and you didn't even bother to call 911."

He grimaces and looks away, unable to meet my eyes.

I pop the door to the Bugatti and put one leg out before pausing and turning back to say, "And if you lied to me about what really happened that day, you can be sure I *will* find out the truth, and when I do, I'll come after you with every power at my command, family or not."

I leave him with that as I turn and start walking back to the hotel to get my Prius.

After a few minutes, Sujit passes me on the other side of the street, slowing down. I ignore him, and he drives on.

As I turn into the hotel lot, something catches the corner of my eye.

I stop and look off up the street.

At the far crossing, on the turnoff, at the corner of the main street, just barely visible, is a vehicle.

It's hard to be sure at this distance, but from the elevation, it has to be either an SUV or a pickup truck.

A red pickup truck?

Haven't I seen that red truck before?

Was it behind me earlier today when I left the command center and drove home?

Was it passing by the high school near my house, slowing as it went past the turn to my street?

Did I see it maybe once or twice the day before?

It's not that uncommon a color but it isn't common either.

And that silhouette, that shape, it's definitely vintage, something from another era when aerodynamism was less important than solidity and masculine ruggedness.

I squint, but it's really too far and barely visible.

I shake my head, admonishing myself.

Nah, it can't be.

Just my exhausted, over-wired brain playing tricks on me.

Still, I know better than to take a chance.

Better safe than dead.

I step off the road onto the dirt shoulder. There's a pine tree a few feet away and I position myself behind it.

My backup piece, the same Glock I used on Sujit, is in my hand, magazine reloaded and ready for use.

I tend to use the Glock after hours, and the Sig Sauer during business hours, because technically, once an FBI agent is off the clock, they're supposed to safekeep their official firearm. Although, as I've learned over time, an FBI agent, like all law enforcement, is never really off the clock. Crime doesn't do business hours.

Seconds later, the light at the intersection changes and the vehicle takes the turn onto Miracle Mountain Parkway, heading toward me.

It's moving slowly, which is reason enough to be suspicious in a state where driving a few miles *over* the speed limit is normalized. I pivot my body from the hips, moving on the balls of my feet as I use the tree as cover while preparing myself for a sudden burst of gunfire from the approaching truck. It is a truck, isn't it? It's still hard to see because there's a light flare from the streetlamp behind and above it which is dazzling my eyes.

Then the truck is right on me, passing within a few meters, close enough to make it hard for a killer with an automatic weapon to fail to see me as I step out from behind cover, gun raised in both hands, ready to return fire.

And it's not a truck at all. Or even an SUV.

It's a frigging utility van, a deep red panel van with a logo for *Rocco's Rooter: 24 Hour Plumbing*.

As I watch, the light at the crossing changes and the truck crosses the intersection, turns and goes the other way, disappearing into the night.

I resume walking into the Hyatt parking lot, arriving in time to see the valet walking back after parking Sujit's Bugatti.

I hand him my parking ticket without a word and wait as he fetches my car.

In the Prius, I pause to look at my phone.

It's blown up with messages over the past few hours, while I was busy dealing with one thing after another.

One of them is from Kayla and it's urgent.

Where r u? Call me asap!!!

THIRTY-FOUR

There are well over a dozen people in the command center, waiting for me when I walk in at just after 4 a.m.

I come to a full halt, taking them all in. Kayla warned me to expect a crowd when we spoke a few minutes ago, but this is still more than I was expecting.

They're all young, a few in their late teens but most in their early twenties, two or three in their early to mid-thirties.

A few are siblings, the resemblance obvious, but most aren't related. Yet it's clear they all know one another.

They all share a common look, something that isn't in their features or their clothes or ages. A look in their eyes. Like they've looked into the heart of the world and what they saw was too horrifying to endure. Their glances are evasive, their expressions masked, their emotions withheld. A few are stringy thin, bones jutting out, hollow-eyed with the familiar haunted gaze of the chronic addict. Others are nervous, fingernail chewing, forearm rubbing, unable to make eye contact. They've all been through stuff; they're all scarred and marked for life.

This sense of loss, desolation, shared despair is what they have in common.

They're a squad, a tribe, or as Urduja called them, a posse.

"Hi," I say to them, raising a hand. "I'm Susan."

A chorus of nods, and hellos greet me.

Urduja comes forward, taking the lead.

Almost shyly, with the air of the introvert who's stepping up because she has to, because no one else will, she says, "These are my sibs. We're all family here. He *made* us family. When he took our moms. They were all we had. He murdered them in their beds, orphaned us. None of us have ever known a dad, not really. A couple of us who have..."

A young man shifts uncomfortably, looking down at the floor between his feet.

"...they were better off not knowing them. We found each other afterwards, those of us who survived. We're only about a third of all the survivors. The others... didn't make it. We found each other, we clung together, we made solidarity. We're all we have now. This found fam. And we're here to ask you, Susan Parker, for your help. You're the first person who's actually listened to us. Believed in us. The cops in this town don't care. As you can see, most of us were dirt poor, trailer trash, people of color, marginalized to the edge of society. The decent citizens, they'd be happier if we stopped breathing. It's no surprise we lose an average of one of us every couple years to suicide. It's easier than continuing to live in a world that doesn't want us, doesn't care. Our moms were forgotten even before they were murdered. Nobody knows them, nobody cares. Except us. And now you, Susan. You care. I've seen it in your eyes. That's why we're here."

I take the bottle of water Brine hands me, thanking him with my eyes. He touches my arm, letting me know he's here for me, the whole team is here for me. I'm grateful.

I take a sip of the water. It tastes cool and delicious, like elixir. How precious are the little things when we have almost nothing. Suddenly, I'm parched, like a wanderer in the desert. I upend the bottle and drain it in one continuous swallow.

I wipe my mouth with the back of my hand and look at Urduja, then at each of the others in turn, making eye contact, connecting with each one.

"I don't know what to say, Urduja. I'm... moved. What you kids have suffered. What you went through. What you've been living with all these years. It's monumental. You've carried the world on your shoulders."

I wipe away sudden moisture from my cheek. I must have spilled some water when I drank too quickly.

"I can't speak for this town. All I can say is as a fellow woman of color, as a person from a marginalized minority group, I know something about that. I was a foster kid myself, an orphan. At least I think I'm an orphan. You see, I don't even know that for sure. My own parentage, family background, is a dark shroud. It's the one mystery I might never be able to solve. What I know is, the world treated me as an orphan, a person of color, and let's just say that love and care were not the things that greeted me growing up. But I survived. And you guys have survived, too. By hook or by crook. Because that's all we have, right? We endure. We overcome. And now I have a shield and a gun, and the power and might of the world's most powerful law enforcement agency behind me. I have a team of the absolute best fellow officers anyone could ever hope for. And I can tell you this. I'm going to get the man who did this to all of you. I'm going to get him and I'm going to drag him out into the light, into justice. That, I promise you. So help me god."

There's a long, silent pause.

I don't know if my words have landed hard or soft. I don't know if they believe me.

But *I* believe me.

Because I meant every word.

And then, after that long, unspeaking pause, they surge forward.

They come at me.

In ones and twos and then all at once.

To hug me.

Touch my hand.

Bump my fist.

Look into my eyes.

Mumble thanks.

Speak a word or three.

Each in their own way, they communicate their gratitude, their love, their support.

Urduja comes last.

She looks at me hesitantly, silently asking permission.

I nod, hold out my arms, and reel her in.

We hug tightly.

I wonder if this is how it will feel, ten or twelve years from now, when Natalie is her age, and I'll be that many years older.

It feels good.

As we disengage, I tell her, "Any mother should be proud to call you her daughter—I know I would."

Her eyes fill at once.

"Thank you," she says.

After they're gone, I look at my team.

"Guys," I say, "I know you must be exhausted after working twelve-to-fourteen-hour days this week, way more than that yesterday and today, and now I'm about to ask you to continue pushing this rock up the mountain, but—"

"Hey, boss," Raman says, "sorry to interrupt you, but we all just wanna say something."

"Yeah?" I ask.

"Let's nail this *pendejo!*"

I bump knuckles with him, miming the kaboom. "Okay then. Let's catch us a serial killer."

THIRTY-FIVE

She doesn't sleep on the job. I can say that about Susan Parker.

I don't just mean that she seems to work around the clock. Back there at the intersection, she almost made me. I thought I was doing a pretty good job of staying out of sight while tracking her. But from about 2 a.m. until about 5 a.m., this burgh is a ghost town. Almost every commercial establishment shuts down by 9 or 10 p.m. There's only a couple restaurants downtown that stay open until after midnight. By 2 a.m. even the transit workers who commute to LA are in bed, and the ones on the early shift don't start moving until five-ish. The streets are deserted, making every vehicle instantly noticeable.

Still, I managed to stay on her trail without being tagged.

Until she decided to get out of the Indian dude's car and start walking up the street back to the hotel.

Who even does that!

I only just managed to duck out of sight, reversing and pulling a quick side turn onto Cinema Drive. Almost rearended a plumber's van. Twenty-four-hour service. Lolz. Clogged drains and killers don't keep business hours!

I was glad I did because when that plumbing service van

went past her, she looked like she was ready to shoot it up. Dayem, the woman really has eyes in the back of her head. She ought to have cards printed up: *Susan Parker. Justice never sleeps.*

She would have shot me down in a heartbeat and there wasn't a damn thing I could have done about it.

The hunting rifle with the scope is great for people watching but it's too cumbersome to use in a close encounter. Besides, I don't even know if I have ammo for it. I bought it mainly for the scope and to give me cover while I hung out in the woods to stake out the Chen place. Nice piece of craftsmanship, cost my sponsor a pretty penny, too, but I hate guns.

I'm a hands-on kind of guy.

Give me a piece of rope in my hands. Something a man can put his own strength behind. I need to feel bones and cartilage crunching when I bear down, that last life gasp being expelled, the rush that comes from taking a life with your own hands.

It was educational to watch SAC Parker at work. She meets interesting people. Billionaires. Wannabe billionaires. Pizza delivery kids. At first, I thought all those kids were there for some kind of outreach program. An addiction counselling and support group, maybe.

But when I saw the Filipino girl, U as the other kids call her, it snapped into place.

They're all *my* kids.

I created them.

You could even say, I *fathered* them.

Their moms gave birth to them, sure.

But they lost their privilege by being neglectful, abusive, bad, bad moms.

They paid the price for it.

And I became the new father for these orphans, giving them new lives, a do-over.

I freed them from the tyranny of bad parenting.

What were *they* doing with Susan Parker? *My* Susan Parker?

Does this mean she's found the connection between Derek Chen and the bad moms? She now knows that I'm the same killer responsible for those ones as well?

She's a sharp tack, my Susan.

Sooner or later, she's going to catch up with me.

I've known that from the moment I first laid eyes on her.

I've never had anyone like her coming after me, sniffing up my trail, and now that she's on the scent, it's only a matter of time before our paths cross.

I've begun looking forward to it.

Or I *was*, until she went and did something really, really stupid.

She got involved with *him*.

I couldn't believe it when I saw her get into his car. His fancy-schmancy jalopy. His look-at-me-I'm-so-rich-I-need-a-ride-that-costs-millions-to-pick-up-women Bugatti! And then she spent hours with him, and then she goes to dinner, arriving on his arm, like his latest trophy date.

That made me so freaking mad. If I was that kind of guy, I would have gone into that restaurant and shot the whole place up. Active shooter? Let me show you *hyper*active shooter, you assholes!

But I don't do guns.

So I had to swallow my mad and figure out another way.

It's not a big leap.

I already have cameras in her house. I have her sister-in-law and her daughter on camera at the press of a button, anytime of day or night. And Susan herself, when she does get home for a few hours, which seems to be less and less each day. Even her most intimate moments.

She's a bad mom.

Good moms don't get involved with guys like *him*.

I mean, she could have gotten involved with anyone, I wouldn't have cared. Not much anyway.

But to get involved with *him*?

That is unacceptable.

So I've decided.

I'm going to go in again today.

Into Susan's house.

Not just a visit this time, but an *intrusion*.

When she's least expecting it, least prepared.

I even have my clothesline ready.

It's around my waist right now, of course, as it always is, as it's been ever since I was a kid, and *she* used it to tie my hands to the flush tank and locked me into the toilet of our grungy trailer to teach me to stop wetting the bed.

And then she went out and got high and forgot about me for a whole day and night, leaving me in that cold, tight space without food or water or warm clothing.

I couldn't even reach the washbasin faucet to drink water. I was naked, hungry, thirsty, desperate. So desperate that I ended up drinking the water from the toilet bowl.

My dad found me when he finally came home from wherever it was that he went to try to pick up a few bucks.

It made him really mad.

When she came home, they had a huge fight over it.

Their worst yet.

She said she did that because *someone* had to teach me to stop having "accidents" and wetting the bed, and it sure as fuck isn't going to be you because you're never around, you fucking loser.

He got really mad at her that day.

He killed her that night.

Strangled her with this same length of clothesline, the one I now wear around my waist.

He thought I was asleep when he did it. He even said my

name and shook my shoulder once to check. I pretended to be dead asleep. But when he did it, I was awake and watching every second of it.

I felt glad he did it.

She deserved it.

I was so happy when it was over.

I thought he would come, wake me up, carry me out of that shitty trailer, take me somewhere that he and I could be a family together. Dad and son. A *real* family.

But instead, he bailed!

He just upped and left me, with her corpse next to me.

Like I was dead, too. Except I wasn't.

And now here I am.

And this time, I have my sights on another single mom.

Susan Parker.

Are you a good mom, Susan Parker?

I guess we'll find out real soon.

Tonight.

THIRTY-SIX

The Santa Carina branch of the Department of Public Social Services is located off Golden Valley Road. The Department of Child and Family Services is in the same premises. The posted notice outside states that their office timings are from 8 a.m. to 4 p.m., Monday through Friday.

I enter their offices at 8.14 a.m. the next morning and request to see Brook Wentworth.

The receptionist asks me if I have an appointment.

"Mr. Wentworth came by my house yesterday for an unscheduled visit. He left his card. I'm just following up."

She looks at the card I've handed her, hands it back, then makes a call.

"Please have a seat," she informs me when she finishes talking.

I'm too restless to sit so I stand and scroll on my phone.

I check the team's WhatsApp group for updates. I texted Ramon and David last night. Then Kayla with a separate assignment. We're scheduled to meet up at the command center at nine.

After I've been waiting for almost eleven minutes, a middle-aged Black woman with dreadlocks and steel-rimmed spectacles appears. She seems very conscientious about her appearance, and speaks carefully and precisely.

"Susan Parker?"

"Yes."

"What business do you have with Brook Wentworth, may I ask?"

I repeat what I told the receptionist earlier.

"Could I see the card he left you?"

She looks at the card, turning it over then examining it again as if trying to make sense of it.

"Is Mr. Wentworth not available to see me?" I ask.

She looks at me as she pushes her spectacles up her nose with her forefinger. "He is not."

"I see. When is he expected back in office?"

She looks away for a moment, as if considering her response. "I'm afraid meeting Mr. Wentworth won't be possible, Mrs. Parker."

"It's Miss Parker, actually. I kept my maiden name after marriage."

"It won't be possible, Miss Parker. I really don't understand how he left you this card. It was yesterday, you said?"

"Yes. He came by our place when I was at work," I lie. Technically though, while I was in McD's lock-up, I was still at work. "I was concerned and wanted to meet him and clear up this misunderstanding."

"Misunderstanding?"

"I don't know who lodged the complaint but there's not an ounce of truth in it. I'm sure we can clear this up very quickly if I can just speak to Wentworth, or his supervisor."

"I am the supervisor for that department, Miss Parker. My name is LaShanda Jackson."

"Could we talk privately, Mrs. Jackson?" I ask.

She looks around uncertainly as if trying to make sense of something. I'm puzzled by her responses.

She finally seems to come to a decision. "Would you like a coffee, Miss Parker?"

I'm surprised by the question. "Sure. I was going to stop by the diner just up the road and get one after I finished here anyway."

"Marge's?" she asks.

"Yes."

"You have a car, I assume?" she asks.

Another strange question. "I do," I reply.

She walks over to the reception desk and speaks briefly to the receptionist then returns to me.

We leave the building together and walk to my Prius.

She notices the FBI sticker in the windshield as we get in.

"Is that official?" she asks, pointing.

"It is," I say.

I reach into my jacket pocket, take out my badge and ID, and show them to her.

She looks at them curiously for a moment then hands them back.

"Thank you," she says.

We don't speak again for the three or four minutes it takes me to drive us a few blocks down to Medal Coffee. I park and we go in. The large blonde with the hairdo that looks like it came straight out of the seventies greets us both with her customary rasp.

"Susan. LaShanda. I didn't know you two knew each other!"

"Hi, Marge. We just met actually," I say.

"Well, come on in, make yourselves at home. Name your poison."

We order our coffees and take a seat at one of the diner-style booths by the window. All the booths run in a straight line by the window, looking out onto Golden Valley Road. A steady stream of morning traffic flows by.

"There's something about Brook Wentworth, isn't there?" I ask LaShanda.

She looks at me. "Is the FBI investigating him?"

"What makes you think that?"

She takes out the card I gave her in the reception. "Brook Wentworth worked with us for about two years and four months. That was roughly nine years ago."

"He left?"

"He was suspended at first, pending an inquiry. Then later, he was fired. There was talk about pressing charges, but for one reason or another, all the aggrieved parties finally decided not to go ahead. I think it was because most of them have been in trouble with the law themselves all their lives, so didn't want to have anything to do with law enforcement. They let it go. But I wager if they had been able to get their hands on Mr. Wentworth, they would have done some prosecuting of their own. Quite definitely."

Marge brings over our beverages. "Spiced chai for you, Susan. Caramel mocha for you, LaShanda. Donuts compliments of the house. So, ladies, what's cooking?"

We both make perfunctory noises, not wanting to encourage Marge who has a very vague notion of boundaries when it comes to private conversations.

But she does have the best coffee and donuts in the valley, and the best gossip, too.

"How's the FBI treating you, Susan?" Marge asks now. "I hear McDuck's been bustin' your balls over some case."

She probably knows about my spending the day in the holding cell yesterday, but at least she's discreet enough not to say so. "You know old white men these days, Marge. It's the only thing they can do anymore."

Marge jabs a ring-laden finger at me. "What she said!" she

tells LaShanda. "You know she's the one caught that psycho killer last year? Splinter? Right here in our own backyard, can you believe it? Hell yeah. Susan Parker's one to watch."

As Marge walks away, LaShanda looks at me. "You were the FBI agent on that one? I read about you. I didn't connect the name."

I shrug. "I've put away a few. Splinter was a bad one though. One of the worst."

LaShanda nods. "I respect what you do, Miss Parker. Takes guts to go after men like that. No ordinary task."

"Call me Susan, please. Do go on. You were telling me about Brook Wentworth."

She tells me how Wentworth was a diligent worker at first, how he seemed to genuinely care about the work they did. She was the one who had interviewed him and approved his application. "He didn't just treat it as a job. It was personal to him. I think he'd been a foster child himself, so he'd been in the system, he knew how it worked. At first, that came across as a good thing. But later, it turned out that he had his own personal agenda."

"How do you mean?" I ask, sipping my masala tea. Hot and spicy, just the way I like it. I nibble at a donut, the sugary sweetness offsetting the tongue-tickling spices.

"You have to understand, most of these homes we go into, they're low-income families. Rock bottom remainders of society. People who've been chewed up and thrown out of the system. They don't have health insurance, college degrees, professional qualifications, they're forced to take minimum wage shifts doing drudge work. Whatever they can get, and however long they can hold on to it, which isn't long usually. They're often alcohol and drug addicts, or both. Most of them have done some jail time or been up against the justice system. Some are illegal immigrants without official documentation. A few are career criminals. The petty stuff usually, fraud, passing bad checks, identity theft, phone scams, solicitation, dealing, it's a long list of misdemeanors and some felonies. And they're also parents. Which is where we come in."

I think of all the houses the Murder Club killer went into on the videos. The rundown houses with booze, pills and needles lying around in plain sight, within reach of little children. The poverty and squalor. The misery of human lives struggling just to get through the days. I think of those eight mothers he strangled to death. Of their kids. It makes my chai taste sour.

"Wentworth started getting over-involved emotionally," LaShanda says, cradling her coffee between her palms as she sips. "Coming back to the office and telling me we had to go in there, *right now*, and get those kids out. I kept trying to explain to him that we had a system, protocol to follow. As long as the mothers or caregivers, though it was almost always single mothers, stayed in their lane, there was nothing we could do. The system is overburdened. There aren't enough foster homes. There are places with seven and eight or more kids living in three-bedroom houses."

"Factories," I say.

She looks at me. "You were one of them, weren't you? A foster child."

"Tell me more about Wentworth."

"There's not much more to tell. He couldn't take it. He started going out and doing his own thing, violating ethical guidelines, abusing regulations."

"How?"

She makes a gesture. "He got into a physical altercation with one family. The woman had several boyfriends—we had suspected her of turning tricks, but could never prove that she was actually soliciting. We can't declare a woman unfit just because she sleeps with more than one man. Wentworth beat up one of her male friends, damn near killed the man. The mother got mad at him, came at Wentworth with a kitchen knife. He broke her arm in three places, and damn near strangled her to death."

I perk up. "Strangled? With his bare hands?"

She nods. "It was a godawful mess. Triggered an internal investigation. We found out that he had been over-reaching with multiple houses that he had been inspecting. Threatening women. Intimidating. Encouraging the kids to talk back and fight back."

"The kids? Why the kids? Were they being abused?"

LaShanda sighs. "It's a very thin line between discipline and abuse, sometimes, Susan. These aren't people raised to believe in kindness and good parenting. They're often abused kids themselves. A mess of issues, psychological, physical, medical conditions. They may not be ideal caregivers, but they *are* the biological parents. We do everything we can to try to redress their shortcomings before making a recommendation of removal."

"Because it's not like the foster homes are such heavenly sanctums either, right?" I say.

She looks up at me through the top of her bifocals. "It must have been hard for you."

"Did the woman he attacked file charges against Wentworth? Or her boyfriend maybe?"

"Like I said before, these are people who distrust anyone in authority. Filing an official complaint would mean exposing themselves to charges, too."

"So nothing happened to Wentworth?"

"He was suspended first, pending an inquiry as I said. But this time, I fired his ass," she says. "And put everything on record. By law, I'm required to inform SCVPD which I did."

"What did they do?" I ask, but I already know the answer.

"Nothing officially, but they did go down to give Wentworth a good talking-to."

"And?"

She shakes her head. "His apartment was cleared out. All his things gone. Rent unpaid. Landlord didn't have any forwarding address."

"Did they put out a BOLO?"

A Be On the Look Out warning sends a picture, name, and description to law enforcement.

"They didn't have an official complaint other than my report, and none of the people involved were willing to go on the record, so it was literally just my word. Detective Brennan said they'd keep an eye out for Wentworth, but they couldn't afford to tie up resources searching for him. Besides, since he was fired, he had no authority to go into people's homes and harass them anymore. Chances were, we'd never hear from him again."

I look at her grimly. "And yet, he turned up at my place yesterday, clipboard in hand, still acting like he's with the DCFS. It's almost like he was sending me a message."

"The message being?"

"Catch me if you can."

LaShanda thinks about that. "Is it true that they do that? Reach out to law enforcement, send them clues. Like the killer in that movie, the case where they still haven't found him."

"The Zodiac Killer. Technically, he was identified as Gary Poste via DNA and appearance, but the Bureau hasn't confirmed that officially. Your point is valid, though. Serial killers often want to be caught. The hunt is part of their thing."

She sips her coffee.

I lean forward. "About Wentworth. Has he done this before? You said all this was nine years ago. Have there been any sightings or similar incidents in the intervening period?"

She shakes her head slowly. "Nothing that's come to my attention. I always assumed he had moved on from Santa

Carina. That's why I was so surprised when you showed up today and gave me that card."

The card reminds me of Lata and how shaken up she was after Wentworth's visit. "Um, I think it's fairly obvious now but just to be certain, there was no complaint filed about me or my family with DCFS? No investigation into us?"

She smiles. "Susan, until you showed up this morning, I didn't know the first thing about you. But now I know that you're a woman of color and an FBI agent who kicks ass. And whatever else you may be, you're not an abusive, neglectful mother, or a crack addict, or any of the other red flags that require us to intervene. You're good here."

A weight slips off my chest. I can't wait to tell Lata. She's going to be so relieved.

My phone vibrates. I glance at the screen. My phone has been buzzing with notifications and missed calls. I've been checking my screen every now and then to be sure I'm not missing something urgent. Now, I see that it's Kayla calling.

"Excuse me," I tell LaShanda. "I have to take this."

Kayla sounds breathless and tense. "There's been another murder."

THIRTY-SEVEN

McBean Ranch is the white elephant of Santa Carina Valley. The biggest and most expensive property, yet it's been struggling to find a buyer for as long as I can remember. Out here in this part of the valley the houses are few and far between. This area was all ranches and farmhouses until half a century ago. Now, it's gradually being converted into housing subdivisions, as the old families die out or sell out, one by one.

I'm among the first to arrive. The large open space in front of the main ranch house is occupied by only two vehicles. One is an SCVPD cruiser, the other is yet another of those supercars. I'm starting to get sick of the sight of these ridiculously expensive luxury cars around our middle-class suburb.

The SCVPD uniform is Officer Sanchez. He's standing by his vehicle, speaking on the car radio. He breaks off and walks over to me as I pull up.

I identify myself to him.

"Inside," he says.

The main ranch house is typical of its kind out here in California. A single-story mid-twentieth-century ranch-style structure. Expansion over the decades has added new rooms and sections, causing the house to sprawl in all directions. I don't recall exactly how many bedrooms and bathrooms it has, but judging from the sheer size, I guess upwards of ten of the first at the very least. On the inside it seems to go on forever.

"Victim's a Jake Perkins," Officer Sanchez informs me as he leads me through yet another hallway. "A realtor named Stacey Schwimmer says he owned the place."

"Where's the realtor?"

"On her way."

Our quest through the maze finally ends in a bedroom. Officer Sanchez stops at the doorway and lets me pass.

There's nothing particularly spectacular about the room or its furnishings, which are at least a half century out of date.

A man's body lies on the bed.

The face is one of six on the whiteboard back at the command center. Jake Perkins, billionaire, known for his over-sized cowboy hats and rhinestone suits. It seems fitting that the rich cowboy whose person and brand image was built on the Old West should end up dead in a traditional ranch house, quite literally with his boots on.

I look around. The two windows both look out onto the rear of the property and a hill. On the access road coming in, I esti-mated that the nearest occupied residence was a good two miles away.

"Who reported it?" I ask Officer Sanchez.

He's still standing by the doorway.

"Realtor lady called it in," he says. "Dispatch asked me to check it out. I just got here five minutes before you showed up. Just went in to confirm that it was for real, then backed right out. I know how particular you feds are about crime scene cont-amination."

"How'd you know it's our case?"

He gives me a knowing grin. "Word from upstairs is that

you guys want it, you're welcome to it. Say, you the fed that sassed the chief and spent a day in lock-up?"

I ignore the question as I look around the scene, trying to take in as much as I can.

"You can go back out and secure the property, Officer Sanchez, I'll take it from here."

I spend a few more minutes examining the crime scene before going out. By accident, I take a wrong turn and find a door leading to a small kitchenette and pantry. Another door leads out of the house. I find myself standing in a backyard looking onto an empty horse corral ringed by a wooden fence. Beside it is an empty stable large enough to house at least two dozen horses. The smell of hay, old leather and horse droppings is still strong enough to make me sneeze three times in a row.

I back out of the stable, my sinuses already irritated enough to put me in need of a tissue.

The sound of a door slamming makes me turn around, hand reaching for my Glock. It's drawn, cocked and pointed in the direction of the sound. I scan the rear of the ranch house, seeing nothing.

A moment later, a gust of wind wafts across the yard, and a loose screen door swings ajar and slams shut on its frame.

I walk over to it slowly, Glock still held at the ready.

Another gust of wind.

Again, the screen door repeats its motion.

I uncock my pistol, slide it back into the holster, and reach for the screen door. I check it, opening and closing it. It's slightly off its topmost hinge, causing it to swing open under air pressure.

I shake my head and grin at myself.

"Almost shot up a screen door."

Another bout of sneezing wipes the grin off my face.

I'm dabbing at my leaky nose with the back of my cuff as I answer my phone.

It's Kayla.

"Mancini's on her way," she informs me. So is the rest of the team. She's also tracked down Perkins' executive assistant, a very pushy young man single-named Plush, who seems to be in denial about his boss's death.

"Tell him he's welcome to come down here and check for himself," I say sarcastically. "All he has to do is take one look at all the blood and he'll shut up."

"Blood?" Kayla asks.

"Yup. Unsub broke his MO. Or it was a different unsub altogether. This one looks like he was stabbed to death, in the back, quite literally. I'll need Marisol to confirm, but it definitely doesn't look like death by strangling."

"So weird," she says.

It is weird. Serial killers don't change their modus operandi. Not unless they're interrupted during the course of the crime or under some duress. This has all the hallmarks of a rage killing, not the coldly methodical strangulations of the eight mothers we have on video, or Derek Chen. I'm not saying those weren't driven by rage—all murder has some element of anger involved—but this is out-of-control mayhem, which is totally unlike our Murder Club killer.

Kayla and I talk some more, then I hang up. My allergy seems to have subsided now that I'm away from the offending place.

I hear a car pulling up and go back to the front of the house to see who it is. Again, the hike through the endless maze of rooms. This time, I notice that a certain pattern repeats itself: living room, kitchen and dining area, hallway, bedrooms and bathrooms, then it all starts over again. The ranch house is subdivided into apartments. I make a mental note to ask about it.

A forty-something woman in a peach jacket and skirt is talking to Officer Sanchez.

He sees me and points, saying something to the woman.

"Special Agent in Charge Susan Parker," I say. "We met earlier, Stacey. I'm sorry to have to do this now but you reported Jake Perkins was dead."

Stacey Schwimmer manages a nod.

"It must have been a shock, finding him like that. Were you close?"

She bites her lower lip. "I only knew him from his visits here, which were infrequent. Our association was purely professional. He was very gung-ho about investing in local properties, even talked about buying a ranch here to use as his SoCal base. That's how I came to show him this spread. He loved it. Said it was perfect. We just closed escrow on it yesterday. Jake, I mean Mr. Perkins, had all sorts of plans. He wanted to restore it to its original glory. Those were his words. He's like a twenty-first-century cowboy, you know."

"So I gather," I say.

"He had a dream of restaging rodeos and horse wrangling competitions, that kind of thing. He would say this and go Yee Haw, even when talking on the phone. I had to hold the phone away from my ear, he was so loud. He could be quite colorful. Quite a character."

She doesn't seem to be aware of it but she's crying. Tears are streaking down both her cheeks, ruining her mascara.

I inform her of this discreetly.

She looks surprised and oddly guilty, fishing out a tissue from her handbag and dabbing at it.

"I'm sorry," she says. "Must be the shock. I've never had a client die on me before."

"Maybe you should sit down," I suggest.

I don't want her in the house, so I help her into the front seat of her own car, leaving the door open so we can talk.

Other cars start arriving.

When I see Brine, I hand Schwimmer off to him and go to talk with Kayla, Ramon and David.

"So that was the killer?" David asks when I tell them about the screen door incident.

"Most likely. The house is a maze. The unsub could have gotten in without Perkins even knowing. It's the kind of place you could play hide and seek in and not find someone for hours." I pause, thinking. "I think the realtor, Schwimmer, might have slept with Perkins. Kayla, you try and see if you can get her to talk about it. Don't push, let it come out naturally."

"We sure this is the same guy, jefe?" Ramon asks.

"Be a hell of a coincidence otherwise," I say. "And you know how I feel about coincidences."

Ramon nods. "I checked out the other stuff you texted about last night."

He turns his laptop around to show me the screen. "None of the guys they put away for the three murders match our unsub. Different body types, for one thing. The timelines don't match either."

I figured as much but had to ask him to confirm it to be sure. No stone unturned. "That's good but I think the game just changed. I'm pretty sure our unsub paid me a visit yesterday."

They stare at me.

"When you were in the lock-up?" David asks.

I feel my jaw tighten. "Bastard came to my house, spoke to my sislaw. Broad daylight, bold as anything. Threatened to take my daughter away from me."

I explain about Brook Wentworth's visit the day before, my morning trip to DCFS, my coffee-chai chat with LaShanda Jackson.

"Son of a bitch!" Ramon says, muscles jumping under his tight tee shirt. "He came into your crib, jefe. Dissed your fam. That's a friggin' throwdown. You gotta pay him back for that!"

"I intend to," I say, calmly and coldly. "But first, we have to catch the asshole."

"We can try pulling his prints off that card," David suggests. "Print your house, too, if you're okay with that. Might get lucky in the system."

"We can do all that, sure," I say. "But he's clearly moving fast here. Five nights ago, he kills Derek Chen. Yesterday he pays me a visit. The same night he kills Jake Perkins. This guy's entering the Frenzy phase."

Serial killers all follow a certain pattern of behavior that the profilers at the Bureau's Behavioral Analysis Unit or BAU in Quantico classify into seven distinct phases: Aura, Trolling, Flirting, Capture, Murder, Totem, and Depression. Some describe an eighth phase that applies to a few rare ones—they call this Frenzy. It's an extension of the Murder phase, except that this time the killer enters into a self-destructive spiral, committing kill after kill, not merely to satisfy his ritualistic urges, but as a response to the pressure of law enforcement moving in. Like the last throes of an animal that senses imminent death and starts lashing out wildly in all directions.

"Makes sense," Kayla says. "Coming to your house was reckless. Now we have a name, an ID, even a physical description. Killing Jake Perkins last night was an even bigger risk."

"That's what worries me," I say. "Something had to have triggered this downslide. He didn't just go off on his own."

"Jefe's right," Ramon says. "Dude was meticulous before now. SCVPD didn't even figure they had a serial. They thought it was domestic violence, random killings. Even the Chen murder was by the book. Clinical. Why mess it all up suddenly?"

"He wants to be caught?" Kayla suggests. "He has a death wish? From what DCFS told you, he was always erratic. Trigger temper. He went crazy attacking that woman and her boyfriend, screwed up his own job and career. If he hadn't done that, DCFS probably wouldn't have cottoned on to his abuse of his position for years, maybe never. Sounds like he was his own worst enemy there, too. Maybe that's a pattern? Self-destructive behavior?"

I frown, shaking my head as I think. "I don't think so. It doesn't fit the pattern. Serial killers are clinical, precise, methodical. By the time they get to the stage of committing multiple murders, they've acquired a certain psychological armor. Built up a persona to shield themselves from scrutiny. The rage, lust and madness is still there, but it's channeled into those carefully planned and executed acts of murder, torture, rape, whatever. Structure, repetition, predictability, habit, these are their best friends. This kind of deviation only happens when there's external pressure, either from close family or from law enforcement closing in."

Even as I say it, it clicks.

"Eureka?" Kayla says, seeing my expression.

I turn to David. "David, did you finish up those data maps?"

"Sure," he says, tapping out one-fingered commands on his laptop. He points at the screen above my head. It displays a map of SCV overlaid with dots and lines of different colors.

"You asked us to map out all the key data we have on the Clothesline Killer's victims."

"The mothers," Brine says.

David points to different colored lines and dots on the screen as he talks, "Birth dates, places, residential and work addresses, social security numbers, driver's license numbers, vehicles' make and model, license plate number, etc. Then we took their cellphone numbers and overlaid their GPS signal pings to show their most frequent locations. Each black dot marks a victim's house. Red dots are their workplace locations. Each of these lines connecting them signify different deets. And placed over them is the word cloud."

I look at the screen. The word cloud is grayed out to allow

the other text to show. Out of the jumble, two words jump out at me.

Medal Coffee.

Marge's place. Where I met LaShanda just this morning.

I find Medal Coffee on the map. The red dots all overlap there to form one big red dot.

I tap the dot. "That's it."

Everyone peers at the screen, trying to see what I see.

"A coffee shop?" Brine says. "Customers?"

"Staff," Naved says, intuiting my theory.

I nod at him. "Marge is known for her bleeding heart," I say. "She's a sucker for a lost cause. Especially women trying to clean up their act. A former junkie herself, she's probably sponsored more young, alcoholic and addicted mothers than the priests at St. Agnews."

"I see it," David says slowly. "She puts them to work. Dozens of young women, all of them hurting, that she's helped to go straight again."

"And LaShanda said that all the DCFS employees go to Marge's for coffee. It's right up the street. Wentworth must have frequented it, too. That's where he met the mothers. Maybe even flirted with them, heard their life stories."

"That means Marge would definitely have known him," Kayla says.

Ramon whistles softly. "Maybe she even knew who the dude was, for real? Marge knows everyone in SCV, right, jefe?"

"Pretty much," I say. "Let's head out there ASAP."

THIRTY-EIGHT

Marge takes a deep long drag of her cigarette, the tiny muscles surrounding her mouth puckering up in a smoker's smooch. When she releases it into the cool spring air, her eyes are glazed, staring back into the past.

"Yeah," she says. "Sure, I know who you're talking about."

I'm on the balls of my feet, ready to run with the information as soon as I have it. We're close. I feel it. *I'm coming for you, you creep.*

Kayla waits with the infinite patience of the seasoned investigator, knowing that suggesting anything could prompt the wrong response from the witness. It's always easier to agree with a prompt rather than do the hard work and remember the real detail yourself. That's why we're trained to wait and let the wit arrive at their own word choices.

"Would you recall their name?" Kayla asks at last.

Marge shrugs. "What you said before. Wentworth something? Brooks, maybe? Yeah, that's it. Wentworth Brooks."

I feel a pang of disappointment. I was hoping to get more out of Marge. "Do you recall him ever going by another name?"

Marge frowns at me. "I served coffee to the man, I didn't date him, if that's what you're asking, honey."

"Of course, Marge. I just thought maybe you might have recognized him from around. Back when he was younger, maybe? A kid?"

Marge shakes her head. "I know he lived around here somewhere."

"Here as in SCV or...?"

"As in Canyon Country," Marge says.

I feel a prickle of hope again. "Did he ever mention a neighborhood maybe? Any local establishments? A corner store?"

"Why would he, honey? All he did was order coffee and breakfast, eat, pay, leave, just like the Julia Roberts movie. Say, wasn't that a book, too? Why don't they make movies like that anymore? I liked that one."

I can see Brine opening his mouth to tell her it's *Eat, Pray, Love*, not pay or leave, but at a look from me, he shuts his mouth with a teeth-click.

"Anything else you recall about him, Marge? It would really be a big help."

"Sorry, honey, I know it must be real important to your case, but like I said already, he'd just order, eat, pay, leave. Man of few words."

Looks like we've gotten more or less all we're going to get out of Marge. I gesture to Ramon who shows her the pics of the mothers. Marge looks at them with a deep, sad sigh and then hands them back with a shudder.

"Poor women. Poor babies, too. What kind of monster would do that? Kill mamas in their own beds, next to their sleeping babies? I hope you catch this one, Susan. And I hope he can be tried in Texas. Even lethal injection's too good for the likes of him."

"Did any of those women ever work here, Marge?" I ask, working hard to sound casual.

Marge looks at me with a Duh Yeah expression. "All of them, sweetheart. Just not all at once."

"Did you ever see any of them talk to Brook or maybe go out with him?"

Marge squints, trying to remember. "To the second part, nope. But sure, they chatted him up some for sure. He was the quiet type. My girls, especially the ones who are in recovery, they can be a bit chatty. I don't mind it. Keeps the customers engaged. Longer they stay, more they order. Good business."

I ask a few more questions but at the end of another half hour, it's clear that Marge isn't quite the magic bullet we were hoping for.

Just before we're about to wrap up, Marge stubs out a cigarette and points at a spot in the parking lot. "Always parks his truck in the same place though. Right there. Real proud of that truck, is the boy. Only time I saw him come alive was when some long-haul trucker passing through asked who the owner was and sang its praises. It's some kind of antique, I think."

A jolt of excitement surges in my chest. She's just used the present tense when speaking of him.

"You're sure he drove a truck?" I ask.

"Not at first," Marge says. "Back in the day, during the time you're asking about, he had some old jalopy. Nothing special. But more recently, he comes in the red pickup. At least that's what he was driving last time I recall. Must have been, oh, maybe a few weeks ago."

All of us on the team are dead silent.

"You mean he still comes here? Like recently?" I ask.

"Well, like I said, it was a few weeks ago. It's not like he's a regular. But every once in a while, he does drop by."

I look at my team. Their eyes are shining, too.

Not long after, we're back in the van with the hard disk dump from Marge's parking lot camera, forwarding through footage.

"There it is," Ramon says, munching a snack. He offers me the bag. I decline. He offers it to Naved who takes one.

All of us try hard not to stare.

When Naved bites into it and chews, he starts coughing almost at once. The coughing worsens for a few minutes before stabilizing. When he recovers, he takes the bag of Cheetos from Ramon and looks at it.

"XXX Flaming Hot with Jalapeno Kick?" Naved says hoarsely.

"Did you feel the kick?" Ramon asks innocently.

"Like a mule kicked me in the gut," Naved says sourly.

"Focus, people," I say. "We've got him in that truck again here at Medal Coffee. And Marge says she believes he lives right here in Canyon Country. Put the pieces together. Let's do it."

I walk away, leaving them to do their thing, while I dial Trevor Blackburn's number.

"Susan," he says, answering on the first ring. "Are you calling about Jake? I just heard."

"Tell me about Brook Wentworth," I say without preamble.

Dead silence.

I walk across the dirt yard. Mancini's trailer is already there, her white-clad team tracking in and out of the ranch house. Other FBI and SCVPD vehicles are there, too. When Kayla called me at Marge's, I told her to initiate standard protocols, which includes door-to-door questioning. With a neighborhood where the residences are as far apart as they are here, that requires local knowledge and coordination. Chief McD may not want to have anything to do with this case, but like it or not, he has to cooperate.

"I probably know as much or as little as you do," Blackburn says at last.

"Bullshit," I say.

"What is it you're expecting of me?" he asks. I detect a note of amusement in his tone.

"Full cooperation, remember? That was the deal. We shook on it."

"I told Chief McDougall not to get in your way, hand over all files, offer whatever support you require."

"Yeah, well, that's his job. He works for the county, not for you. He's expected to do all that by law. I'm talking about what you know about this guy Wentworth. And don't give me that bullshit about not knowing anything. Your little billionaires Murder Club somehow managed to track this guy down, hacked his intranet which he set up to illegally spy on his victims, and you've been doing it for years. How did you do that?"

"We just got lucky, I guess."

"Come on, Trevor. Serial killers don't go around advertising their services. You don't just stumble across them while browsing the internet. You found this guy somehow, and you did that a long time ago. You've been watching his kills for at least eight years. You know his real identity, not this fake Brook Wentworth cover. I need to know everything you know, and I need to know it now."

"What makes you think Brook Wentworth wasn't his real name?" he asks.

"Because it's a dead end. It took my people all of five minutes to learn that Brook Wentworth's social security number, driver's license, lease agreement all lead nowhere. The real Brook Wentworth is a junior high basketball coach in St Paul's, Minnesota. He's sixty-four years old and he's never set foot in California."

"So he committed identity theft, used fake IDs. That's not unusual for a serial killer."

"I'm not playing this game with you, Trevor. Tell me how you found him."

"What makes you think I was the one who found him? Not Derek, Jake, Riley, Cara, Zeus?"

"Because they aren't the ones willing to risk their lives to spend two hours alone with a serial killer. Because you clearly have something going on with this guy that's personal. I asked you about it before. You put me off then. No more games. What is it, Trevor?"

He's silent for a long moment.

When he comes back, he says, "We profiled him. The same way your guys do at your BAU in Quantico. That was how our Murder Club, as you call it, started out. As an exercise in seeing if we could track down an active serial killer."

"The Behavioral Analysis Unit is the most respected in the world. Don't insult it by comparing it to your amateur hour. Profiling requires evidence to work from. An actual case, ideally more than one. That's how we find a pattern, a ritual, look at the details, build a profile."

"Well, we might not meet your high standards, Susan, but believe me when I say, we weren't just pursuing a hobby. Each of us had a genuine, shared interest in serial killers for personal reasons. We had all spent years, decades studying the phenomenon intensively. We each had very deeply personal reasons for doing so, and we went about it as methodically and scientifically as possible. Sure, we might not measure up to your BAU, but believe me, we weren't amateur hour either."

"What personal reasons?" I say.

"Personal," he says, "which is why I'm not going to tell you about them. But I can tell you this. We looked at thousands, maybe tens of thousands of cases, looked for patterns, similarity in MO, murder weapons, wounds, victims, etc. That's how we found the first two mothers he'd strangled."

"The first two on the videos?" I ask.

"No, these two were from before. No videos of their murders. Thanks to U, we knew there had probably been

Clothesline murders even earlier, so we kept digging. We found them the old-fashioned way, by going through law enforcement files. They were the ones that helped us identify other similar, potential victims. After that, we knew what to look for. When he struck the third time, we knew we were onto something. It still took us another two victims before we finally figured out that he was using cameras, recording them and sending the recordings back to himself through an intranet. That's when we started to hack his intranet and tape our own copies off his video feed. After that, we began recording copies of all his kills."

The watchers watching the watcher watching his victims. "So before these eight, he had killed, what, five times that you knew of?" I ask.

"At least. There might have been more, earlier kills, while he was honing his craft, that went unreported. The victims he picks tend to be the lowest strata of society, the dregs, so law enforcement doesn't expend a lot of resources on solving their murders."

"Santa Carina Valley has one of the lowest crime rates in LA County, among the lowest in the state," I say. "Not to mention probably the lowest murder rate. That doesn't sound like something that would go unnoticed."

"If you're asking me why Chief McDougall didn't realize that he had a serial killer operating in his backyard, well, that's a question you'll have to ask him, Susan. You asked me how we tracked down the Clothesline Killer, I'm telling you."

There's something else there that he's not telling me. Something personal again?

"It's a little convenient that you happened to find a serial killer so close to home, isn't it?" I say. "I mean, of all the places in this great big Golden State, why Santa Carina Valley?"

His tone is different when he answers this time. "Because when we began searching, we decided to only look at a certain area."

"Which was?"

"Southern California," he says.

I frown. "That's an oddly specific area."

"We were operating on the theory that there are anywhere from twenty-five to fifty unidentified serial killers active in the United States at any given time, responsible for around one hundred and fifty murders each year. Those are FBI estimates, right?"

"More or less. Nobody knows exactly."

"Okay, Susan. We theorized that if there are fifty active serials right now, that's about one in each state, so we decided to look for our local California serial killer. They do say buy local, right?"

I ignore the tasteless joke. "Why not northern Cali? Why only SoCal?"

He makes a sound. "Because we're all from there, okay? If you want to get personal about it, that's the reason. We all came from the area. That's one of the things we had in common."

Now we're getting somewhere. That explains a lot. "All six of you were from Santa Carina Valley?"

"Either born there, or grew up there, or were there for a significant part of our growing years. And don't start psychoanalyzing us. It was just a starting point. If we didn't find one in our neck of the woods, we were going to widen the net. We just happened to luck out, that's all."

You sure did, Trevor. You hit the jackpot. "We have people in the Bureau whose job it is to comb through murder files from across the country, cross-referencing MOs, murder weapons, victims, all that stuff. We don't just find serials that easily. I find it hard to believe a bunch of amateurs did it in their spare time."

"Yeah, well, you'd be surprised what having almost unlimited resources can do for you. Are we done here, Susan? I do have a business to run, you know. I'm really sorry about Jake. He was a good guy. Bit of a redneck, but basically heart in the right place. He'll be missed. I hope you get the son of the bitch responsible." He hung up.

I walk around the yard for a few, thinking it all through.

Someone approaching me from behind makes my self-preservation antenna kick in. I turn around.

"Hey," Naved says.

He looks tired, the dark circles beneath his eyes more pronounced than usual. Not for the first time, I can't help noting the similarity, slight as it is, to a familiar showbiz personality. Even Lata noticed it when she described Naved as 'a South Asian Benicio Del Toro'.

"Hey," I repeat.

"You still mad at me from last night?" he asks.

"I'm not mad at you, Naved. I was mad at Sujit. I'm sorry if I wasn't able to make that clear last night before I took off."

"You have nothing to apologize for. I get it. You had every right to be upset. Anyone would be upset at finding out such a thing. I'm just sorry that I had to bring you that news, and that all this happened to you."

"You did the right thing, Naved. It was a lead that had to be followed up. And I did. I spoke to Sujit last night, as you know."

Naved perks up. "What did he say?"

I shrug. "Nothing earth shattering. He admitted that Amit had called him to the Rao house that day, but by the time Sujit landed up there, Amit was already dead."

"That's it?" Naved looks disappointed.

"That's it. And I believe him. Sujit lies through his teeth about almost everything but this time, I believe he was telling me the truth. Besides, I can't think of a single reason why he would want to kill Amit."

"What about the big deal he's working on? The redevelopment plan for downtown?"

"He'd love to kill Trevor Blackburn to get him out of the

way, but Amit? No way. That doesn't compute. Naved, I think you did amazing work, tracking Sujit's GPS showing that both Amit and Sujit were there around the same time, but I think it's another dead end."

THIRTY-NINE

Lata listens to me without saying a word for the duration. When I'm done, she spits out a single expletive. It's a word she would never use in front of Natalie but as an ex-Marine who served three tours before decommissioning, I'm sure there's a lot more where it came from. I second it.

"He came into our house, Suse," she says. "Why the fuck did he come into our house?"

"I don't know, Lata, but it's the biggest mistake he ever made," I say, then pause. "I think maybe he wanted to send me a message, tag me so I'll come after him. Serial killers do that sometimes, as you know—we've talked about this over the years."

"A serial killer? I can't believe it. He played the part so beautifully. I really believed every word. And I'm not exactly a pushover for con artists."

"He actually did work for DCFS once upon a time, so he knows exactly what to say, the protocols, the forms, the lingo. He's fooled a lot of people before, Lata. Don't take it personally."

"Hell with that. This is fucking personal. *He came into our house!* Threatened to take Natalie away from us!"

"And I'm going to get him for it," I reply, meaning every word of it. "I'm on this, Lata. My entire team is working only on tracking this guy down and nailing him."

"That's good. But why, Susan? Why did he come into our house? Why us?"

"Because he knows I'm leading the case. It's his way of taunting me with a 'catch me if you can' challenge," I say. "That's my theory."

"If that's true," she says, "then challenge accepted. You goddamn better get this bastard. Because, God help me, Suse, I'm so mad right now that if this dude actually dares to make the mistake of coming back here, I swear I won't be responsible for what happens next."

I know she means every word of it, too.

This isn't just Natalie's aunt speaking. It's a decorated Marine who's taken down jihadis in the 'stan. Most people who interact with Lata every day see only the likeable, attractive, deeply affectionate caregiver and aunt.

Even I can't claim to have seen Marine Gunnery Sergeant Lata Kapoor, not really. That's a side of herself she saves only for combat tours and her training and refresher camps. Her 'away' side, as she calls it. But it's there. Under the woman who always has a smile, a kind word and an Indian biscuit—no, they're not cookies, she always insists, these are Indian *biscuits* —lies a tough-as-nails, hard-ass, American soldier who's taken lead, shed some of her blood and spilled a helluva lot more enemy blood to defend her country. Our country.

If the man who calls himself Brook Wentworth makes the error of returning to our home, it will be the last mistake he ever makes.

I'm betting she's walking to the upstairs hall closet even as she's talking to me on her cellphone, using the ladder to climb up to reach the built-in gun safe where we stow our weapons and ammo when at home. We never open or close it when Natalie is around to see, and never make the mistake of leaving either around the house. As career professionals who use weapons and deal with violent antagonists on a daily basis, we know the dangers of guns and are hyper alert about such precautions. She'd never be careless about such a thing but as co-caregivers it's my job to remind her just as it is hers to watch out for me, and so I say:

"Remember safety protocols."

"Always," she replies. "Okay, Suse. I'm good now. Thanks for updating me. He'd have to be a real dumbass to even attempt that kind of stunt again, but if he does, I'm afraid you're going to have one very dead serial killer."

"Just the way I like them," I say, "well done and crispy, riddled with holes."

I'm only half-joking.

I'm not a fan of vigilante justice. I don't even support the death penalty. But if a man who's killed over a dozen young mothers in their own beds is idiotic enough to come visiting my family home again, my sislaw and I have every right to defend ourselves and may the consequences be on his head.

I hang up and look at Kayla, who's just climbing back into the van, looking like the cat who just brought home a nice fat rodent to drop at her mistress's feet.

My instructions to Kayla earlier were simple and clear: "Schwimmer's lying. I want you to break her alibi. Find out what she's hiding from us."

"And?" I ask Kayla now.

She grins at me. "You're on fire today, boss. You were so right. She broke down in a New York minute. Gave me every-thing. I didn't even have to browbeat her or break out the mind games."

I'm not surprised to hear that. Upscale real estate agents

like Stacey Schwimmer come mostly from the blue blood families of SCV. Generationally wealthy families who can afford not to work the rest of their lives and simply live off the fat of their trust funds. When they do choose to work, it's usually something like upscale real estate deals, using their upper-class contacts and access to deal with high-end properties. They get to move in the same social circles, meet and negotiate at the same clubs and chic bistros, and when they close a deal, the commission check is respectable enough to pay for their weekend spa treatments and vacations in Belize. They're not hardcases capable of holding out under interrogation; if they get into a jam, they leave that to their thousand dollar an hour attorneys to handle.

"She was sleeping with Jake Perkins. Nothing exclusive for either of them but if he was in town, they usually hooked up. He started out as a client, contacted through a mutual acquaintance, and he's been sniffing around looking for properties in the valley for a couple of years now. She actually closed escrow on the McBean Ranch with him just yesterday, but they were able to keep the whole deal hush hush because the buyer of record was one of his shell companies. Anyway, he wanted to celebrate here, at his new property. He came in late last evening; she had opened up the place and changed the sheets. They ate out at Bella Trattoria on Sierra Canyon Road, then came back here for a quick tumble. She left to go home just after one because she's having a new infinity pool put in and the contractor was going to show up bright and early this morning. She says Perkins was alive and well when she left, and I believe her. She was with him when they heard the screen door banging, and he went to check it out but said it was nothing, just the wind. She came in around eight this morning, found him dead, panicked, and ran. She pulled over a couple of miles away, came to her senses and called it in. She says she didn't mean to lie to you or the cops, she was still in shock. I kept expecting her to ask for her attorney, but she said no, she wanted to help us find whoever did this. For what it's worth, Suse, I think she had real feelings for the guy. Woman's a mess."

"Okay," I say, "good work, K. Did you ask her about the back door I found? The one with the loose screen door?"

"Seems the McBean family began to fight bitterly among themselves in the second half of the last century. They all wanted a piece of the ranch because for one reason or another, all their other businesses and plans went sour. This parcel of land was all they had left; that, and the family name. The various siblings each had their own partners and kids and needed more space, so they kept expanding the original structure, adding apartments for each new family. They wanted to maintain the illusion of unity, so there was only one entrance and door, but they couldn't stand to see each other, so they built separate entrances at the back, one for each apartment. They all had keys and came and went that way."

"How many apartments in all?" I ask.

"Fourteen, plus the original house."

"Wow. That's a lot of front doors. Or back doors in this case. That means there were fifteen separate ways for an intruder to get in?"

"Pretty much. But she says all the others were kept locked. I had SCVPD do another sweep. The locks are still intact. We're dusting them all for prints to check if they've recently been tampered with or changed. But it looks like the only doors used recently were the front door and that one back door, the one with the loose screen door."

"That's probably where the killer got in," I say, thinking. "Okay, K, you did good." I turn to David. "David?"

He holds up his tablet, showing me the screen filled with legal documentation in fine print.

I wave it away. "Summarize."

"Like the realtor said, escrow was closed yesterday. The

property was officially Jake Perkins'. I suppose it's fitting. He got to die under his own roof, in his own bed."

"With his boots on," I add, "like a true cowboy."

"And the birth and schooling records for Perkins and the others?"

David nods, tapping his tablet. "It checks out. Five of them were born right here in or very near SCV. Only Hamilton was born in Norfolk, California, and his family moved here when he was two. They all spent at least a good part of their school years right here. But here's the thing. Trevor Blackburn wasn't going by that name then. He's the only one who changed his name."

"What's his real name?" I ask.

"That's the weird part, boss. I don't know."

I stare at him. "What do you mean, you don't know? How did you even find out he changed his name?"

"I didn't."

David doesn't talk much, unless you get him on a topic that floats his boat, which is usually some bit of arcane trivia. Sometimes, it can be hard to get him to say more than is absolutely necessary. This is a very useful trait for him when he's called on the witness stand at a trial, but it can be a little frustrating when I'm trying to keep the momentum going with a free exchange of info.

"Um, David, I'm going to need you to be a little more clear," I say.

He taps the screen of his tablet, swiping and enlarging to show me documents and forms, trying to explain the intricacies of legal name changes.

"Okay, okay," I say at last. "What you're saying to me is that you know he changed his name because there isn't any conclusive documentation proving that he did change his name? Did I get that right?"

He beams. "Yes."

"Color me very confused. How do you prove a negative?"

"Because there is no birth record of any Caucasian male named Trevor Anthony Blackburn, fifty-seven years old, anywhere in the United States," David says.

Now we're getting somewhere. "But I thought you confirmed that he was born right here in Santa Carina Valley?"

"That's what his school transcripts show at SCV High, and before that, at SCV Junior High, and even SCV Elementary. But there's no birth certificate in any of his transcripts."

"How is that possible?" I ask. "Isn't a birth certificate mandatory for admission to any school?"

David shrugs. "It is, but if you're transferring, the previous school records are usually sufficient. The onus is usually on the first institution to capture your birth certificate."

Translated from David-speak that means the elementary school. "And you're saying that SCV Elementary doesn't have the birth certificate on record? How did they verify his age then?"

"Probably from his medical and immunization records. Those are on file with them."

Something I read in an issue of *The Signal*, the local SCV newspaper, comes to mind. "Wait. Wasn't SCV Elementary shut down a few years back? Because of the building predating earthquake standard construction or something?"

"Yes," David says, "four years ago. The old school building was demolished and a new structure erected. That's now called the Celine Woodruff Elementary, apparently after its founder and benefactor."

That makes sense. Celine Woodruff was a silent movie star who gained fame for playing a popular cowgirl heroine in a series of films, all shot right here in Santa Carina Valley. At that time, SCV was Hollywood's backlot for westerns, and the majority of the cowboy movies of the first half of the twentieth century were filmed right here.

"Okay," I say, "so the records must have been digitized at

some point, right?"

"Right. Most of the records predated computers. They digitized them before the demolition and reconstruction. That's the archive I accessed for this information," David says.

"Maybe they somehow missed the birth certificate?" I suggest.

"It's plausible," David says.

Plausible, but not likely, is what he means.

"David, do me a huge favor," I say. "Go down there and search their physical archives for the Blackburn file. See if you can lay your hands on an actual birth certificate. I know it's a long shot, but it's worth a try, right?"

"Oh yes," he says, agreeing wholeheartedly. "Because all his other documentation is consistent with that birth date and location. Which is why it's very odd that I couldn't find a birth certificate anywhere."

"You checked all the county records?" I ask. "And hospital records, too? Because sometimes, almost never but still it does happen, hospital records go missing before the mother can register with the county and get an official birth certificate issued. There's always the slight possibility that's what happened here. It would explain the missing birth certificate."

"That it would," he says, not looking convinced. "All right, I'll go check it out."

"Thanks, David, you're awesome," I say.

Ramon speaks up. "Jefe, I have a question."

"Shoot, Ramon."

"This dude Brook Wentworth doesn't exist, right? That's why nothing we found on him is authentic. Fake address, social security number, driver's license, the works. So how the hell did he get the job at DCFS? I mean, they're a government organization. They have direct connections with all other branches of government. They can verify these things instantly. So how did he pull one over them?"

I frown. "That's a great question, Ramon. I've asked Kayla to follow up with LaShanda Jackson there. Add that to the list."

Kayla nods, making a note. "I'm heading there now actually if you don't need me."

"Go for it," I say.

David and Kayla both head out. Ramon is the only one still here in the van with me. Brine is busy coordinating the crime scene work with Mancini's field investigative team as well as the door-to-door with SCVPD.

He pokes his head in shortly after.

"Mancini wants you," he says.

I walk over to the mobile lab. The meeting is short and sweet.

"You are sure this is same killer?" Marisol asks me without preamble.

"What does the evidence say?" I ask.

She nods approvingly. One of her favorite phrases is, *Listen to the evidence, it knows more than you do.* "Evidence very confused today. MO is different from Derek Chen killing. Multiple stab wounds, bludgeoning on head, no strangulation, no polypropylene traces. But!"

She raises her finger, pointing at the white ceiling and blindingly bright fluorescents. I don't think there's a single shadow in here. "But he use nitrile glove again. And same Tyvek suit."

She shows me the tablet screen. This time, I'm reminded of an Indian abstract artist's work, S.H. Raza.

"You see?" she says, after spending several minutes explaining the chemical compositions of the trace elements found at the scene.

I take her word for it. "So what's your theory based on the evidence?"

She looks troubled. "It is quite unusual. Seems like different killer. But then we have the nitrile gloves and Tyvek suit. So maybe it is same killer trying to make us think it is different killer?"

"But then why use the exact same type of nitrile gloves and Tyvek suit again? He'd have to know we would be able to match them."

Marisol nods, her hand working the button on her wheelchair to roll a half inch forward, then a half inch back. It's a nervous tic she has when thinking sometimes. I've seen her outside the mobile unit, smoking furiously, while doing the same forward-back motion for several minutes.

"Good question. Maybe he not sophisticated enough to think we will find out? He underestimate Mancini ability?"

I smile at her. "Nobody in their right mind underestimates your ability, Marisol."

She smiles back.

Not for the first time, I'm charmed by her classical beauty. In another life, she could be gracing the covers of fashion magazines, or filling the silver screen. "You flatter me too much. But yes, I not think that. He sophisticated, that I already know. Interesting killer you have here this time, Susan. This unsub intrigue me much."

"He intrigues me, too," I say. Though 'intrigue' might not be the exact word for the sick feeling this killer evokes in me.

I tell her about the videos of the eight strangulations we found, and about how badly SCVPD botched up the investigations.

She clicks her tongue as I describe how at least three of the cases ended in the wrong unsubs being convicted.

"Our great justice system," she says. "World famous. When it work good, it work very, very good. When it fail, it fail totally. We Americans, we are masters of the extreme."

She asks me to follow her as she wheels herself out of the van.

"Come, let me tell you something," she says.

FORTY

Outside the mobile lab, Marisol Mancini unzips the top of her bio suit, digs out a pack of Italian cigarettes with just the letters MS printed in front.

She taps one out, and lights it with a Bic lighter.

She takes a small drag and exhales, holding it in her long fingers.

The smoke smells pungent, even spicy, and very strong.

Even mostly covered in the bio suit with the mask dangling from her ears, she's stunning. It's hard to believe she spends most of her days elbow deep in blood and guts and body parts.

"In these videos," she asks, looking not at me but into the distance, the smoke drifting around her hair like an ocean haze, "unsub is wearing the Tyvek suit and gloves?"

"Gloves, yes, though I can't tell what kind. But definitely no suit."

"So maybe these things are new. He has changed his, how you call it, *equipaggiamenti*?"

I search for the right English equivalent. "Accoutrements? Yes, seems like it. His victims are very different, too."

"Yes, yes, that is good point," she says. "Maybe he not feel required to use such elaborate precaution for his female victims. Because he know police not pay close attention too much. But with these *miliardari*, how you say it, billionaires? He know lot more attention be focus on their murders."

"That makes sense," I say, thinking about it.

Until just now, when Marisol asked me about it, I never realized that the unsub wasn't wearing the biosuit in the eight recorded murders. Maybe he knew their deaths wouldn't warrant the A-team attention that Derek Chen and Jake Perkins are now receiving.

"So he is strategic, yes?" she says. "Like a good generale militare, he change to match his victims."

"How do you explain the change of murder weapon and MO?" I ask.

She takes a deep drag and exhales slowly. "I think he do it on purpose. I think maybe first murder was mistake."

"Derek Chen's murder was a mistake?" I ask, hearing the surprise in my own voice. "How?"

She waves a hand. "Not murder itself. I am saying, MO of that first one might be mistake. He intend to do it some other way maybe. But some reason, he unable to. So he fall back on old tried and tested method. Do strangulation like before times. But intention was to use new MO."

"New MO like the way he stabbed Jake Perkins?"

"Maybe..." she starts to say, then waves a hand again. "No. I think he want do Derek Chen some other way. And I think next one he do, is being third MO."

"So he's switching up his MO for these Murder Club murders," I say, thinking it through. "But why? That's not how serial killers usually operate."

"Something else going on in this man's head. He in some new space now. Way he killed Jake Perkins, it not just new weapon, it look like rage killing. Force of wounds, number, way he keep stabbing even after victim is dead... all suggest he angry with this Perkins. It become personal somehow."

I frown. What personal motive could the unsub have for Jake Perkins which he didn't have for Derek Chen? It's an odd observation, a very unorthodox way of looking at the evidence, but my gut instinct tells me Marisol is onto something. It resonates somehow. I saw Jake Perkins lying there in his bed, the sheer amount of blood, the wounds on his body, the splatter patterns across the wall behind him, the bed, the floor, it all suggests a crime committed in a violent rage, not the usual methodical, clinical, serial killer's ritual.

She's finished her cigarette and turns her wheelchair to go up the ramp.

I look at her.

"Marisol, I know I've told you this before, but I'll say it again and not for the last time. You're awesome."

"Yes, this is fact," she says, unselfconsciously. "You pretty awesome yourself also, Susan. You go catch this bastardo now, okay?"

My phone buzzes as I'm walking away.

Sujit Chopra calling.

The hell does he want now?

"Sujit?" I say as I pick up. "I'm a little tied up right now."

"I know, I know, bete," he says. "I heard. Jake Perkins. That is a second big blow for Trevor Blackburn and his Silicon Valley South."

The glee in his voice is unmistakable. I roll my eyes impatiently even though it's a voice call and he can't see me. I'm not really interested in hearing him gloat over his business rival's problems.

"I'll call you back when I have a minute," I say, and start to hang up.

The word "Amit" stops me.

"What did you say?" I ask.

"I said, I remembered something else about the day Amit died," he says.

My heart skips a beat.

"Tell me," I say.

"I should have thought of it last night but you had a gun pointed at me. That made it hard to think. It came to me just now and I thought, I should tell Susie. I do not think it has any real importance, but I did not want you to get upset in case you spoke to her and found out afterwards."

"Found out what, Sujit?" I ask impatiently. "Just spit it out."

"The day Amit called me and asked me to meet him at Dr. Rao's house, he asked me if his mom was with me. He knew we were partners in the business, of course. I told him no, she was with Kundan."

"And?" I ask, feeling my pulse quicken.

"And he said he had tried her already, but the call went straight to voicemail, so he left her a voicemail and a text."

"Saying what?"

"Asking her to come, too."

"To the Rao house?" I ask.

"Yes, yes."

"And what had she said?"

"She had not replied by the time he called me. That was why he asked if she was with me. I told him that she would probably just turn up directly. If he had sent her a voicemail and a text, she would definitely call him back or come directly."

"And did she?"

"She never came to the Rao house. Not while I was there. I cannot say if she came before me and left or afterwards, but I do not think that happened."

"But what did she say when you talked to her about it after

Amit's death?" I ask. "You must have talked to her about it, right?"

He's silent for a moment.

"Sujit? Did you or didn't you talk to Aishwarya about Amit calling both of you to the Rao house that day?" I ask.

"I tried to bring it up once in private," he says. "But she acted as if she didn't know what I was talking about. I thought maybe she was upset about it and did not want to discuss it. You know Aishwarya. She can get moody at times."

"So you never really talked about it with her?"

"Not after that one time," he admits.

"And that's all you remember?"

"Yes," he says. "That is the whole story. Amit called me, asked me to meet him there, would not tell me what it was about, then he said he was trying to get Aishwarya to come, too. I went there at the exact time he had specified, on the dot. I found him already dead. I left. That is all that happened."

"Okay," I say. Hard as it is for me to say the words, I reluctantly concede. "Thanks, Sujit, I appreciate your calling."

"You're most welcome, bete. Now about Jake Perkins' murder. Can you tell me anything about it? Is it true he was sodomized before he was shot?"

I hang up.

FORTY-ONE

"Okay, let's review," I say.

We're back at the command center, later the same day of Jake Perkins' murder. It's been a long, grueling day of interviews, canvassing, pounding the pavement—figuratively as well as literally—researching and deep-diving, analyzing and processing.

We're all getting a little burned out by this stage, though a new murder often means the investigation clock is reset and the 'first forty-eight' starts all over again. Unfortunate as it is for the victim, that's what passes for a lucky break in our line of work.

The whiteboards are filled with pictures and evidence, questions, and connections. Colored lines and arrows zigzag, crime scene photos vie for space with victim head shots.

Screen grabs from the eight videos get their own separate section. That's the one with the least amount of hard data.

Ironic, given the number of murders and victims and the sheer heinousness of the crimes.

In contrast, the two Murder Club murders boast an abundance of evidence and data, each with their own whiteboard, packed with crawling handwritten notes in every possible color.

The color codings reflect individual team members, one for each one of us.

I run down the facts in all ten murders. I'm leaving out the other murders that Trevor Blackburn told me about because we haven't been able to officially confirm them or find case files on them. Even Urduja's scrapbook and posse haven't been able to confirm them. Urduja suggested that perhaps they took place in another town nearby before the killer moved here to Santa Carina Valley? That's definitely one possibility.

I don't doubt they happened, because I believed Trevor when he told me that was how the Murder Club tracked down the Clothesline Killer. I just can't confirm it yet. The fault doesn't lie with him; it lies with law enforcement letting these unfortunate women slip through the cracks somehow.

It makes me mad to admit it, but it happens all the time.

The system is overburdened.

Cops are human, too.

There's simply too many crimes and not enough time.

Under a mountain of stress, the system defaults to its own brand of unofficial triage, letting public attention, the media, influencers decide which cases get the highest priority.

In our lopsided celebrity, wealth and fame-obsessed world governed by toxic social media, two famous dead male billionaires win hands down over eight (plus who knows how many more) unknown trailer trash women.

It sucks big time.

But that's how it is in the real world.

"Let's start by looking at where we are on the unsub's real name and likeness," I say. "Kayla?"

Kayla points out the pictures of the man who posed under the name of Brook Wentworth that she's stuck on the whiteboards. He's surprisingly good-looking with clean cut features, a strong jaw, sharp probing black eyes, heavy eyebrows, and medium-length brown hair.

"We got these off LaShanda Jackson and her colleagues' phones. Taken at various office events or enlarged from pics where he was accidentally clicked in the background. They all seem to say more or less the same things about the guy. He was friendly, outgoing, charming, a very good talker, attractive to women and liked by the guys as well. A good worker, he did all his assignments, is said to have the most organized workspace, and worked really hard, often coming in early and working till all hours. He took the work seriously, maybe a little too seriously, and seemed to genuinely believe in what DCFS does."

"Sounds like employee of the year!" Ramon says sarcastically.

Kayla points at him. "Which he was, actually, the second year there. And of the month several times, too."

"So it was all an act?" Brine asks. "I mean, this dude has killed a dozen people or more that we know of, he's seriously sick. That doesn't gel with the bio you just gave us."

David speaks up mildly. "It's possible his psychosis wasn't full-blown at the time that he worked at DCFS. His colleagues could have been seeing a psychopath in the making rather than an active serial killer at that time. Perhaps it was while working there that he was exposed to experiences that triggered and accelerated his descent into psychosis."

"The Making of a Serial Killer. How Da Boogeyman Got His Game On!" Ramon recites, imitating a documentary promotional voiceover.

"I'm with David on this," Kayla says. "From what LaShanda and his other coworkers said about him, he wasn't a Jeffrey Dahmer type. No creepy vibes coming off him. He could be pretty intense, and it was obvious the job was taking a toll, but they all chalked it up to his getting over-involved emotionally. It's an occupational hazard and they've all seen their share of burnouts on the job. In fact, LaShanda could only find three people in the entire department of seventy-seven who were working there nine years ago when Brook Wentworth was there, herself included. The employee attrition and turnover rates are high. So is the suicide and depression rate. I got contact details for almost two dozen other ex-employees who she thinks are probably still alive. I could talk to them, too, if you want, but I think LaShanda and the others pretty much covered it all."

"Did any of them have a relationship with Brook Wentworth that LaShanda or the other two knew of?" I ask.

"In the two and a half years he was there, nobody saw or heard of Wentworth ever dating anyone," Kayla says. "At first, a couple of women assumed he was gay, but there was another gay employee who shot down that idea, said he'd openly propositioned Wentworth and the guy turned him down flat, saying he wasn't sexual."

"He wasn't 'sexual'?" Brine asks. "Is that, like, an actual quote?"

"It is," Kayla says. "And I think we can officially confirm that our Brook Wentworth is definitely not a sixty-four-year-old junior high basketball coach from St. Paul's."

"No," I say, "but other than that, there's not a whole goddamn lot we do know about him." I look at the pictures on the Wentworth profile board. "Ramon, have you had a chance to—?"

"No go, jefe," Ramon replies, cutting me off before I can even finish asking the question. "Ran his mug through all the databases, turned up nada. Guy's a ghost. No social security. No driver's license. No passport. Not even a public library card that I could find anywhere in the system."

"You didn't find a single Brook Wentworth?" David asks.

"I found a bunch of Brook Wentworths, bruh," Ramon replies. "Except for a half dozen, the rest are all too old, too young, too sick, or too dead. I ran the half dozen down through Carlotta just in case the dude had plastic surgery or somehow managed to change his features, but nothing gives. Our Brook Wentworth doesn't exist. He never did."

"So how do you explain his getting the job at DCFS?" I ask. "They come under the DPSS and they take employee vetting pretty seriously, especially since that division is responsible for child welfare."

"Yup. They use Homeland Security. All the government agencies do. Somehow, this Wentworth dude ponied up all the official documents, driver's license, social, you name it, that checked out in the system. But get this, jefe, they're all fakes. Not just fakes, they're Grade-A fakes. Gold plated. Even I'd be proud to take credit for those forgeries!"

"Let's not get too excited about committing felonies, Ramon," I say dryly, knowing he's just trying to push my buttons by implying he might be involved in forging government IDs. Does he know people in that line of work? Absolutely. Might some of those people be related to him by blood? Very possibly. But Ramon himself hasn't messed with the law since his 'banger days and the only time he flirts with stuff that walks the line is at my behest.

"Actually, forging IDs is what prosecutors call a 'wobbler' offense," David says. "It can be charged as either a misdemeanor or a felony. Unlike counterfeiting which is an automatic felony charge."

"Thanks, David," I say. "Speaking of official documents, what did you find in the SCV school archives about Trevor Blackburn?"

"I had to go to the school district board office," David says. "They sent me to the archives, which is basically a storage facility. That's where it gets interesting. Turns out they have files from every year predating computerization, since the school district started."

Here he holds up his finger.

"Except for the specific year when Trevor Blackburn was admitted. That entire year is gone."

"What do you mean 'gone'?" Kayla asks. "How can one entire year's worth of files just be 'gone'?"

"There was a break-in around eleven years ago," David says, not bothering to look at his notes. He has a phenomenal memory and can recite reams of figures off the top of his head after scanning them for a short time. "It was never quite clear what the thieves were after, since there was nothing of value worth stealing at the site. All they took were some boxes full of files."

"And in those boxes are the files we're looking for?" Brine asks. "Trevor Blackburn's school admission file?"

David spreads his hands as if to say, go figure.

"There's something going on here," Kayla says. "We've got Brook Wentworth living off fake IDs, and now we find that we can't verify Trevor Blackburn's identity either. Isn't that a little crazy?"

"Maybe we need to come at this another way," I say. "Let's re-examine what we know. If he's *not* Trevor Blackburn, then what was his birth name? Why can't we find his birth certificate or any records of his parents or family? Why is there a gray area in his past? I mean, he's a public figure. One of the richest men alive. Why isn't more known about his beginnings, his child-hood, his birthplace, his parents, family, etc? I've done online searches on him myself, even AI deep searches—it's all pretty sketchy as far as I can tell."

"You mean sketchy as in thin on facts, or sketchy as in shady?" Brine asks.

"Both," I say.

"Well, his official bio gives us a pretty detailed history of his childhood, family, early years, youth, etc," Brine says, turning his tablet and flipping through browser tabs to show me a Wikipedia page, an official website bio, and then a search list of several hundreds of thousands of articles on Trevor Blackburn.

"Yes, but how many of those bothered to actually corroborate those details, ascertain if they were hard facts or just embellishments wrapped around a core of truth?" I say.

"Are you saying Trevor Blackburn made up his own life story?" Kayla asks.

"Not the whole thing, but what if he made up a fictional past? I mean, he's not one of the generationally wealthy billionaires. He was rich to begin with, according to the online lore, but it's only recently that he became *uber*-rich. Almost his entire wealth was amassed in, what, the last six or seven years?"

"Eleven years, to be exact," David says, looking over Ramon's shoulder as Ramon works his keyboard.

"That's the time Blackburn struck gold in the markets," Ramon says. "That's how I was able to crack his encryption key. Everyone knows the story of how Trevor Blackburn and a small group of upstarts stormed the gates and got rich almost overnight, right, jefe? Twelve years ago, Trevor Blackburn was just another successful but nothing-special businessman, jefe. Then overnight"—Ramon snaps his fingers—"he strikes gold on the markets and rides the boom. Nobody's ever become that rich that quick before. It ain't the kinda thing that happens every day."

"Right," I say. "And he did it all based on some kind of value investing algorithm that he came up with, right?"

"When you're right, you're right, jefe," Ramon says. "Cholo pulled a GameStop ten years *before* GameStop."

"In all, the total net worth accumulated by the group was estimated at over $5.7 billion," David says. "Nothing like it had ever been done before, and it probably will never happen again. They've plugged the loopholes in the system that the Murder Club used. But yes, what Trevor did was impressive, bootstrapping himself into a billionaire."

"So he's a self-made man," I say. "The question I'm asking is, is his background also self-made?"

"I still don't get where you're going with this," Kayla asks. "Like what do we achieve by proving that Trevor Blackburn made up his life story? This is America. Reinvention is like a mantra. He wouldn't be the first American success story to rewrite his past to suit his present. It's an American tradition to take a new name, new identity, and start over from scratch. So what if Trevor Blackburn did that?"

"Nothing wrong with it," I say. "I'm simply saying that isn't it strange that Trevor Blackburn's past is sketchy on verifiable factual details? And he's obsessed with this other guy, who we know as Brook Wentworth, who also shares the same problem? Don't you think that's a bit too much of a coincidence?"

"Okay," she says. "Then you *are* comparing the two?"

"I am," I say, "in this respect. How is it that one of the world's richest men has no officially verifiable past and that he happens to be insanely obsessed with a serial killer who also has no officially verifiable past? That's no coincidence. That's a freaking bizarro story, don't you think?"

FORTY-TWO

Naved calls in. I asked him to review all the door-to-door interviews and area checks conducted by SCVPD.

"Anything?" I ask, keeping my fingers crossed but not really hoping.

"Nothing. It's hard getting anything out of those OG settlers, the big ranching families. Even their neighbors are afraid of saying anything that might be seen as backbiting them," he says.

"Sure. Most of these rancher families have been here since the first settlers came west and drove out the Native Americans. They're pretty deeply dug into the community here, even if their glory days are long gone."

Until the European immigrants came, Santa Carina Valley was the home of the Tataviam tribe of Native Americans since around 450 CE. The White settlers who rolled west in their wagon trains slaughtered the entire tribe and stole their lands. From time to time, a local SCV historian laments the loss of that ancient culture, language, and history. Whatever little chance there might have been of preserving them vanished forever when the last full-blooded Tataviam, Juan Jose Fustero, died in

1921. Valley families can get very defensive about the provenance of their lands. Especially these days when that provenance is frequently being challenged. There's even a bill for reparations in play at the California state assembly.

Naved tells me about one young rancher, a woman, who reacted when he told her that her neighbor—if a house two and a half miles away could be called that—had been killed. "She says to me, and I quote, 'Didn't even know there was anyone living at the old McBean place. But if there was and that's what really happened, then they probably deserved what they got. Those McBeans have always had it coming.' I'm guessing she wasn't a fan, but she had nothing helpful to offer."

Apparently, that pretty much sums up the general tone of the interviews, with just one exception. Naved has a habit of saving the good news for last. Just as we're winding up, and I'm ready to write off a full day's efforts by some thirty uniformed SCVPD patrolmen, he throws me a lifeline.

"A Hispanic gardener working a leaf blower on the sidewalk said he might have seen a red pickup truck blow past," Naved says.

My skin prickles.

That red pickup truck again.

The Clothesline Killer was driving a red pickup truck in the videos. Thanks to his Spielbergian colorization, we knew its color and from screengrabs, we'd been able to confirm that it was an old Dodge D/W truck, the precursor of the present day Dodge Ram trucks which had been introduced in 1993.

Unfortunately, despite his amazing skills, Ramon still hasn't been able to track down a DMV registration for a possible owner here in SCV or find any link to Brook Wentworth.

Not yet, at least.

"Did he see who was driving?" I ask.

"Not exactly,"

"What's that mean?"

Naved explains that the gardener wasn't paying attention. The wind was blowing into his face, and he was bundled up to protect himself from the dust and leaf particles. That's common for the guys who mow lawns and work the leaf blowers; they wear bandana-style scarfs around their necks, covering all but their eyes which are protected by sunglasses.

"The truck blew past really quickly, too quick for him to look up in time, but he got the impression that the guy was also a gardener," Naved finishes.

"Why's that?"

"Because the gardeners all drive old pickup trucks, and he thinks that the driver's face might have been covered with a bandana, too."

"That makes a lot of sense. We're all used to seeing gardeners' and landscapers' pickup trucks around. If the unsub covered his face with a bandana, and threw a few gardening implements in the back, nobody would give him a second look. That could explain how he got in and out of Derek Chen's property and the McBean ranch."

I tell him about noticing that the grass had just been cut at the Chen cabin.

"All he'd have had to do is finish work at the end of the day, pretend to drive away, park his truck in the woods, and wait until Margaret Chen and Fiona Worthing left later that afternoon for her show. We already know there wasn't any other staff on duty that evening, so Derek Chen would have been home alone."

"That sounds good, Susan, but I wouldn't bet the farm on this gardener's testimony. He really doesn't want to testify. Most of these guys are undocumented transients. He didn't even want to talk to the officer who questioned him. The officer noted down a number and address, but I'd bet you twenty to one we'll never be able to track the witness down again."

"Let the DA's office worry about putting the case together

later, Naved. This is great news. We have a witness who placed the unsub's truck at the scene of Jake Perkins' murder. That's a major win. If we find that truck, it could be full of evidence linking him to Perkins, Chen and even the earlier murders. That's a big step forward from where we were this morning. I hate to say it, but Jake Perkins dying might be the big break we've needed."

I feel a pang of anxiety. Even though Lata is with Natalie and it's near impossible that the Clothesline Killer would go after them again, I still feel acutely anxious about them. It's a feeling I'm probably going to have to learn to live with from now on and I hate it.

Naved hears something in my voice that conveys my anxiety. He's good like that, at picking up the unsaid.

"You okay, Suse?" he asks.

"I will be once we catch this mother," I say, my voice catching.

"Okay," he says. "You need me to come back to the command center? I'm basically done here. If you don't need me there, I thought I'd head out to your place now."

The team has insisted on taking turns to stake out my place in case the unsub calling himself Brook Wentworth returns. Naved has an SCVPD patrol car doing a drive by every hour or so as well, as a deterrent. He's also insisted on taking the first shift, starting now. I'm grateful for the support, especially since I can't afford to stand watch myself with the case gaining momentum.

While I know Lata is armed and more than capable of handling any situation, the ideal situation is for the unsub not to be allowed to enter the house at all. In close quarters, if he's also armed, then things can get very hairy very quickly. I'm more concerned about collateral damage than him actually succeeding. A stray bullet can kill, maim or injure just as devastatingly.

"Okay," I say. "I really appreciate you doing that."

"Hey, this is professional courtesy, not a favor. This bastard came into your house, threatened your family. That makes him everyone's problem now. If he's stupid enough to show up again, he'll find more than just polite answers this time."

"Thanks, pardner. You're a champ."

I hang up and think for a minute about what Naved just said.

It is pretty stupid of Wentworth, or whatever his real name is, to have visited my house. He had to have known that I would break his cover instantly and then he would be bringing the wrath of SCVPD and the FBI down on himself.

Why take such a huge risk?

And for what?

It's not like he tried to attack Lata or Natalie—thankfully—so what did he really achieve?

It doesn't make sense, yet he must have had a good reason. Serial killers are generally gifted with above average intelligence. That's how they're able to operate as lethal predators claiming multiple victims over years and decades without being caught.

Everything I've learned about Brook Wentworth and how he goes about his evil business has only confirmed his intelligence and cunning.

He's eluded me and my team brilliantly so far, leaving almost no trail for us to follow, and given our own brainpower and investigative abilities, that's saying something.

And then he goes and deviates drastically from the norm, showing himself.

Why?

I put the question aside, knowing the answer will come when it's time.

I go over to Ramon.

"Ramon, we need to press harder on the red pickup," I start.

Ramon grins, winks, and taps his laptop screen. "We got it,

jefe. Just now while you were on with Naved. Take a look. Ain't she a beaut?"

He shows me the picture of a classic red Dodge pickup with a distinctive engine hood and bumper. It's featured on a vintage car site.

"It's a 1949 four-door D/W," Ramon informs me. "A classic. Not too many of these babies out there in running condition. This site tracks vintage cars and records sales."

He taps a screen that shows columns of dates, dollar values, and other details. "Only three of them sold in California in the past decade."

I stare in astonishment. "Are those the actual resale prices?" I ask. "Just for an ugly seventy-five-year-old truck?"

"Hey, watch it," Ramon says, "just 'cause you're not a fan don't give you the right to diss other people's loves."

"Oops, my bad," I say.

"S'okay, jefe, just watch it next time." He winks. "These babies sell for anywhere from thirty thou upwards depending on their condition and how many original parts they have."

He taps his screen again. "This particular one, the one our unsub rides, was sold about ten years ago for $431,000 from a vintage dealer in Pomono. That's not including any later additions or customizations he may have added on. I say, tack on another sixty grand for power steering and windows, seatbelt, air conditioning, tints, accessories, etc, and you've a sweet-sweet badass ride."

I stare at the dollar figure on the screen. "You've got to be kidding me, Ramon? Ten years ago would make it just before he joined DCFS. Even assuming he worked for some other similar job, how the hell would a guy like that afford a truck costing almost half a million?"

Ramon shrugs. "He saved up a long time, maybe? She's definitely worth it."

Kayla's on the phone.

I call out to her. "Kayla, did Wentworth ever talk about his truck to his coworkers?"

Kayla says something into her phone, takes it off her ear and says to me, "He didn't drive that truck. He drove a beat-up old Caprice."

"A Chevy Caprice?" I ask. "You sure about that?"

"LaShanda said he gave her a ride once when her car was in the shop. She said the interior rattled so loudly and the engine was so noisy, they had to shout to make themselves heard."

"Do we have any pictures of the Caprice?"

"Hang on a sec. It's on one of the pictures, I know."

She rummages through the stack of glossy printouts she printed earlier from the digital files that Wentworth's coworkers forwarded to her.

"This one." She holds up a print.

I move toward her, she toward me. We meet midway.

She hands me the photo. "My cousin had one just like it back in the day. It's a 1990 model."

I only have to turn and look at Ramon for a second before he says, "That old-school ride? Get you one for seven, maybe eight grand max, jefe. Australian Shamu."

"What does that mean, 'Australian Shamu'?" I ask.

"What they nicknamed the new model after 1991. Chevy moved production to Australia. The 1990 was the last year they made 'em here in good old US of A."

I look at the picture of the Dodge pickup on the laptop screen, then the selfie picture of one of Wentworth's coworkers taken in the DCFS parking lot. Wentworth, at the wheel of his Caprice, was visible in the background, pulling out.

A spark sizzles in my head.

"He buys American," I say. "A 1949 Dodge truck. The 1990 Caprice. Both American classics."

Ramon makes a throaty sound of disgust. "'Cept one's a half million beaut, the other's an eight thou nobody."

"Sure, but he needed a car for work. He could have bought anything. A brand-new Honda or Hyundai wouldn't have cost much and would probably have been cheaper on gas and maintenance. Yet he bought the last model of a classic American car company before they moved production of the line overseas. This guy is proud of being an American. He drove the Caprice to avoid attracting attention, but he couldn't resist sticking to Detroit."

I snap my fingers. "Track down that truck. He would have had to have bought the Caprice with his Wentworth fake ID to keep his cover intact. But the truck was a vanity purchase. It's his pride and joy. You can see the gleam on the bodywork even in the videos. I'm willing to bet he bought that truck in his own name. Find it and we'll know who he is."

"Great going, girl," Kayla sings out.

The others nod acknowledgment and heap praise at me, too.

I wave it away. "We still have a long way to go. Time for victory laps later. Let's keep at it, people."

My phone trills.

Trevor Blackburn calling.

I look at the screen for a long moment as it buzzes.

Kayla notices me staring at my phone and raises her brows.

I shake my head, pretending it's nothing, as I walk outside to take the call. The April evening air is crisp and cool, with a hint of wetness. The sky is clear, that lovely, deep Mediterranean blue that I've only ever seen in California, but a gentle breeze carries a memory of rain.

"We should meet," he says. "Let me take you to dinner."

I look around at the parking lot.

On the corner beside the front door of the old sheriff's

station is a big blue metal receptable shaped like a mailbox. It's a drop box for the public library.

A mother and her three small children of different ages are taking turns reaching up and inserting their library books in the slot. The mother holds the slot open as the youngest child, a little girl no more than five, reaches up on tiptoe and uses both palms to push the large picture book in.

From the picture on the cover, I recognize it as John Klassen's *I Want My Hat Back*. It slides in and I hear it land with a hollow thump. That book used to be one of Natalie's favorites when she was around that age. I used to read it to her, acting out the various animals with exaggerated physical gestures and expressions; she would roll on the floor in hysterics.

The memory makes me wish I was home with her right now. These early pre-pubescent years are so fleeting, so precious. Every minute I'm not with her is lost forever. It's a constant reminder of how precious this time is, and how important it is that I use it wisely. Because it doesn't last. Nothing ever does, does it?

"What for?" I ask.

A moment of silence. I'm guessing Trevor Blackburn isn't accustomed to having his offers questioned, especially by single women.

The five-year-old sees me watching and waves at me.

I wave back with a smile.

"Because we all have to eat?" Trevor replies rhetorically. "It doesn't have to be dinner. We could drive and talk instead. I just thought I might grab a bite to eat and that you might be similarly inclined."

I make him wait another long minute and then say, "Okay."

There's a brief pause, as if he isn't sure I really said that. But he's smart enough not to ask for confirmation.

"Great," he says, "how about—?"

I cut him off. "The parking lot in fifteen minutes," I say crisply. "I can only spare a half hour."

I hang up without waiting for an answer.

I go back in and catch Kayla's eye.

"I'm going fishing," I say. "Could use a little help baiting the hook."

FORTY-THREE

Kayla and I are in the restroom of the command center. She's helping me with my face.

"Girl," she says, "you're so pretty. You learn to put on just a little bit and you'd slay."

I smile. "Thanks, but I don't really use makeup. Never have."

She pauses what she's doing to lean back and make eye contact.

"Not at all? What about a face wash?"

I shrug. "Just soap and water. I use a light facial cleanse every night, just to get the day off my face, and if I remember, maybe a little moisturizer because of how dry this desert climate makes my skin, but that's it."

She shakes her head in disapproval as she continues to work on my cheeks with the soft brush.

"That's a crime, woman."

She tells me how I need to take care of myself better, especially now that I'm approaching my mid-thirties, and the sheer wear and tear of the job is going to show. "Just a little light touch-up. A few lines of Indian kajal, some eyeliner, a primer, a lightly tinted mineral sunscreen, and if you have time, a light dusting of concealer. And of course lip color."

"I use lipstick sometimes," I say. Though the truth is, I almost always forget, and when I do, I end up eating most of it when I chew my lips out of anxiety. Occupational hazards.

She shakes her head severely. "Lip color," she insists.

I don't argue the point.

My phone screen lights with a notification and I notice the time. "Could we speed this up a little?"

She sighs, leans back, looks at me and shrugs. "We're done."

"Great. Thank you so much for this, Kayla!"

"Suse, listen to me," she says.

"Yeah?"

"You're a woman."

"Um. I know *that*."

"So use it."

I look at her.

She shakes her head. "You think men don't use their masculinity? We only have what we have. There's no shame in using it to get the job done. You're a beautiful woman, Susan Parker. And that's all you. God given and woman made, courtesy of the mother who birthed you and the Creator who carved you. Never hesitate to use it. It's your greatest weapon in this patriarchal shitshow of a world."

I nod slowly. "You know that? You're absolutely right. Why should I be embarrassed to be a woman just because I'm an FBI agent?"

"You said it."

"Okay, Kayla. Great talk. Gotta run."

"Give him hell. But make him want to live in it forever because you're the one escorting him there," she says as I go out of the restroom.

Urduja is coming in as I go out the front door. I hold the door open for her.

She thanks me and then pauses, stopping in the doorway with a stack of pizza boxes in her hand. She looks at me with a strangely intense expression that makes me curious. She's about to say something when my phone buzzes.

Sujit Chopra calling.

I make a silent gesture to Urduja, twirling my finger round, to indicate that we'll talk later. She nods and manages to free one hand to give me a thumbs up.

I go out into the parking lot.

I take a deep breath of the cool spring air.

Time to nail a billionaire.

FORTY-FOUR

This time, it's not the Bugatti.

From the double RR monogram on the front of the hood, I deduce that he's driving the Rolls-Royce Boat Tail that he was featured with on the cover of *GQ* when he was voted Man of the Year a few months ago.

I'm not a fan of ultra-super hyper-rides or extravagant 'look-at-me-I'm-rich-and-cool' cars but the luxuriousness is undeniable. I sink into the soft leather seat like it was made for me and once I'm embedded in it, I feel like I could stay here forever.

And that smell!

It smells like fresh, crisp hundred-dollar bills fresh from the mint. Everyone loves that new car smell, I guess. But $28 million new car smell is something else altogether.

Trevor steals a quick glance at me as I get in the car but doesn't say anything.

I know that look well, even if it's been a while since I paid attention to men who give me that look. It's the kind of look that tells me he thinks I look good.

I know that I'm a little flushed after the bathroom talk with Kayla and that it shows even through my melanin-rich skin, thanks to my white Irish nana, God rest her soul. It makes my cheeks pink and my eyes light up. It's as close as this brown girl gets to a 'glow on'.

"What did you want to talk about over dinner?" I ask as he takes Miracle Mountain Parkway north. I'm determined to set the tone for this 'meeting' and keep it businesslike.

A trio of young men in a Honda Accord do a double take as we go by, then whistle and exclaim at the sight of the Boat Tail. They look like they could die happy right now.

"We'll be there in just a couple of minutes," Trevor says. "It's better if we talk over dinner."

The drive really does take just a couple of minutes, although that involves driving well over the speed limit.

I look through the windshield at the façade of Trois Meuf, the most expensive fine dining restaurant in Santa Carina Valley, and feel a shiver go through me, right down to my bones.

Trevor doesn't notice.

He's already walking around to the passenger side. He holds the door open for me, then frowns.

"Are you all right?" he asks, leaning in.

A small sound escapes me in lieu of words.

I regain control of my vocal cords and manage to say, "Fine."

I get out of the car, trying very hard not to stumble or fall.

I feel like my heart's racing at thrice its resting rate, and if my face looked flushed before, it's probably turned red as a balloon right now.

Trevor shoots me a quick glance, this time not the same look he gave me when I entered his car. It's a look of concern.

"What is it?" he asks.

I stare at the lit sign for a moment, shaped in delicate neon script.

"We had a reservation for that weekend," I say at last, my

voice sounding strange to my ears. I can barely hear over the sound of the blood pounding in my head.

"Amit and you?" Trevor asks gently.

I glance at him. It sounds very strange to hear my husband's name coming from his mouth.

But of course he knows my husband's name was Amit Kapoor. Why wouldn't he? Anyone with a device and an internet connection can look it up in a minute. His death was a news headline. *FBI agent's spouse found dead in Splinter murder house.*

"It was our anniversary," I say. "Or it would have been. Our eighth."

He waits for me to go on.

When I don't, he says softly, "If you want me to take you back, just say so."

I take a moment. Not to think. I'm beyond thinking at this vulnerable moment. I'm too full of feelings, memories, conflicting thoughts, warring impulses, a hodge-podge of instincts, sensations, electricity, and nausea. Emotional jambalaya. My heart is fat with pain.

"I'm hungry," I say and climb the steps without waiting for him.

The maître d' is obviously expecting Trevor. So is the manager and the owner who is also the chef. At least that's who I assume they are, the three men with polite smiles poised. They barely glance at me, a fact I'm grateful for, because I'm definitely not dressed right for dinner at a French fine dining restaurant run by a celebrity chef.

I don't need to be self-conscious about the other patrons because there are none. Apparently, we've either arrived too early for dinner—unlikely, since they only open from 6 p.m. to 11 p.m. and it's 7.25 p.m. now—or business is terrible, which is even less likely for SCV's only Michelin-starred restaurant.

After a brief flurry of hushed 'kiss-the-ring' greetings, we're seated at a table for two. A lit candle burns steadily in the center of the round table.

As Trevor sits down, I turn my phone screen toward him, showing him the time. "Twenty-five minutes? They must have the fastest service in the world."

He smiles. "We can make it to go if you prefer."

I smile back. "Nah. A girl's gotta eat, right?"

"We'll save time deciding and ordering," he says. "I've asked them to just go ahead and serve us their chef's special dinner. I hope you're okay with that?"

"As long as there aren't any snails," I say. "I don't do snails."

He grins. "You can relax. Neither do I and Chef Claubert is aware."

Look at that. Five minutes in, and we already have something in common.

The first course is the aperitif, which tonight happens to consist of mousse de saumon canape and a small glass of wine which the chef calls Pouilly-Fume. I make a note to look it up later for Lata because it's to die for and she loves white wine.

The canape is just enough for a single bite and is very delicious. I hesitate before picking up the sauvignon blanc but then I remember that I'm not driving and it's barely a gulp anyway.

"Someone is picking off my partners," Trevor says just before the entrées are brought out.

Apparently in French cuisine, l'entrée is the starter or hors d'oeuvres, not the main course as it is in America. Tonight's entrée is French onion soup. The serving is small but lip-smackingly good.

I wait till the servers are out of hearing then say, "To kill your deal?"

He looks impressed. "You're good," he says. "Yes, exactly."

I shrug as I take a spoonful of soup. "It's not rocket science. You're on the cusp of this massive deal. You and your six partners are looking to bet big on Santa Carina Valley with Silicon

Valley South. You have a lot at stake. You're all joined at the hip, wedded together in a complex, very complicated financing deal that I won't even pretend to understand. Someone, or several someones, realizes that all they have to do is kill you guys off one by one until there aren't enough of you left to keep the deal afloat. Goodbye, Silicon Valley South."

"And hello to SCV Downtown, the next big tech destination in Southern California," Trevor says, raising his wine glass. "Good work, Susan."

"Thank you, Trevor. But you didn't ask me here just to compliment me on my work," I say, looking at my small, empty bowl with genuine regret. I wonder if asking the chef for seconds might be viewed as an insult. The French can be weird. "Let me guess. You have a very good idea who stands to benefit from your failure. Someone who's invested almost as much as you have in securing the contract for SCV Downtown. Someone with strong ties to the local powers that be. Someone who's been doing business here long before SCV was a tiny mote in your ambitious eye. I'm talking, of course, of Sujit Chopra and his partner Aishwarya Chopra."

The chef announces the fish course, sole meuniere, with the pride of a father announcing the birth of his first born.

Trevor takes a bite of fish, chews it appreciatively, and looks at me. "You seem to be a step ahead of me tonight, Susan."

"Here's your chance to catch up. Tell me the information you wanted me to have so urgently."

He sets his fork on his plate and sits back.

"Oh, wait," I say. "That was it? You wanted me to know that Sujit and Aishwarya are behind the murders of your partners and friends Derek Chen and Jake Perkins? And that if I don't do something to stop them quickly, they'll continue their murder spree and kill off the remaining three members of your billionaire serial killer Murder Club? Good gosh. I'll get on it right away, Mr. Blackburn, sir."

The chef is headed to our table, probably to ask if everything is to our satisfaction. When he hears my tone, even though I'm speaking quite softly and politely, and sees Trevor Blackburn staring at me, he turns around and retreats to his inner sanctum.

"Susan," Trevor says. "If I've offended you in any way—"

"*If*," I say with quiet intensity, "*if?*"

He exhales silently.

I put my fork down. This fish is so, so good, just melting in my mouth.

"Did you really think it would be that simple, Trevor?" I ask him. "Did you believe you could manipulate me like a marionette? Put on a nice little puppet show with SAC Susan Parker occupying center stage? What was the plan? You heard that I'd been called in to head the case and you assumed at once that because I'm related to the Chopras that I would of course be in cahoots with them? Which, in the current scenario with the power dynamic being what it is here, would mean I was on the opposite side to your own? So you sicced your pet bulldog on me, invented obstacles where there really were none, made yourself the elephant god sitting to block my way, just so you could graciously and kindly agree to move from my way, on the condition that I worked with you, toeing your line. You didn't expect me to do so willingly or wholeheartedly, of course, but you thought I would be pragmatic enough to know that I should keep a foot in both camps. That's how it's usually done, isn't it? Pay homage to both opponents, so no matter who wins, you're in good graces with the winner. That is what you expected, isn't it?"

I sense movement behind me and glimpse the chef and servers emerging from the kitchen with two steaming plates.

It looks like some kind of gratin.

The chef even says, in a quizzical tone, "Tartiflette au poulet, monsieur?"

Trevor makes a curt gesture that translates the same in all languages: not now.

"Mais oui," I hear the chef say, in an injured tone.

I feel bad for Chef Claubert. Well, maybe not.

He expected to host a billionaire and his lady friend for a night of fine French dining they would remember and talk about—ideally to all our high society friends and media interviewers. Instead, he got Special Agent in Charge Susan Parker and the person of interest who thought he could twirl her around his little finger and is now understanding he made a big mistake.

"Susan," Trevor says, on the defensive now. "I would never underestimate you that way. I know you're not the kind to play political games. Give me some credit. I researched you very thoroughly. I know you don't even like your in-laws. Especially Sujit Chopra. Because nobody likes Sujit Chopra. I never expected you to be my or anyone else's marionette. You're a strong, tenacious agent. A brilliant investigator. You have an A-grade team. You're able to use their combined resources in ingenious, exceptional ways, achieving what other teams can't in a tenth of the time and with a fraction of the resources, under incredible pressure and against formidable odds. You're one of a kind. The last thing I would dream of doing is treat you with such disrespect."

It's my turn to put down my fork, sit back and look at him.

He's still lying to me.

"Okay," I say, taking my napkin off my lap and dropping it on my fish. "Okay, let's say I take you at your word. You're saying that you've been upfront with me until now? That you haven't tried to manipulate me to serve your own goals? That you're offering me full cooperation as you promised me?"

"Yes," he says quietly and firmly. "*Yes*."

"All right then," I say. "Tell me the truth about yourself and the Clothesline Killer. What's your connection with him?"

FORTY-FIVE

Trevor Blackburn flinches.

"What do you mean?" he says, reaching for his water glass to take a sip.

I gesture impatiently. "Brook Wentworth. The Murder Club Strangler. The Clothesline Killer. Call him whatever, it doesn't matter. I know he's connected to you somehow. Personally. Because I don't buy your bullshit explanation that you and your billionaire Murder Club were obsessed with serial killers and randomly chose him just to watch over his shoulder while he made his kills. This guy, this Brook Wentworth, or whatever his real name is, he's *someone* to you."

"Why would you think that?" he asks.

"Because that's the only explanation that fits," I say.

I hold up one hand in a fist, sticking up one finger.

"One, why *him*? Why this particular serial killer? Sure, he was the first one you said your search threw up. But that's not entirely true, is it? Because all six of you in the Murder Club are from right here, Santa Carina Valley. So it can't be a coincidence that you picked a serial killer who happens to be operating in your old stomping grounds."

I stick up a second finger.

"Two, it's a very bizarro coincidence that your childhood and parentage are so obscure, especially for a major celebrity in this information super-era. What did you do? Use your power and money to have people go into the servers and archives and erase or disappear every piece of paper or file that lists your real name, mentions your parentage, or any other personal details about you from those first twenty-five or thirty years of your life? And could it be, gasp, that you used your money and resources to buy the same erasure package for him as well? But wait, why would you do that? For a serial killer!"

Third finger up. "Three, how convenient is it that all of the Clothesline Killer's previous kills, the genuine serial killer ones where he was clearly following his inner voice, his dark passenger, and acting out his psychotic ritual, went undetected for almost a decade by SCVPD, the very PD that just happens to be in the pocket of yours truly?"

Trevor shoots back. "Isn't that FBI jurisdiction? Your agency was sleeping through these murders, too. You don't seriously believe I was able to corrupt the entire federal system?"

"Uh-huh, Mr. Blackburn. You shoot, but you don't score. The Bureau needs hard evidence to justify looking into a local PD case. Your man made sure that evidence was either mislaid, lost, or never collected in the first place. I did my homework. I checked the detectives assigned to those cases. They were all McD's pet bulldogs. Guys who do his bidding, no questions asked. And they all got promotions and raises during this same period. Despite overlooking one of the deadliest serial killers ever to operate in the region!"

Trevor's eyes are bright. He's still outwardly calm but I know he must be seething inwardly by now. I doubt anyone's been able to talk to him this way in a decade and gotten away with it. Well. He's going to have to get used to it. He's got a lot more coming. I'm loaded for bear tonight.

"Four, and this is the kicker," I say, "a serial killer who has a very specific victim profile, a very specific ritual murder that he acts out, very specific kinks and MO, suddenly ups and switches everything just like that? Instead of picking single, addicted, impoverished white mothers with questionable parenting skills and strangling them to death in their own beds at night, the entire ritual videotaped by him in a very particular sequence, this guy now decides to go after a bunch of billionaires? How convenient!"

He's glowering now, but I push on regardless.

I now have my whole hand raised, all fingers splayed. "Fifth, and this is my favorite part, both these last two murders, Chen and Perkins, as well as the other three Murder Club members, whom I presume are also on the to-do list, happen to be partners with you in this big development deal with the city of Santa Carina Valley. If our friendly neighborhood serial killer continues to oblige, and Cara Brin, Riley Walling, and Zeus Hamilton also fall prey to his new creatively eclectic murder spree, then the whole deal would be in danger of falling apart, wouldn't it?"

Trevor leans forward. "Exactly. And that is the opposite of good for me. I need these guys. What possible motive would I have for killing my own biz sibs? That's where your whole wild ass theory falls to pieces, Susan."

"Maybe," I say, "or maybe, as a little birdie informed me just before you picked me up, that you do have an excellent motive for wanting them dead?"

"Enlighten me," he says in a challenging tone.

"With all five dead, or maybe even with just two dead, and the others pulling out because the murders scare the heck out of them, your deal would die a natural death. That sounds like a helluva motive right there to me."

"Why would I want out?" he says. "This is the biggest deal I've ever negotiated. I've worked years to get it."

"Of course you'll say that. But the word on the street is that you're over-extended in the market. Word is that you're bleeding cash and at the current rate, you're incapable of meeting your commitments to SCV for the project. But if your partners, your biz sibs as you call them, pull out, then you're off the hook and can walk away, lick your wounds, and live to fight again another day. That sounds like a very strong motive to me."

"So I, what, hired a serial killer to kill Chen and Perkins for me?" He laughs. "You're reaching, Susan. That's a wild theory."

I'm about to retort to that when my phone blares with the distinctive jarring tone of an emergency alert. It breaks the tension at once.

It's from SCVPD, which means it's been triggered by a random 911 operator who believes they have a credible report of a public life-threatening situation.

My heart freezes as I read the all-caps text.

> ACTIVE SHOOTER ALERT. ARMED SHOOTER
> REPORTED IN RESIDENTIAL HOME VICINITY
> OF CENTURION HIGH SCHOOL ALL
> AVAILABLE UNITS RESPONDING RESIDENTS
> ARE URGED TO SHELTER IN PLACE AND
> AWAIT FURTHER ALERTS.

That's my neighborhood.

And I'm betting it's my home.

I'm up and moving even as I finish reading the text.

I yell at Trevor. "I need your car!"

FORTY-SIX

From Trois Meuf to my place is less than two miles if I take a shortcut up Dry Canyon Road then swing down Centurion Street. I usually avoid that route because Dry Canyon Road is steep going up and even steeper coming down and my long-suffering Prius doesn't handle gradients well.

But in Trevor Blackburn's luxury tourer, I'm able to do it in under a minute.

He sits silently beside me, not saying a word as I treat his expensive toy like a go-kart, taking corners at a speed that would probably make my Prius flip over and barreling downhill fast enough to make my stomach drop because of the momentary loss of gravity.

I bring the RR to a standing halt outside my driveway. A part of me is probably impressed by the car's handling and sheer muscle power but I don't give a shit about what that part thinks right now.

The only part of me currently functioning is the mother and agent part, and right now, both are on the verge of freaking out.

I take a second to check my Sig Sauer and get out of the car, turning right and left, scanning the entire area for movement or silhouettes, gun at the ready.

The quiet side street is empty. Most of the daytime traffic here is due to Centurion High School just around the corner, and with school having closed hours earlier and all the residents back from work, you can go all of ten minutes without seeing a single car go by.

Naved's Camry is nowhere in sight.

He's supposed to be watching the house. Where the hell is he?

The promised police car that's supposed to drive by is not to be seen either. Great!

I clock Lata's Jeep Cherokee parked at the curb in front, in its usual place. No other car is parked nearby, except for a Toyota and Hyundai that belong to our left-side and right-side neighbors. I don't see any other strange car that sticks out, but the intruder could have parked nearby and come here on foot.

I try Lata's number on my phone, but it goes straight to voicemail. I check my messages and see the one she must have sent seconds before the emergency alert went out:

> Someone's in the house!

I curse myself for being so absorbed in my diatribe to Trevor Blackburn that I failed to see that text message instantly.

In a life-or-death situation, seconds count.

I'll never be able to live with myself if I was too busy working while a psychopath was attacking my daughter and sislaw.

But now's not the time to dwell on that.

I run quickly and silently up the driveway as Trevor calls out something from behind me.

I ignore him and stop to take a peek around the corner of the garage.

The living room blinds are open, and I can see the couch, carpet and flatscreen. Beyond it, adjoining the kitchen, is our dining table. Natalie and Lata should either be at dinner or have just finished around now. Neither of them are visible. The living room and dining area look deserted.

I know better than to go in through the front door.

I go up the side of the house to the garage door and find it already ajar.

I push it open with the sole of my boot, enter, and do a quick sweep with my weapon, heart pounding like a jackhammer.

All I want to do right now is run into the house and sprint upstairs yelling out to Natalie and Lata.

That would be a terrible idea and a great way to get them both killed.

I force myself to breathe in slowly through the nose and out through the mouth, re-centering myself, and let my training guide me.

It's empty except for a bunch of cardboard boxes and assorted stuff we've accumulated over the years. Like most people, we started out using our garage to actually park our car, but over time, it's become a storage area.

I've restrained myself from putting on the overhead light to avoid alerting the shooter if he's still in the house, but there's enough ambient light coming in through the garage windows up by the ceiling for me to see the huddled shapes and outlines of all our junk.

I almost trip over something that's in the way but catch myself in time. I make a note to check what it is tomorrow and move it out of the way.

A door leads into the house, via a small hallway which serves as the laundry room, and the downstairs toilet. A second door opens onto the mud room and the kitchen area.

Before I go in, I take my boots off slowly and carefully.

While all the rooms in the house are carpeted, the hallways are all bare wooden flooring, and my boots would make a noise loud enough to alert the Clothesline Killer no matter where in the house he is right now.

The floor feels cold to my bare feet as I pad across the laundry room, which smells of detergent and the fabric softener I use on all Natalie's clothes and blankies and her soft toys.

I go through both doors without meeting resistance or hearing anything out of the ordinary.

In the kitchen, I stop and listen.

Sirens are audible in the distance, approaching us but still at least three or four miles out, and as many minutes away.

The new sheriff's station is way over on the far side of the valley, a good seven or eight miles away, so I can't fault them for taking that many minutes to respond.

Still, I'm surprised that there aren't any cruisers closer by that could respond. I'd have expected at least one to have beaten me here.

And Naved. Where the hell is Naved?

My phone vibrates in my jacket pocket.

Keeping the Sig Sauer ready, I use my other hand to check the text message from Lata.

> He's upstairs. v r in master closet rear

Those first two words send a chill into my bones.

The thought of a deadly killer, armed and ready to kill, within reach of my daughter, makes my stomach clench.

I grit my teeth, forcing myself to slow down, and start up the stairs.

I try to remember the ones that creak and step over them.

When I reach the halfway point, I swing out, keeping the gun raised and turning left and right to check the visible areas of the second floor.

Still no sight of him!

Where the hell is he?

It's a fairly small house.

There are three bedrooms upstairs, but really only one is a full-sized bedroom, the master. The other two can barely accommodate a double bed.

That's at the end of the hallway to my left, behind me.

Ahead of me as I come up the last few stairs, is Natalie's room in the corner, and an even smaller spare room.

I have to check them out before I go to the master bedroom, but impatience gnaws at me like a living thing.

The sirens are a little louder now but still a couple of minutes away.

In active shooter terms, that's a long time. Long enough for several dozen people to get shot, as more than one PD or SWAT unit responding to a school shooting has learned the hard way.

And for the two people who matter more to me than anything else in the world, it's an eternity.

Natalie's bedroom and the spare room are clear.

From the Elsa plushie and open picture book on her bed, I'm pretty sure that Lata was reading her a bedtime story when the shooter broke in.

The thought of how my daughter must have felt in that terrible moment scalds my heart.

I'm here now, sweetie, I'm going to protect you. Mommy won't let anything bad happen to you, that's a promise.

I move up the last hallway to the master bedroom.

The door is slightly ajar, but I'll have to push it in to enter.

If he's in there—and he *has* to be in there, because there's nowhere else left—he'll see that door being pushed in and have the drop on me.

But that's not the only thing that's worrying me.

This is a nightmare scenario.

If I go in and he shoots, as he almost surely will, I'll have to shoot back.

"Wentworth," I call out.

No answer.

"Brook Wentworth, I know you're in there. This is Susan Parker. I'm the one you're after. If you come out, I promise I won't shoot."

A slight sound, like the rustle of fabric.

"I just want to talk, that's all. We can go downstairs, sit, and have a chat. I give you my word that I won't shoot you or let you be shot."

Is that the sound of him breathing? Or is it just my own breathing, sounding so loud in my ears that it seems to fill the entire house?

"There's no way for you to escape. My people are outside, and they've got the house surrounded," I lie, knowing that he can't see out of the bedroom window with the blinds drawn and even though the sirens are still a minute or so out, that doesn't mean my squad isn't already here. "SCVPD is seconds out and the entire area's been locked down, so there's no escape. Give yourself up now, and I promise I'll see that you're taken in alive and treated fairly. I'll even suggest a good lawyer. You haven't done anything yet that we can pin on you, so chances are you could walk out a free man just hours from now."

I'm flying solo and blind, and the chances are he knows it, too.

"I'm going to lay my gun down here in the hallway. It's within sight of the doorway. I'm going to leave it here and go downstairs now. Please follow and don't shoot."

I match actions to my words and start down the stairs.

My actions are in direct violation of FBI protocol and all my training. By surrendering my weapon, I'm putting not only my family but also myself at risk. If this ends up being an officer involved shooting and I'm put under scrutiny, I'll lose my shield and be kicked out of the Bureau.

Right now, I don't give a damn about any of that.

All I care about is keeping my family safe and alive.

And after reviewing all options, this is my best bet.

So I continue down the stairs.

This time, I deliberately step on all the squeaky ones to make sure he hears me.

I don't look up till I reach the bottom, but my ears are peeled and listening as hard as I can.

I glimpse the bedroom door move.

He's checking the hallway.

I pause for just a second then walk over to the living room sofa and sit down on the edge.

Natalie's *Encanto* blankie and Mirabelle stuffy are beside me, along with her Nintendo Switch controller.

I feel the overwhelming urge to lift the blanket and inhale my daughter's smell.

I hear a heavy footstep upstairs.

I glimpse movement near the place where I left my gun.

A sense of elation balloons in my chest.

I've got him out of the master bedroom at least!

That's several feet farther away from Natalie than he was just a moment ago.

This might actually work.

I know the chances of him shooting me at any second are pretty high.

I'm willing to take that chance.

It's part of my job.

All I care about is getting him away from my daughter.

"I didn't have a gun," he says.

My skin prickles at the sound of his voice.

It's a medium tenor, not particularly deep and throaty, but not too thin. It's a perfect balance of full, masculine sound but with just the right intonation to sound friendly, pleasant, harmless.

It's a voice anyone would want to trust, unless the man using it happens to be standing in your living after he's broken into your house with the intention of killing you and taking your daughter.

"But I have one now, thanks to you," says the Clothesline Killer.

And then he's standing behind me, behind the sofa on which I'm seated.

I glimpse his hand coming up and see my Sig Sauer held in his gloved fist, aimed at me.

He points it at my head and fires.

FORTY-SEVEN

The Sig Sauer goes off with a dead clicking sound.

Of course I took the clip out before putting the gun down. I'm shocked that he didn't have a gun already but there was no way I was going to give him another one to use!

And I still have my backup weapon.

The Glock Gen 5 that I pulled on Sujit the other night.

It's out and in my hands as Brook Wentworth reacts to the sound of the clicking Sig Sauer.

"That one isn't loaded," I say, holding up the clip in my free hand. I flex the Glock. "This one is."

He stares at the Sig Sauer, then at the clip and the Glock in my hands.

He's tall, with short, close-cropped brown hair, black eyes only partly masked behind geeky glasses, dressed in a checked shirt with a jacket, and pleated trousers. It's easy to see why Urduja's mother, and all those other moms, would have believed on sight that he was a government employee. He looks the part.

He lowers the gun, then shrugs.

A small grin plays across his face.

"Smart," he says. "But then you are a smart one, Susan. You're a real pistol, aren't you?"

He grins at his own pun.

I don't smile or react. I'm still pissed enough to want to shoot him in the chest where he stands.

"You came into my house," I say. "You threatened my family. But that was your last mistake."

He shrugs. "Win some, lose some."

The shift from friendly, geeky, government employee to athletic, lightning-reflex serial killer is so sudden, it almost takes me by surprise even though I'm expecting it.

He throws the Sig Sauer at me.

A deadly throw, the pistol aimed to strike me in the forehead and nose with full force from barely ten feet away.

I'm forced to duck it, and he's already moving as I duck.

I dodge the flying handgun, feel it miss my cheek by a hair's width, strike my collarbone hard enough to make me grunt with pain.

It distracts me long enough for him to throw himself at me.

He must weigh 170, maybe 180 pounds, almost all lean muscle mass. It lands on me like a ton, knocking me backwards, on the floor.

I hit my head in a glancing blow on the floor. Even though it's wood flooring, the impact stuns me. I still have the Glock in my hand, but his knee is on my wrist, crushing it. His other knee is on my chest, shoving the breath out of my lungs.

And in his hands is the least likely weapon I've ever been attacked with in my career.

A length of nylon clothesline.

Double braided.

It's wrapped around my throat and constricting my airway before I can fully react.

Powerful hands, muscled forearms bulging with wiry

sinews, pull the rope tight enough to make me see blue dots flashing.

I'm struggling to throw him off, get my hands up to snag the rope, to stop him somehow, but he's got me pinned down under his superior weight and brute strength.

There's a death's head grin on his face and a cold fish-eye look that are terrifying. Somehow, it feels worse than if he were wearing a Boogeyman mask. At least with the mask, you could imagine you were being killed by a supernatural force, something beyond control. But to see another human being, a relatively normal, mild-looking guy choking the life out of you, is bone-chilling.

I feel the life draining out of me.

My vision blurs.

My chest heaves, unable to get the oxygen it desperately needs.

I kick out, wriggle, flail, but my efforts are flagging.

I'm dying.

Something flickers above him.

For an instant, some oxygen-deprived part of my brain sees it in slow motion, as a hand descending from high above, like an angel reaching down to smite him from heaven.

I feel the impact of the blow, hear the crash and tinkle of the vase as it smashes against the side of his head. Stray fragments of porcelain fall on me, forcing me to shut my eyes to avoid injury.

The killing pressure on my neck is gone suddenly.

So is his crushing weight.

I gasp, reach up with fluttering hands, and pluck the nylon rope from my tortured throat, yanking it free, gasping in breaths.

Lata stands over the fallen intruder, the base of the flower vase still in her hand.

She's starting to lean over, the look on her face telling me that she's capable of using the shard of vase to slash his throat if he so much as moves an inch. I know she's killed for her country before on her tours. She won't hesitate to kill for her family now.

I gasp involuntarily as breath refills my lungs, causing her to glance at me.

That's when his feet lash out, kicking hard at the backs of her knees.

Lata grunts and falls forward, twisting to avoid landing on me. That costs her because she falls sideways at an awkward angle, landing on her hip, crying out as she hits the floor with a thump.

Brook Wentworth is on his feet, already racing across the room.

There's a gash on his temple, dripping blood, but it clearly isn't stopping him.

He's headed for the back door.

I fumble the Glock in my hands as I pull myself up, still pulling in breath, and take aim.

The wall that separates the kitchen area from the playroom blocks my view of the back door, giving me only a fraction of a second to get a clear shot, and only one shot at that.

I take the shot.

The sound of the Glock firing in the house is very loud.

FORTY-EIGHT

The shot misses him by barely an inch, ripping a hole in the side of his jacket and missing his chest, which is what I was aiming for. Central body mass.

Then he's gone. Through the back door and into the backyard.

I chase after him.

I emerge into the backyard, hearing the sirens closing in as I do. They must be less than thirty seconds away—this has all happened very fast.

I turn just in time to see him on top of the back wall.

"Freeze!" I yell. "Freeze or I'll shoot!"

In the dark, he's just a silhouette. A dark man-shaped thing cutting out the stars.

He doesn't respond.

Back in the house, my heart was in my mouth when I let off that shot, even though I was downstairs and Natalie was upstairs. I know from long and bitter experience how easily a stray bullet can go through walls and floors and ceilings to hit an innocent bystander several houses or streets away. Every shot is a life risk.

But out here, with only the sky as a background, I have no hesitation.

I fire at him, letting off several shots in rapid succession.

The gun is loud in the quiet night.

I think I see him flinch just as he drops off the wall, disappearing. I might have hit him but I'm not sure. If I did, it wasn't a fatal shot.

I run and leap onto the flowerbeds, crushing Lata's marigold plants.

As I heave myself up, I hear a motor engine start up. It sounds like a truck.

Behind our house runs the Bouquet Canyon Creek. At some point it was probably just a large muddy ditch that carried the run-off from the annual few inches of rain that we get some years if we're lucky. Before Amit and I moved in, the city had expanded and deepened it into a concrete conduit about twenty-five meters wide and almost as deep.

There's a service road that runs on either side of the creek, for maintenance vehicles.

He must have broken the lock on the gate access to the service road and parked his pickup truck on that road, right behind our house. That's how he got in so easily.

When I reach the top of my back wall and look down, I see the service road some twenty feet below me.

The red pickup truck is on that road directly behind my house. He's already moving up the service road, toward the wide-open gate and the street. Toward freedom. I can see the lights of the arriving SCVPD vehicles on the street, coming to my house. They won't know to look for him or stop him. He's going to drive right past them and get away.

I take aim and fire two more shots.

I hear one strike glass and metal, but the other one goes into the creek.

The gate is only about a dozen meters from where I'm sitting on the wall.

I watch as the red truck hits it and it crashes open. I see the lock that was previously cut, probably with a bolt cutter, hanging loosely, and the truck goes out onto Centurion Street, swings left and heads toward Bouquet Canyon Road, picking up speed.

On the other side of the street, three SCVPD cruisers fly past in the opposite direction, screeching as they slow to turn into my lane.

I should reach for my cellphone and call it in. But I know that by the time I do that, he'll be half a mile away and once he reaches the junction, he could go anywhere.

Instead, I jump down from the wall, run barefoot to the side gate, shove it open and run out into the street, and see the Boat Tail parked askew where I left it.

Trevor is standing beside it, staring at me as I come running up.

"What—?" he starts to say, but I don't hear it.

I jump into the car and get in, slamming the door shut.

The engine is still running. I throw it into gear and accelerate, shoving off like a NASCAR driver at the start line.

Trevor jumps in, landing sideways in the passenger seat with his head sticking out. Somehow, he manages to pull his head in and yank the door shut just as I swing the RR around the rear of Lata's Cherokee, narrowly escaping decapitation. He fumbles himself into the seatbelt as I round the curve and accelerate up Centurion Street to Bouquet Canyon Road.

My phone buzzes and I grab it out of my jacket pocket and all but throw it at Trevor. "Put it on speaker!"

He pauses his seatbelt strapping-in long enough to do as I ask, and Lata's voice screams at me.

"I can still see him. Heading south on Bouquet Canyon

Road, almost at Central Park now. Natalie and I are fine. Get the son of a bitch, Suse!"

The RR leaps like a gazelle at my merest touch, zipping up the arterial road, weaving around and leaving behind a Mustang like it was standing still. In another few seconds I spot a flash of red up ahead.

"You bet!" I yell back.

Trevor has managed to click in his seatbelt, but he still holds on to the hand loop as I zigzag through a trio of vehicles, putting the hypercar through its paces.

On the other side of the divider, one, two, three and then a fourth SCVPD cruiser fly down Bouquet Canyon headed back to my house. Too late the heroes.

"You're bleeding," Trevor says.

The pain in my collarbone is a ringing throb, the pain coming and going in waves. I feel wetness on my chest, too, dripping.

"It's nothing," I say as I feel the blood dripping off me as I change gears. "I'm getting blood all over your upholstery," I then blurt out.

"It's just a car," he says. "It'll clean off."

About a half mile ahead, I see the red pickup truck make a turn onto Golden Ranch Road. I blow through a red light.

"It's him, isn't it?" Trevor asks.

"It's your Boogeyman Brook Wentworth," I say. "What the hell was he doing in my house, Trevor? What aren't you telling me?"

He's silent.

I don't have time to interrogate him, so I settle for swearing.

I'm approaching the turn to Golden Ranch Road but now I have a complication. Two SCVPD cruisers pull up directly across both sides of the street, blocking traffic.

The uniformed officers get out of their vehicles and hold up their arms, shouting something at the nearest oncoming drivers who are forced to slow down.

They're both armed and I know they won't hesitate to shoot with an active shooter alert out, but I have no choice.

FORTY-NINE

The uniformed cop sees me and frowns, holding up his hand to stop me. His other hand drifts toward his holster. He talks into his shoulder radio.

"How the hell do I get the windows down?" I yell at Trevor as I jab at a button that accidentally turns the high beams on, blinding the cop and alarming him enough to make him pull his weapon out of the holster.

Trevor speaks in a conversational tone, "Rosie, lower the driver's side window and switch off the high beams."

My window disappears instantly, as if it was never there. Neat trick.

I hold my shield and ID out the window as the officer squints at me suspiciously. I spit out words like bullets.

"Federal agent in pursuit of a suspect. He's in the red pickup truck headed east on Golden Ranch. Call it in. Tell McDougall Susan Parker called it in. Send everyone that way. Do it now!"

He's still taking this in as I push forward, using the front right end of the RR to shove the back right end of his cruiser aside just far enough to make a hole for me to slip through. The Boat Tail elbows the cruiser aside like it's a go-kart.

"Hey!" the uniformed cop calls out, startled. "You can't—"

I can and I do, accelerating and taking the corner in one smooth slingshot motion. Then I'm flying up Golden Ranch Road as fast as Rosie will let me. Somehow, my window has miraculously reappeared.

"Rosie?" I ask Trevor.

"Rolls-Royce. Rosie," he says.

Billionaires!

I spot the red pickup truck three quarters of a mile ahead. The brief stop by Officer McSlow cost me but Rosie is a good girl. She eats up the road like it's cotton candy.

The Clothesline Killer's red pickup truck is going all out now, but I'm coming up in his rearview fast enough to knock him into tomorrow and he probably knows it because he suddenly takes a hard right onto Soledad Canyon Road. Ramon was right, he must have paid extra to have power steering put in otherwise I doubt that antique would be able to pull off that maneuver.

"Tell me the truth, Trevor," I say as I take the same turn with the ease of Natalie leaning sideways to turn her Radio Flyer scooter. "You ponied up the half mill for Wentworth to buy that jalopy, didn't you?"

I glance over at him to see his face.

He just nods. "Yes."

Good. We're finally getting somewhere now.

"One more question, and I want the truth again. You protected him during those years, when he was strangling all those single mothers in their beds, didn't you? You made sure McD kept his bulls from connecting the dots and looking too closely at them. You erased all his public records somehow, and gave him his new identity as Brook Wentworth, didn't you? All so this bastard could continue his sick sport and not get caught, isn't that right?"

This time, there's a moment of hesitation before he says again, "Yes."

I look over at Trevor again. "If he had harmed so much as a single hair on my daughter's head tonight, or even my sislaw, I swear, Trevor, I would have come after you and put you in the fucking ground. And if he survives tonight and tries to do it again, I'll still come after you and put you in the fucking ground. I don't care what they do to me afterwards. I'll hold you personally responsible for the Clothesline Killer's actions, and I'll make sure you pay for them with your life. Do you hear me?"

He stares at me. "I believe you."

"Good. At least now we both know where we stand," I say.

I'm on Soledad Canyon Road but I'm starting to get worried. There's no sign of the red truck anywhere for a couple of miles ahead, which is about as far as I can see on this stretch. There's no way he could have gotten farther than that in that old jalopy. Where did he—?

And then I see him.

In my rearview.

Almost a mile behind.

He took the turnoff one traffic light back and I was so busy questioning Trevor, I blew right past him. I see him there now, stopped at the crossing.

The one across the rail tracks.

It's the same crossing Lata, Natalie, and I took when we finished at the go-kart track a few days ago and went to lunch across the street.

The red pickup truck is at the crossing, just standing there, waiting.

I swing the RR around in an impromptu U-turn with a screeching of tires, cursing loudly at having missed seeing the truck. That's what comes of driving a car that's too fast too furious.

I see the goods train creeping up beside me as I drive back on the wrong side of the road, ignoring the honks and yells from startled drivers.

It's one of the mile long specials that go through every night, carrying the thousand and one things that we Americans absolutely positively must have five dozen of *right now*. The train is less than a hundred meters from the crossing now, and the engineer blows the customary series of warning blasts to caution the traffic waiting up ahead.

Like most railroad crossings in the country, there aren't any barriers on either side to hold the traffic back safely, probably because that would require an attendant and would slow the traffic down. We Americans don't want to wait for an attendant to raise a barrier. We want to go *now*.

Suddenly, I glimpse a thought and accelerate, the RR leaping again like a jaguar going for the kill.

"He can't be..." I say aloud, voicing the thought. "Is he?"

I only need to cover about a hundred meters, swing a sharp right, and I'll be right there on his tail.

I'm going much faster than the goods train and will easily beat it.

But Brook Wentworth has other ideas.

As I come roaring up Soledad, I see the red pickup truck accelerate forward, turning right to face the oncoming goods train head on.

The Clothesline Killer drives the truck onto the tracks, directly at the train.

The engineer sees this and hoots frantically again, the sound filling the night. He's probably already reaching for the brakes.

But that's a good mile plus worth of containers behind him, each one weighing something like ninety tons or more.

That's, I don't know for sure, but at a wild guess, I'd say at least twenty thousand tons barreling along at thirty or forty miles an hour. It's not the speed of all that deadweight, it's the sheer mass and density of it.

There's a reason why people use the phrase 'like a freight train' to describe an unstoppable force.

I yell out loud as the RR takes the turn and races up the rise toward the crossing.

Just as the red pickup truck slams headlong into the goods train engine, doing maybe eighty miles an hour in the opposite direction. The combined speed brings both together in a devastating kiss of death.

Metal meets metal in a deafening impact, screaming and scraping and ripping and rending before the truck crumples like a slow accordion and explodes in a blinding orange ball.

FIFTY

It's an unholy mess.

I look around the mass of official vehicles at the Soledad crossing. Chief McDougall is here along with about half the SCVPD.

There are fire trucks, ambulances, and private vehicles, too. There must be a hundred in all, all clustered around the site of the accident, clogging up both sides of the tracks. People are going crazy, stranded on either side of the stalled goods train, asking when they can pass through so they can get home. Cops and first responders are talking on radios and cellphones nineteen to the dozen. Someone is asking if the insurance investigators are coming. A cop is telling McDougall that the FRA and NTSB are both here and both are claiming jurisdiction. It's an orchestra of chaos.

McDougall is losing his temper, trying to organize this clustermess into some semblance of order.

From time to time, he glances at me, glaring as if I'm responsible for it all.

I can see how he might see it that way.

I was pursuing the unsub who probably realized he didn't

stand a chance in hell of escaping, not from Trevor Blackburn's hypercar *and* all of SCVPD as well. So he took the easy way out, or the hard way, depending on your point of view.

I look around, running my hand through my hair. I'm still barefoot and it's starting to get more than a little uncomfortable. People keep giving me strange looks. I can only imagine what I look like, barefoot, blood dripping down the front of my jacket and shirt, wild-haired, makeup mussed up.

I go back to the Boat Tail. Trevor is standing beside it, talking into his cellphone. He sees me coming, says something into the phone, and hangs up.

"Let's go," I say. "This time you drive."

He looks bemused but gets in as I click in my seatbelt.

Through the windshield, I see McDougall staring in my direction with a frown. There are half a dozen people talking to him from all sides, and he looks lost in a semi-daze.

When Trevor starts the Boat Tail and starts to maneuver through the crowd, McDougall snaps awake. He starts toward me, his mouth working.

"Parker! The hell are you going?" he yells.

I say, "Rosie, roll down passenger side window."

The window disappears.

I stick my head out and yell back.

"You know where to reach me."

He yells something back, but Trevor has managed to make the crowd part like Moses parting the Red Sea. I think the $28 million car with the billionaire driving has something to do with that.

He gets us onto Soledad Canyon Road and heading back in the direction of the command center within seconds.

My phone buzzes again.

Lata's voice says in a very quiet tone, the way she sounds when she's very, very angry. "Our house is on fire."

I take a deep breath. "Look, I'm sorry about what happened,

Luts. I'm just glad you and Natalie are okay. But we got the guy. He's toast. I'm heading to the command center now to wrap this up."

Lata repeats in the same quiet tone. "Our house is on fire."

I frown, staring out my window.

In the distance, I glimpse a small red glow to the northwest.

Just about where our neighborhood is.

It occurs to me that maybe she isn't speaking metaphorically.

"Say that again," I ask.

She repeats it for the third time.

"Our house is on fire?" I say aloud. The words simply don't make sense to me.

Even as she's telling me this, I hear sirens and a red fire truck passes us, heading back toward my home. Two more trucks follow. They've been diverted from the train wreck to deal with the fire.

Lata's voice is quiet and calm, the voice of an ex-Marine who's been in hairy situations in foreign lands, surrounded by strangers wanting to kill her. "He must have left some kind of incendiary device in the garage. We were out on the street, Natalie and I, while the cops went through the house to make sure it was clear."

Trevor looks at me as yet another fire truck passes us.

I point at the fire truck.

He understands and pulls right, following the truck.

"I'm coming to you," I say to Lata.

The fire is visible all the way from Bouquet Canyon as we approach the turnoff to Centurion Street. The flames rise above the roofs of the houses all around, lighting up the whole neighborhood.

Trevor pulls into Centurion Street but then has to stop because our lane is jammed full of emergency responder vehicles.

People are out on their lawns in their night clothes, staring at the fire.

At our house.

The first and only house I've ever been able to call my very own, after a childhood and youth spent in a succession of foster homes.

The house that Amit and I bought eight years ago, when I was pregnant with Natalie.

The house where our daughter was born.

Where we lay in bed together and dreamed of a second kid, of a future filled with possibilities, careers paved with success, a shared life packed with boundless joy.

The house that became our sanctuary during the pandemic, when the whole world seemed to be going to hell.

The house that Lata moved into after Amit died, to help me care for Natalie, where the three of us, over that bitter, heart-crushing time, built a new normal for ourselves, a found family, out of the embers of the old.

The house in which we've finally just begun to find our feet again, to rediscover the joy of living, to dream again of the future, of the possibilities that life might, just might, still hold, even though I know now that I'm not meant to have them all.

This house. Our house. The home of my heart.

In flames.

I get out of the multimillion-dollar car and walk down my street, into my lane, past the gawking neighbors, the first responders milling about, the firefighters yelling at one another, hauling equipment, cracking a hydrant, pointing hoses at the fire, battling the monster that's steadily digesting the precarious edifice of wood, fabric, brick and stone in which my family and I lived until just a short while ago.

Lata and Natalie see me and come running.

Natalie's face is flushed from the heat and excitement, but she looks otherwise unharmed and whole.

She raises her hands in the universal gesture of daughters to mothers since time immemorial and I pick her up.

She fills my arms.

My heart is already full with sorrow.

Natalie signs furiously to me, asking me a dozen questions.

I shake my head, trying to communicate to her that I don't have the answers.

I feel the tears rolling down my cheeks and let them speak for me.

She understands and stops, then leans in, smelling of the fruity mint toothpaste that she loves, and kisses me on the cheek.

She lays her head against my shoulder, snuggles in tightly, and holds me as only a daughter can her mother.

We stand in wordless sorrow, watching our dreams burn.

FIFTY-ONE

We're back at the command center.

Lata has taken Natalie to Aishwarya and Kundan's condo in Century City to spend the night.

Kayla has organized a round-the-clock security watch for them.

Anyone who's foolish enough to try to come after them again won't live to regret it. Even though I saw the red pickup truck crushed into junk metal with my own eyes, I'm not taking any chances.

Back at the house, I allowed an EMT to patch me up. She said she couldn't do very much for the throat bruising and I needed to come in for an X-ray, since she suspected the collarbone might have suffered a hairline fracture and I might have sustained serious trauma to my trachea and upper spine from the strangulation. She wanted to take me right away, but I said I was capable of making it under my own steam. I made the appropriately reassuring noises, promising to head on to the hospital ASAP. She looked skeptical that I would follow through; she's probably used to dealing with law enforcement.

She offered me painkillers for the throbbing pain, but I declined.

I need to keep my head clear.

Naved is explaining to me how the fire started.

"The cops were clearing the house. Standard procedure. They were just finishing up when there was a small explosion in the garage. Next minute, everything starts burning like crazy. The whole house went up like a box of matches. I talked to the fire chief. He said they would do their best but don't get your hopes up. Off the record, he said he had seen this kind of thing before, and we should expect a total write-off."

From what I've seen of the burning house, that doesn't come as a surprise, but it's still a shock to hear that everything you owned in the world is gone forever, just like that.

Even my damn boots. The boots I took off in the garage when I went in. I'm still barefoot. My feet are now dirty and cold. I have grit between my toes.

I tell Naved, "When I went into the garage, I tripped over something in the dark. We're usually very careful to keep things clear, so it must have been the thing he brought in there. The incendiary."

Naved nods. "That makes sense. I'll pass it on."

I look at Naved.

"Where the hell were you when the unsub got in?" I ask. "How the hell did you let him get past you?"

He sighs. "Believe it or not, I thought I was chasing the unsub. The patrol car had just done a check of the vicinity and was heading back to the station. They called a minute later to say they'd spotted a red pickup truck matching the description we'd put out earlier today, heading toward me, and asked if I wanted them to turn around and check it out. I told them I'd check it out and get back to them. I went around to Bouquet Canyon to see if I could spot it. I saw it driving down the street and went after it. I chased it a few blocks, then it turned in somewhere and just disappeared. I don't know the streets well enough to know for sure, but I think the unsub took a short cut and doubled back somehow. I was out searching when you arrived at the house. I got the emergency alert same as you did, when Lata called it in directly. I reached your house just in time to see you racing off in that supercar with Blackburn."

I nod, accepting the explanation. I've been in enough crazy situations over my career to know that when things start happening, nothing is predictable. The things we all do in those moments seem crazy to others who don't know what's going on, but they're the only things we can do at the time to get through the crisis. Look at me, federal agent with no shoes on! I trust Naved enough to know that he was doing the best he could and made the right call at the time.

Kayla calls out, trying to get our attention.

"Everyone, listen up. That was Chief McD. He says they cut open what was left of the pickup truck. They didn't find a body."

The skin on the back of my neck prickles.

"Maybe he got thrown out?" Brine suggests.

Kayla shakes her head. "Nope. Chief said he jumped out the door just before the train hit the truck. Witnesses saw him. They say he was injured, bleeding and holding himself like he was hurting. They saw him limp away. He was heading up the service road that runs parallel to Soledad Canyon Road, heading northeast."

"On foot?" David says. "He won't get far. They'll pick him up in minutes."

"He's had almost an hour and a half's head start," Kayla says. "Chief says they only just heard from the witness. An old man who was waiting to cross the tracks. There's so much chaos down there, it took a while before the guy was able to find a cop ready to listen to him."

"Frigging hell," Ramon says. "He could be anywhere by

now. Coulda gotten another ride, stolen one, or taken an Uber. He could be at LAX right now, catching a redeye out!"

Everyone starts positing theories and criticism.

Kayla holds her hand up for silence. "One more thing. Fire chief called from your house, Suse. They finally doused the fire. The house is gone, I'm sorry to inform you. They found the incendiary device in the garage. His people also found a similar one in the footwell of the truck. Both were set off using a remote. Chief McD's men found the remote tossed by the side of the tracks. It had blood all over it."

Naved looks at me, stunned.

"He's still alive?" I hear myself say.

FIFTY-TWO

"He came after me personally," I say. "This wasn't just some random thing. I don't fit his profile in any way, and besides, he's suspended his serial murders of bad moms to carry out his killing spree of the Murder Club. Since I don't fit into either category of victim, there was something else going on here. I saw it in his eyes. He was mad at *me*. Susan Parker. That's why he left that incendiary in the garage. He knew the odds were against him carrying through on his plan, he would have known that both Lata and I were capable of taking care of ourselves and were likely armed. Yet he came in without a gun, just that... that rope! The incendiary was his backup to make sure that even if he failed, the whole house would burn down."

Naved stares at me. "But... why?"

"Good question."

"I can maybe understand the animosity toward you. You're trying to catch him. But I don't get the incendiary device. What does he get out of burning your house down?"

"I don't know for sure, Naved. But there's someone who does. I'll bet on it."

I look over at Trevor. One of the richest men in America is

sitting on an uncomfortable wooden chair, sipping our lousy machine-made coffee. He senses me and looks up.

I crook a finger at him and point at one of the interview rooms across the hall.

Minutes later, Trevor and I are sitting across a table from each other. He still has the styrofoam cup in his hand. Naved is beside me.

Trevor takes a sip.

"This is terrible coffee," he says.

"Maybe if you billionaires paid more taxes, we government servants would be able to afford a better blend," I say.

Trevor nods. "Fair point."

"Enough economics," I say. "I need some answers, Trevor, and I need them right now."

He lowers his head. When he looks up, his face is genuinely remorseful. "I'm so sorry for what he did to you and your family, Susan. I swear to you, I had no idea he'd go this far. But I promise you, I'll make up for it. Whatever it takes, however much it takes, I'll make sure you're compensated for your losses. I'll make reparations."

"To hell with your reparations. Tell me about the Clothesline Killer."

Trevor's face registers something at the mention of the word. "What do you want to know?"

"In the car earlier," I say, "you admitted that you've been funding him, protecting him, using your resources to give him a new identity, shield him from the consequences of his actions, corrupting the PD to make sure he wasn't caught or even put on file. Do you stand by those admissions?"

Trevor glances at Naved, who looks back at him, then looks at me. This is the first time Naved is hearing about it. I nod slightly, confirming that I mean what I just said, and it's not just an interrogation tactic.

"I'm not recording this, Trevor," I say. "I just want to know the truth."

Trevor looks into the distance, exhales, and nods once. "I did everything you said, and then some."

I lean across the table. "Why, Trevor? Tell me why?"

He looks at me with an expression of such pure, deep sorrow that I'm taken aback. The handsome, mature, sexy older guy who dazzles the world with his financial acumen and charisma has given way to a vulnerable, wounded middle-aged man. It's a shocking change and to see it happen like that jars me.

"I had no choice, Susan," he says.

And I can see the tears behind his eyes, waiting to be released, held back only by a powerful ego and sense of dignity.

I stare at him.

"Why?" I ask.

He looks at me, then looks down.

I sense multiple emotions: Shame. Embarrassment. Guilt.

"I can't tell you that," he says softly, still looking down, unable to look at me.

I wait several beats.

"Okay," I say, knowing when not to push too hard. "Let's move on."

Naved leans forward, about to say something.

I cut my eyes at him, shake my head once, curtly.

He understands, and sits back, silent.

I turn back to Trevor, who's still sitting with head lowered, staring down.

"Derek Chen. Jake Perkins. Me and my family tonight. What was all that about?" I ask.

Trevor looks up, not at me, but at the wall behind me. At nothing in particular.

"You have to understand, Susan, I'm a regular joe, from the streets, from the projects, from the trailer parks. I grew up hardscrabble. When I make a deal, I honor it. Trevor Blackburn stands by his word. Anyone who does business with me knows that."

"Okay," I say. "Okay. So then what was it? Why did your pet psychopath suddenly start killing off your partners? You tell me."

He sighs. "Because he wants to hurt me."

I stare at him. "Come again?"

"He's being vindictive. He wants to destroy me. He wants to blow it all up, burn it all down, everything I've built."

I stand up, leaning over Trevor, glowering down at him. "Except it wasn't your mansion he burned down, Trevor. It was my little house here in Santa Carina Valley. If he wants to destroy you, why is he setting my life on fire?"

Trevor spreads his palms. "By getting to the people he thinks I care about, who are with me. He probably figures that by killing off my partners, he'll destroy the biggest deal I've ever negotiated. And he's right. He's already set me back considerably. If he were to keep going, I'd be ruined. The six of us are in a consortium. We're already two down and that's a big hit."

"Okay, I buy that. They're your business partners, Trevor. Killing them hurts you bad. But why me? I'm nobody to you."

He shrugs. "I don't know. There was that picture from the other night. The social media posts. Maybe he got the wrong idea."

I frown. "What picture? What posts?"

Naved clears his throat. "The other night at the Indian restaurant. Trevor dropped you off and held the door open for you. Someone clicked a pic of it and posted it online. It kind of went viral."

I remember the young drunk Indian couple who harassed me at dinner. I recall Kayla trying to show me something on social media earlier today and brushing it off saying whatever the hell it was, I didn't care and didn't want to see it or hear about it.

"So what?" I say aloud, trying to put it together. "The Clothesline Killer got the idea that, what? We're boyfriend and girlfriend? That we're involved? All from that one stupid social media pic taken by a drunk stranger? Even if he did, why would that matter to him?"

Trevor doesn't answer.

I stare at him.

Wheels are turning in my head.

I think through everything I've got on this case, on both cases, technically, the Murder Club murders and the clothesline murders. I think about the red pickup truck and Trevor paying for it. I think about the absence of paperwork on Trevor Blackburn's past and for Brook Wentworth, too.

Everything comes together in a rush.

I stand up suddenly, knocking my chair down to the floor with a crash, and walk out of the interview room.

FIFTY-THREE

"Ramon, I need you to go back into the system and look up something for me," I say as I walk out of the interview room.

I see that Urduja has joined us.

She's still in her pizza delivery tee but is probably off work by now. She looks wide eyed. There's a lot going down in our sleepy little burgh tonight, and she knows that she's involved in it, even though only peripherally.

"Name it, boss," Ramon says, fingers poised over his keyboard.

I tell him what I'm looking for, and what time period.

His fingers fly, working their magic, Carlotta doing the heavy lifting.

Naved comes out of the interview room. "Maybe we should arrest him and sweat him," he says. "We might still be able to make a case. Even if he gets it tossed out later, we can use it to leverage the info out of him."

I shake my head. "Never mind that. I'm trying another way."

"You sure?"

"Yep. In fact, bring him out here. I want him to be here if we find something."

By now, I have a sense we are going to find something. It's just instinct born of years of working cases. Just when it feels like everything is hopeless, and we're up against an impossible task, you achieve a breakthrough. The old cliché: It's always darkest right before dawn.

"Jefe," Ramon calls out. "This is what you were talking about."

"Hit me," I say.

I hear the interview room door open again.

Naved returns, accompanied by Trevor.

I ignore him.

My attention is focused entirely on Ramon's screen now.

Everyone else has stopped what they're doing to do the same.

Ramon points to his screen. "This what you're talking about?"

I look at his screen. "That's Wentworth's fake driver's license, the one McD's guys found in his pickup?" I say.

"Right. And here's Blackburn's driver's license, which is as legit as they come," Ramon says.

"Right."

"So, like you said, there's a twenty-year age difference between them, right?"

"Exactly. Look at their birth dates on the two licenses. I'm betting that even though Wentworth's license is fake, like everything else about him, the date is still correct or at least close enough to his actual birth year."

"Makes sense, boss. So you want me to run a check on birth certificates in SCV, looking for all boys born on those dates."

"Yes," I say.

Beside me, Trevor tenses.

"You might have something, boss. Because, look. They're

both the same day of the year. February 11th. That's a mighty big coincidence."

"It's no coincidence, Ramon. That's why I believe those dates are real."

"Sure. But here's the thing. Remember I told you about the key I used to crack the encryption code on Blackburn's cloud account and devices?"

"What about it?"

"That was keyed to the date on which Blackburn and all the other biggies made their raid on the stock market and started raking in the moolah, remember?"

"Sure."

Ramon pulls up another screen, this time a news article announcing the news of the six newly minted billionaires—multimillionaires at the time of the article. "See the date?"

February 11th. Again.

"That definitely can't be a coincidence," I say.

I feel a sudden rush. It's all starting to come together now.

"It ain't all, jefe, stay with me now," Ramon says as his nimble fingers fly over his keyboard. "Like you asked me, I told Carlotta to look up February 11th on different years in this burgh, Santa Carina Valley, going back as far as she could and lookit what my girl found."

"What?" I ask, hardly daring to hope.

"This."

He shows me a scan of a print newspaper report from *The Signal*, the local newspaper.

Soledad Canyon Mother Strangled In Bed While Son Slept Beside Her.

Clothesline from house used in shocking murder.

A shiver goes through me.

I skim the article. It's light on details but even then it's clear that it's the work of the same killer.

The Boogeyman. The Clothesline Killer.

I look at the date.

February 11th. Again.

"That's it," I say. "That's our connection."

I turn to Trevor.

"That was you," I say, pointing to the article on Ramon's screen. "You murdered your own wife, the mother of your son, while she slept, with her own clothesline. Your son happened to witness it. You thought he was asleep, but he wasn't. He just pretended to be asleep because he was scared you might kill him, too. You strangled her and abandoned him. He grew up to become Brook Wentworth, replaying the same trauma he had suffered, inflicting it on other little kids like himself. Like Urduja here. At some point, he figured out that his dad had gone on to change his name and bury his past, and transformed himself into a billionaire. You. Trevor Blackburn. That's when he started blackmailing you, demanding you pay him off. That's how it went down, isn't it?"

Trevor glances around at everyone's faces, meeting their eyes—and facing their judgment and contempt. "He didn't even know. I was the one who reached out. I wanted to try to make amends. I sent him money. I wanted him to be taken care of, have a good life. But somehow, he was able to track the money back to me. It triggered something in him. He'd already killed by then, but he became methodical about it, systematic. Driven."

Kayla makes a sound. Something midway between disgust and horror.

The others just stare blankly at Trevor, arms crossed, jaws tight, eyes cold.

Urduja looks like she wants to claw his eyes out. Kayla is beside her, making sure she doesn't do anything stupid.

"*He sent him money,*" Urduja says. "*Money.*"

Trevor doesn't look at Urduja. He falls silent.

I nod. "Okay, it's all coming together now."

"We now know that Trevor Blackburn was actually John James Kensey," Ramon says. "He had a wife, Sharon, and a son, William John Kensey. When William was seven, he saw his mom strangled to death in her bed by a man in a Boogeyman mask. He grew up. He *became* the Boogeyman. The Clothesline Killer."

I point to the door. "And he's still out there. Still alive and dangerous, and certain to kill again. And keep killing. Until he's stopped."

I point to Ramon's screen. "Now that we know his real name, we should be able to track him down. Find him for me, Ramon. And the rest of you, start gearing up. Once Ramon gets us a location, we're moving out. Full gear. We're taking down this guy tonight!"

FIFTY-FOUR

Ten minutes later, I'm in my Prius outside a condominium in a side lane just off Golden Valley Road.

It's one of the new developments that have started springing up of late, considered an eyesore by longtime valley residents who hate seeing anything over two stories breaking the skyline. I'm inclined to agree with them. I like the endless rows of red-tiled roofs and Spanish-style houses, each with its own little front and back yards, some with actual acreage. It would be a crime to ruin that classic SoCal vibe with a bunch of ugly concrete blocks. They're also irritated that a 1250 square foot apartment in this luxury condo complex goes for more than a house twice that size.

"At least he made good use of your money," I say to Trevor.

He hasn't said a word on the drive here.

He watches as I check my Sig Sauer, slipping in rounds to replace the ones I shot at the Clothesline Killer in my backyard.

"He's my son," Trevor says. "What was I supposed to do?"

I turn and stare at him directly. I'm in no mood for any more of his bullshit. "Not kill his mother for starters."

He flinches. "You don't understand. We were young, poor,

desperate, barely holding our heads above water. She got addicted, she was sleeping around, she was abusive to Billy. I knew I had to get out of there, start over. But if I left her with Billy, I don't know what would have happened to him. I couldn't leave him with her, and I couldn't take him with me because then I'd be stuck forever."

I think of a dozen things to say to that but hold my tongue. "So you killed her, problem solved."

"He was better off without her," Trevor says. "We both were. At least this way, we got to start over clean. He went into the foster system. I busted my ass trying to earn a buck. When I succeeded, I went back looking for him. I did everything I could. But it was too late. He was already messed up. I blame her for that. She treated him like an animal when he was a baby, a toddler. The damage was already done. He grew up to become a psychopath."

"Watching your father strangle your mother to death in their marital bed will do that to a kid," I say.

He holds his head in his hands. "I'm not proud of it, okay? If I could, I would go back and change it all. But I can't. So I've tried to make amends. Do the best I can."

"Okay, you've done the best you could," I say. "Now it's time for me to do what I have to do."

Trevor reaches out to touch my arm.

"Susan, listen to me. I can still save him. I know I can. Give me one last chance."

My radio crackles. "Jefe, we're all in position. Just say the word."

"Hold your positions," I say. "Wait for my go."

I release the talk button and look at Trevor. "What are you asking?"

"Let me go in there. Alone."

I shake my head. "I can't do that."

"Listen to me, Susan. He's hurt, he's scared, he's feeling

cornered right now. If you go in there, he'll try to defend himself. There's only one way that can end."

I don't reply to that. He's right. A part of me is itching for a chance to put another bullet into the man who invaded my family home and burned it down. And this time, I'll aim for a killshot.

"Let me go in and make amends. Give me a chance to talk to my son face to face. I'll talk him into turning himself in. Please."

I close my eyes.

"Susan," Naved says on the radio. "If you're thinking of doing what I think you're going to do, don't do it."

I open my eyes and look at Trevor.

I shouldn't do this. It goes against all my training, my protocol, every rule in the law enforcement rulebooks.

I open my mouth to say no.

Instead, what comes out is: "You have five minutes. Go now before I change my mind."

I watch him get out of the Prius and walk to the building as my radio crackles.

"Suse, what the hell are you doing?" Kayla asks. "Are you out of your mind?"

I pick up the radio. "Kay. Naved. Ramon. David. Brine. This is on me. It's entirely my decision. None of you had any part of it. Whatever happens, it's my responsibility. I'm going in after him. I want everyone to hold your positions for five minutes, then come in after us. Repeat: I'm going in solo after him, everyone else hold five minutes, then follow."

They squawk back arguments and try to talk sense into me, but I ignore them as I drop the radio on the seat and get out of the Prius.

Even though this violates every regulation, every protocol that's been drilled into me, it *feels right*.

I'm only a few steps behind Trevor.

I see him step into the elevator.

I take the stairs two at a time, checking the elevator indicator on the second floor.

There's only three levels.

He's going to the third.

I'm maybe ten seconds behind him. I hear him speaking through the closed front door of his son's condo then the sound of the door opening as I reach the fifth story. I'm out of breath by this time. My throat, which hasn't stopped hurting all night, is making a rasping sound. I feel a little catch in my chest. The collarbone is agony, too. And I'm butt-tired. It's been a hell of a night and a hell of a week.

I ignore it all.

I stand with my back to the front door, which is ajar, my Sig raised in a double-handed grip, and peer in cautiously.

I can hear their voices and glimpse the back of the younger man. There's blood on the front doorlatch and on the floor and on his head and back. Beyond him, I can see Trevor facing me, talking to his son, the serial killer.

I go in carefully, trying not to make a sound.

Trevor is saying, "It can't go on. You know that. They're outside right now. You can't fight them all."

Brook Wentworth AKA William John Kensey makes an amused, bitter sound in his throat. "I'm not armed. I don't do guns. You taught me that, remember? Guns kill people."

Trevor's face reacts to that as if slapped. "You... remember that? You must have been, what, three at the most?"

"I remember everything," William says, and then adds, "*Dad*."

Trevor's face crumples like a paper sack.

"I..." he starts. "I'm so, so sorry."

There's a long moment of silence then William says, "You said we were a team. That we were father and son, and nothing could ever separate us. Well, you did, Dad. You broke us up. You left me!"

Trevor shakes his head, sobbing now. "I know. I *know*."

"Well, guess what, Dad? We're still a team. I've made videos of myself after each kill over the years. I explained why I did it. That you made me do it. That you were with me all along, guiding me, leading me. That we were a team. If they catch me now, they'll find those videos. They'll take you down with me. You won't be able to buy your way out of this one, Dad."

Trevor's face is buried in his hands, shaking.

I come up behind William, the Sig aimed at his back, careful to keep a safe distance in case he turns and throws himself at me again.

"Raise your hands and turn around slowly," I say. "Don't even think about trying anything. This time, I'll shoot the instant you make a move."

William does as I ask.

He turns, arms raised to shoulder height. Blood flows freely down from his chest wound. He's wheezing audibly. One of my parting shots to him from my backyard wall must have punctured a lung. It looks and sounds like the bullet is still in there and his lung's continually filling with blood. I can see a little crimson spray coming out of his mouth each time he exhales. It's possible my shot nicked an artery. Either way, he isn't going to last long without immediate medical assistance.

"I'll call for an ambulance," I say. "You need help."

He smiles at me strangely. That same lopsided grin with the cold fish eyes. Eerie, desolate, lost. The eyes of a little boy who experienced the worst that life could throw at him.

"Don't bother," he says.

Through the open door, I hear the sound of feet pounding up the stairwell.

My guys are coming.

I don't think they even waited two minutes before following.

It doesn't matter now. This is all I needed—wanted—to have. This moment or two with the unsub. To look into the eyes of the man who came into my house, threatened my family, almost killed me, burned my house down.

"Why me?" I ask. "Why my family?"

He chuckles, spraying blood.

"Because... you're the dream. The perfect mom. The perfect family. I couldn't let *him* have that."

I'm still processing this a second later when I glimpse the hand rising up behind William, the elbow crooked, and shout, "Trevor!"

William's face doesn't look at all surprised as his father's arm slips around his throat, grabbing him from behind, pinning his throat in a chokehold.

I can't be sure in that final, blurry moment, but I think I see that grin reappear. That manic grin born of unspeakable pain and suffering. The grin that declares with pride and relief: I did it. I made him do it.

Then Trevor Blackburn's arm yanks his son's neck in a vise grip, while his other hand presses the side of William's head sharply to the side, breaking the neck.

William is dead before his body hits the floor.

Boots come pounding in, through the front door.

Guns and Kevlar vests with *FBI* on them, shields dangling on chains around their necks, guns raised in double-fisted grips, eyes flashing, scanning, taking in everything, voices clamoring.

I hold out my palm to stop them, saying hoarsely, "Hold your fire."

Then I point the Sig at the man standing over his dead son's body.

"Trevor Blackburn, you're under arrest for the murder of William John Kensey."

FIFTY-FIVE

"SAC Parker, hold up a moment, will you?" Deputy Director Zimal Bukhari calls out as I'm walking away from the conference room.

I turn and wait for her to walk over. She says a quick word to one of the other senior agents who were in the meeting with us. Most of them are lawyers.

Bukhari joins me. "This is going to have to come through formal channels which take their own sweet time. This is the Bureau, after all. But I wanted to let you know right away rather than letting you stew."

I look at her, trying to read her face.

She smiles. "Congratulations, you've been formally cleared."

"Thank you, that's great," I say.

I feel a weight lift off my shoulders. While everyone, including my Bureau-appointed legal representative, said that it would just be a formality, I was still anxious about the outcome. You can never tell with these official inquiries.

"It was pretty straightforward," she says, as we walk down the hallway together. "Every single member of your team testified to the same thing. That Blackburn went into the condo against your explicit orders, got there a few seconds before you were able to follow, somehow got into a struggle with the unsub, defended himself, killing the unsub. It was all consistent with the evidence and the SCVPD reports from the scene. All your team members concur. There was no way you could have known he was going to do that, and nothing you could have done to stop him in time. You did everything by the book. Of course, Trevor Blackburn will stand trial for taking the law into his own hands, but he's rich and powerful, and he could spin a pretty convincing case for self-defense. In any case, anything he did isn't on you. It's unfortunate it went down the way it did at the end, but let's face it, nobody's going to mourn the loss of a serial killer who had killed well over a dozen innocent women over the years, ruined dozens of lives and would have probably gone on to kill many more if he hadn't been stopped."

"And Derek Chen and Jake Perkins," I say.

She nods. "Them, too, of course."

"Thank you, Deputy Director Bukhari," I say. "I appreciate you letting me know right away." A thought occurs to me. "I noticed Deputy Director Connor Gantry wasn't at today's hearing. I haven't heard from him in a while either. Is everything all right?"

She sighs. "I'm afraid I can't reveal too much detail about that. But what I can tell you is that there's a full-scale investigation that's ongoing."

"An investigation?"

"Yes. It's been brought to our notice that Deputy Director Gantry might have had certain personal connections with certain parties in Santa Carina Valley that led to certain, um, arrangements, shall we say, that might not have been in line with the Bureau's official standard of ethics. In light of the questions raised by the very unsatisfactory investigative work into the serial murders committed by William John Kensey in SCV over the years, and Chief McDougall's own business interests in the region, the Justice Department has opened an investigation. I really can't say any more at this time, but it's possible, even likely, in my opinion, that Deputy Director Gantry might be taking an early retirement from the Bureau."

"I see."

She sees my expression. "If you're wondering how that impacts you, SAC Parker, let me set your mind at ease. You have nothing to worry about. On the contrary. Moving forward, you'll be reporting directly to my office."

"I'm glad to hear that," I say, and mean it. Even though I've only met her a handful of times, I've seen enough to know that I'd be far better off having Deputy Director Zimal Bukhari as my boss than Gantry.

"In fact," she says, "I'd like very much to talk to you about your future at the Bureau. Maybe you can drop by my office sometime next week to discuss?"

"Sure," I say.

"Good, I'll have my EA call you and fix it up. See you then," she says and flashes one last smile as she walks away.

I ride down in the elevator, exit the building and am in the parking lot when my phone buzzes.

It's Lata.

"Well?" she asks. "Don't keep me in suspense."

I tell her the good news, that the hearing went off smoothly and that I'm completely in the clear.

"Hallelujah," she says. "This calls for a celebration, Suse! You deserve to let your hair down and chill, too. You survived again!"

"Okay, okay," I laugh. "Give me an hour to get there, then we'll figure something out."

"Natalie says she wants to go to the amusement park. She wants to see the dinosaurs. I told her it's Mommy's day, so

Mommy gets to decide. She says she's okay with that, too. She actually said, 'Copacetic'."

I grin as I get into my Prius. I have to slam the driver's side door shut twice to get it to stay shut. "I'm fine with dinosaurs. The amusement park sounds great. I'm happy just being out with crowds and happy kids yelling their lungs out. You figure out the logistics and call me back. Maybe I can meet you directly there instead of driving all the way back to SCV and us driving back."

"You got it, boss, I'll call you right back," Lata says brightly before hanging up.

I smile to myself as I pull out of the parking lot of 11000 Wilshire, the FBI's LA field office.

It's another bright, sunshiney day in SoCal, the sky is that beautiful deep blue that it gets here in this wide-open state, and I can sleep tonight without worrying about my job. From what Bukhari said, I think I might even be able to hope for a possible raise. Maybe? Fingers crossed.

We could definitely use the money.

We're surviving for now.

Camping out at Kundan's and Aishwarya's condo until we can figure out our house situation. It's a roof over our heads at least. Especially since Aishwarya has been shockingly generous enough to let us have the place to ourselves, opting to go stay in her San Francisco condo to deal with business.

But sooner or later we're going to need a house again. Lata and I are hoping and praying that insurance will cover the house, but they won't pay up until the fire investigation is completed. And that's not so simple since arson was definitely involved.

It's a complicated situation, insurance wise.

And even when and if they do pay out, we still have to find a house, and then restart the painful process of rebuilding our lives in SCV from scratch.

But at least for today, I decide, I'm going do exactly as Lata said.

Let my hair down and enjoy a day out with my family.

And dinosaurs!

We all love dinosaurs!

My phone buzzes as I take the turnpike onto the freeway.

"Hey, Lata," I say. "Tell me. What's the plan? Am I meeting you guys directly at the park? I just got on the freeway, I can be there in around twenty-five minutes."

But the voice that replies isn't Lata's. It's a woman with a strong North Indian accent. Lata is North Indian too, of course, but she sounds as American as I do. This woman's voice has a very Delhi Punjabi accent.

"FBI agent Susan Parker?" she says.

"Who is this?" I ask.

I glance at my screen.

It reads:

CBI Delhi calling.

CBI stands for Central Bureau of Investigation. It's the Indian equivalent of the FBI.

What do they want with me?

A LETTER FROM THE AUTHOR

Hi!

You just turned the last page of *The Murder Club*.

Did it chill you? Thrill you? Stir up feelings? Maybe even creep you out or scare you outright? Nothing like a good thriller to get the pulse pounding, heart racing, and adrenalin going, huh? More fun than cardio!

If you made it to these end pages, I'm going to guess you answered yes!

When I started writing the Susan Parker series, I had a clear plan for her life and career, before the series started, and all the way to the end.

The same applies to all the major series characters.

The bad news is, all of them won't make it.

The good news is, the best is yet to come.

In fact, we're poised on the cusp of some huge reveals about Susan and her family, major, life-changing stuff that will throw her (and us) into a tizzy.

So before we go any further, I'm going to ask you to follow the link below and sign up to my mailing list. That way, you can be sure of never missing the latest news and updates about Susan and her adventures.

www.stormpublishing.co/sam-baron

The only thing more wonderful than a great read is sharing

it with another avid reader. I would really appreciate it if you could spare a few moments to leave a review. Even a short review of just a couple of lines and that all-important five-star rating can make a huge difference to an author and book. Sharing is caring, after all! Thank you so much!

At the end of this book, as you saw, we left Susan and her family at a precarious place. Home invaded, family put at risk, house burned down, the mystery of her husband Amit's death still unresolved, and she barely surviving a tangle with some rich and powerful men who could easily have derailed her career. Some of these men should have been her allies—I'm thinking of McD here—instead they turned out to be her antagonists. With allies like that, who needs enemies!

Yet she survived, and closed the book on the Clothesline Killer. Badda-bing badda-boom, one more monster in the iron room!

But now what? Can Susan continue to work in her home territory, Santa Carina Valley, and still trust the law enforcement colleagues she has to work with on a daily basis? Where will she, Natalie, and Lata live now? As we saw in *The Therapy Room* and *The Murder Club*, Susan tends to attract violent men like a water buffalo attracts Bengal tigers. If she and her family were vulnerable before, now they're positively exposed! They literally don't even have a roof over their head. What are they going to do?

And what about Amit's murder? Is she just supposed to give up on it in frustration? Throw her hands up, yell "Gah!," and get on with her life? Ridiculous, right? We both know Susan isn't the giving-up kind. One way or another, she's going to get to the bottom of that. The question is how and when. And when she does, how will the answers affect her mental and emotional state?

Just before the start of *The Therapy Room*, Susan's grief after Amit's death was powerful enough to drive her to viciously attack the man she thought was his killer. What will happen once she learns who the killer really is—and when it turns out to be the person she least expected?

We're going to get some answers in the next Susan Parker thriller. Not all of the answers, maybe not even the ones you were expecting, but we will get some. And the story itself will also stand on its own as a compelling, pulse-pounding, adrenaline-pumping chiller thriller. It's a monster of a case and I'd go so far as to say that it's the best of the series so far.

I promised myself when I started this series that I'm going to tell these stories in as close to real time as possible.

That literally means that if Susan is dealing with a case in a certain month of a certain year, the book will also be published that same month and year. That's how it was for *The Therapy Room* and also for *The Murder Club*. And it's going to continue at the same pace, several times each year, until the entire series is done.

As a thriller reader myself, I love it when the books drop at a fast and furious rate, maintain a high quality, and meet or exceed my expectations.

That's my goal with the Susan Parker series!

Will this be the fastest crime thriller series ever published? Good question!

Will it be the best? That's for you to judge!

What I can say for sure is that you're now aboard the Susan Parker Thriller Express. The train has left the station. There's no turning back now. And we're on a one-way trip to the dark unknown. Brace yourself. Things are about to get crazy!

Love, only love, and happy reading forever!

Sam

KEEP IN TOUCH WITH THE AUTHOR

facebook.com/samkbaron

x.com/samkbaron

instagram.com/samkbaron

tiktok.com/@samkbaron

Made in United States
Orlando, FL
24 November 2024